The Scent
of Fear

The Scent
of Fear

Patricia Matthews
with
Clayton Matthews

Thorndike Press • Thorndike, Maine

Library of Congress Cataloging in Publication Data:

Matthews, Patricia, 1927-
    The scent of fear / Patricia Matthews with Clayton
Matthews.
        p. cm.
    ISBN 1-56054-336-1 (alk. paper : lg. print)
    1. Large type books. I. Matthews, Clayton. II. Title.
[PS3563.A853S32   1992]   92-23099
813'.54—dc20   CIP

Thorndike Press Basic Series Large Print edition
published in 1992 by arrangement with Severn House
Publishers Ltd.

The tree indicium is a trademark of Thorndike Press.

This book is printed on acid-free, high opacity paper. ∞

We would like to dedicate this book to Kristina Brisco and Julie Fisher, The Next Generation!

Patricia and Clayton Matthews

CHAPTER ONE

Midnight.

Midnight had always been a bad time for Casey Farrel.

It had been midnight when she had lost her baby. And the miscarriage had resulted in her losing a good secretarial job in California. It had been midnight when she had come home from working the swing shift in a fast food restaurant on Camelback Road, and found herself locked out of her apartment for non-payment of rent — three months in arrears. And the following night, exhausted and almost asleep on her feet after spending the night in her car, she had been asked to work overtime when one of the girls didn't show. Because of her fatigue, Casey had spilled a whole tray of food into a customer's lap, and she had been fired — at exactly midnight.

And now, as she raised her head from the uncomfortable bed she had made in the back seat of the T-bird, she glanced at her right wrist, forgetting that she had hocked her

7

wrist-watch two days ago for eating money. Peeking over the front seat, she saw by the dash clock that it was exactly midnight. She shivered.

If someone had told her six months, or even three months ago that she soon would be unemployed, spending her days looking for a job and the nights sleeping in her car, she would not have believed them. Thank God the T-bird was paid for! Otherwise she might be sleeping in cardboard boxes. It was terrifying to realize that she was only one step removed from becoming a street person. She vowed to herself that whatever happened, she would not sell the car. It was all she had, and besides, Phoenix was almost as bad as Los Angeles; it was very difficult to get around without wheels.

For the past two nights she had been parking in the alley behind a row of apartment buildings only a few blocks off Central Avenue. Thank goodness the nights in Phoenix were warm, but it wasn't easy to find a place to park without being rousted by the cops. So far, no cop car had prowled the alley. But how long would it be before people in the apartment buildings would call the police about the mysterious car parked every night in the same spot?

She frowned, running her fingers through

her tousled black hair. What had awakened her? Something. Some alien sound. She had been sleeping in the T-bird for three weeks now. At first she had slept only fitfully in the cramped confines of the back seat, but now she had become almost accustomed to the discomfort, so *something* must have disturbed her.

Sitting up, she turned to look through the back window. The alley was dimly lit, only a street light at the far end throwing light along the trash-barrel-lined alley.

Nothing back there that she could see.

She turned back to face the windshield, and saw a black-and-white mongrel dog nosing out from behind a dumpster a few car lengths ahead of the T-bird.

Casey relaxed. That was what she had heard — the dog bumping into something while scrounging for food. Poor thing. She pulled the quilt up as if to shelter her body. She might be forced into doing the same thing soon.

Donnie Patterson stood at the window of his room in the two-story apartment building, staring out. He couldn't see very much, because his eyes were blurred. He gulped, trying to stem the flood of tears. At nine he was too old to cry.

But out there, somewhere, was Spot, his dog. He was probably hungry and thirsty.

9

There was a rule against dogs in the apartment house, but Donnie had found Spot whimpering in the alley just three days ago, and had smuggled him into the apartment. He had managed to hide the dog's presence in his room until earlier this evening, feeding the animal table scraps, and sneaking him out of the building for a walk every evening before supper.

Spot was unusually quiet for a dog, but tonight, for some reason, he had started barking, and Donnie hadn't been able to hush him.

Brent Karson, the man who lived with Donnie's aunt, had heard the barking, and had stormed into Donnie's room

When he saw Spot, he cuffed Donnie alongside the head, knocking him across the room, stunning him. He roared, "You little bastard! Where'd that mutt come from? You want to get us thrown out of this place? You know no dogs are allowed!"

Donnie said, "All the other kids I know have pets."

"I don't give a shit what the other kids have, you're not going to have one. Even if it was allowed, all dogs do is cause trouble and messes."

Karson bent down and picked Spot up by the scruff of his neck.

"This animal goes out of here now, and if

you try to sneak him back in, I'll blister your little butt until you won't be able to sit down for a week!"

Donnie cried out, "No!" and tried to grab Spot, but Karson backhanded him again, knocking him across the bed.

This time Donnie lost consciousness for a few minutes. When he came to, man and dog were gone. Donnie got to his feet, and stumbled out into the hallway, just as his aunt came out of the other bedroom.

She was dressed to go out, in a skimpy dress red as a fire engine, high heels as sharp as ice picks. Her dyed blonde hair fizzed out around her bloated face.

"Where's Spot?" Donnie demanded.

"If you mean that flea-bitten mutt, he's gone for good, young man," she said in her shrill voice. "You knew better than to bring that dog in here. You got poor Brent all upset." She swatted a palm at him, and Donnie shrank away just in time.

"Soon as he gets back, we're going out. You go to your room and stay there. We'll be back when we get back. I want you in bed in five minutes. Into your room, young man. Now!"

Donnie retreated to his room and closed the door. But he didn't climb into bed. He waited at the door, ear to the panel, straining to hear. He heard Brent come back, heard his voice

11

growling at Aunt Edith, and a few minutes later he heard the front door slam as the two of them left the apartment.

He waited a few minutes longer, to be sure they were gone. He knew from experience that they would be bar-hopping until all hours. They rarely came back before the bars closed, at two; and they were always staggering drunk.

When he was certain they were gone, Donnie hurried through the apartment. He had no key, so he left the door unlocked so that he could get back in. He knew that if Aunt Edith and Brent were to come back early, and find him gone, the door unlocked, he was in for a merciless beating; but he had to risk it.

He hurried down the stairs, and flew out the front door. It was already quite late, and the street was quiet. He went along it, calling softly, "Spot! Here, Spot!"

There was no answer, no sign of a small, spotted dog running toward him, tongue lolling, stumpy tail wagging. Slowly, Donnie made his way toward the alley behind the building. This was where he had found the dog before, investigating the smells that clung to the trash bins and dumpsters.

Donnie travelled the length of the block, looking behind every dumpster, behind every box and trash barrel.

No Spot.

Finally, after an hour's searching with no sign of the dog, Donnie trudged back to the apartment, heartbroken, hot tears threatening.

Since then, he had been standing with his face pressed against the window, keeping a vigil, hoping to see the little dog. He had seen the pretty lady park her car in the alley around ten o'clock. He had seen her park there last night as well, and had watched her settle down to sleep in the back seat.

Now, he saw her stir, the white blur of her face in the car window. He saw her lean forward to look out the windshield. Wondering what had awakened her, Donnie's glance jumped to the dumpster not too far in front of her car. Spot! Spot was sniffing the ground around the dumpster. He was probably starving.

Galvanized into action, Donnie ran pell-mell out of the apartment.

Casey was just about to settle back to sleep, when she saw a small boy, about eight or nine, burst through the gate in the wooden fence that separated the apartment buildings from the alley. She watched as he ran to the dog and snatched him up in his arms.

At the same instant car lights swung into the alley, moving slowly. The boy, hidden from view of the approaching car by the huge dumpster, seemed oblivious, nuzzling the dog in his arms.

Casey couldn't see beyond the glare of the headlights, couldn't see if it was a police car or not. Then the car stopped by the dumpster. The headlights went out, and she could see that it was a dark van. The motor was left running.

The driver, stocky, with broad shoulders, got out, walked around the van, and slid open the side door. Intrigued, Casey watched closely. The driver was pulling something bulky out of the van, something in a long, black plastic bag. With apparent effort, he slung it over his shoulder, and stepped to the dumpster with it.

Casey felt the muscles along her spine tighten. The newspapers had recently been full of articles on the "Dumpster Killer." Over the past two weeks the bodies of two women, both prostitutes, had been found in plastic bags, in dumpsters.

The man lifted the lid of the dumpster with his left hand, and, lifting his heavy shoulders, rolled the bag into it.

The sound of the lid falling back into place must have alerted the boy. Still holding the dog in his arms, he stepped out from behind the dumpster just as the man turned and saw him. Both the man and the boy stood still, staring at one another.

The man took a step toward the boy, hands reaching out, and Casey snapped out of her inertia. Although she had not had time to analyze the situation, it seemed obvious to her that the man meant to harm the child.

Moving quickly, she threw herself over the front seat and fumbled for the headlight switch. The high beams struck the man full in the face. She had a brief glimpse of a round, surprisingly boyish countenance, before he threw his hands over his eyes. Attention diverted from the boy, he took an uncertain step toward Casey's car.

Casey slammed her hand down on the horn button. The sound was loud in the walled alley.

The man broke then, running around the idling van to throw himself into the driver's seat. Within seconds he had put the vehicle into gear and was backing out of the alley.

Casey, blessed with a near-photographic memory, got a good look at the Arizona license plates as the van swung around before exiting into the street. The letters and numbers of the plate burned themselves into her mind.

She reached for her ignition key. She had to get out of here in the event the man came back. Then she saw the boy still standing as though frozen in place, staring at the alley entrance where the van had disappeared.

Casey rolled down her window. "Kiddo, don't stand around out here. Get in the car!"

The boy's head swung toward her.

A window banged up in the apartment house opposite the dumpster, and a male voice yelled. "What the hell's going on down there?"

Casey shouted. "Call the police!"

Now the boy was running toward her. She reached over and pushed the right-hand door open. The boy tumbled into the car, holding on to the dog.

"Close the door," Casey said.

He slammed the door. She pressed the lock button.

The boy stared at her out of round, blue eyes in a pale, slender face. "Who was that man. Was he going to hurt me?"

She nodded grimly. "More than likely. Do you live around here?"

"Up there." He indicated one of the apartment buildings. "I'm Donnie Patterson. Spot here got out." He stared toward the end of the alley. "Will that man come back?"

"He may." Again Casey reached for the key, then paused as she heard a siren in the distance. "That'll be the police."

She hesitated. Of course they would want

to know what she was doing parked here at this time of night, but her code of ethics would not let her consider leaving. If, by some chance, that man had been the dumpster killer, the police would need her information. She turned to the boy.

"I guess we'd better wait here for them," she said.

CHAPTER TWO

Ordinarily, Detective Sergeant Joshua Whitney would not have been riding in a patrol unit. The uniforms usually got their shorts in a twist when a plainclothes guy decided to ride with them. Josh suspected that it was because they were nervous that the ride-along might be a member of Internal Affairs. However, they couldn't very well complain; and today Josh wasn't in the mood to worry about their feelings. There was a new killer on the streets, and Josh had drawn the case. So far he didn't have diddley-squat to go on, and this made him nervous, irritable, and not a joy to be around.

What he had so far, was two killings with identical MOs. At a meeting earlier in the week, Lieutenant Wilkins, commander of the unit investigating the killings, had told the assembled detectives: "Look, guys, we've got two cases with similar MOs, but I don't want any of you mentioning the words 'serial killer,' okay? Particularly to the media. You know how those people run with something like that. The Mayor doesn't want a panic. It's bad for business. Besides, it's still too early to tell what we've got. There may well prove to be two perps. So keep your mouths shut. Okay?"

Josh bit back a wry smile. Yes, a serial killer could put a real crimp in the tourist business. There was nothing like it to keep people off the streets and out of the stores and places of entertainment. But Josh felt, deep in his gut, that this was what they were dealing with. Two killings within two weeks, both on a Saturday night. And tonight it was Saturday night again.

Each of the two victims had been hookers, on the stroll on Van Buren, and some of the detectives on the case couldn't get too stirred up about it. As one had commented, "What's another hooker, more or less? Hell, the killer could be doing us a favor, clearing out some of the scum."

But Josh cared, very much. Maybe it was corny, old fashioned, but to him, murder was the ultimate crime; and anyone who willingly committed that crime deserved to be put away where they could never harm anyone again. That was the reason he had chosen to become a homicide officer.

The radio on the dash squawked. Josh

leaned forward to hear the call. Another body, a woman, in the alley off 7th Street and Thomas Road.

The young officer in the front passenger seat turned to look at Josh. "I'll bet you a fin that it's the Dumpster Killer. What do you say, Sergeant?"

Josh winced. So much for the lieutenant's words of caution.

They were only a dozen blocks from the location, and they were on the scene within five minutes. Several other prowl cars, dome lights throwing light on the alley walls, were already parked in and around the alley-way. In the alley, the curious, most of them in robes and pajamas, were gathered, held back by a uniform. Already, a yellow crime scene tape had been stretched around the perimeter of a large dumpster, crouched against one wall.

As he got out of the cruiser, Josh noticed a lone civilian vehicle parked up the alley about fifty feet from the dumpster. As yet, no other plainclothes detectives were in evidence.

Josh nodded to one of the uniforms. "Tony. What have we got?"

"A dead woman, Sergeant. A hooker from the look of her."

"Strangled?"

"Until the coroner says otherwise. Looks

like the same MO as the other two."

Josh shook his head. "You first on the scene, Tony?"

"Yeah, I was only about two blocks away when I got the call. A man in one of the apartments heard a commotion down here and called 911. I got here in two minutes, not more than ten minutes after the body was dumped."

"How do you know what time the body was dumped?"

Tony smiled. "We got lucky this time. There's a witness. Two, in fact."

Josh's gaze jumped to the civilian vehicle. "Who? Where?"

Tony's gaze followed Josh's. "Yeah, that's it. There was a woman in the car, saw the whole thing. The other witness, a kid, is with her."

"Did she get a good look at the perp?"

"Says she did. Got the license number too."

"Did you call it in?"

"Just finished when I saw you turn into the alley. It should be on the air by now."

"Thank the Lord for small favors!" Josh took a deep, grateful breath. "Maybe we'll get lucky this time. It sure as hell's more than we have on the other two."

Tony jerked a thumb in the direction of the body. "Want to take a look? We're waiting for the guy from forensics before we take her

21

out of the dumpster."

Josh shook his head. "No, I think I'll wait too. You've seen one, you've seen 'em all, right?" It was a lame joke, eliciting only a meager smile from the other officer. Josh had learned, early in his career, that cops were prone to bad, often tasteless jokes. They seemed to help stave off burn-out, which came soon enough, God knows.

"But I think I will have a talk with our witnesses."

Walking over to the civilian vehicle, he approached it on the driver's side. The window whirred down, and Josh found himself looking down into a pair of large brown eyes set in a young, lightly tanned, feminine face, framed by short, curly, black hair. He took a good look. It was an attractive face, strong, but delicate. The eyes showed intelligence. On the other side of the seat sat a small towheaded boy, with a small spotted dog asleep in his lap. The space between the front and rear seats, Josh noted, was crammed with boxes of all shapes and sizes.

He nodded, and gave what he hoped was a reassuring smile.

"I'm Detective Sergeant Josh Whitney. I understand that you and the boy are witnesses to what happened here."

The young woman returned his nod, tried

for a smile, and didn't quite make it. "I'm Casey Farrel, and this is Donnie Patterson." She swallowed.

"Can you tell me what you saw?" Josh prompted gently, taking out his notepad and pen.

She swallowed again, and looked at the boy. "I saw a man drive up next to the dumpster, in a dark van. I saw him take something out of the back of the van, something fairly large, covered with black plastic. He put it on his shoulder, and . . . and then he put it into the dumpster." She hesitated. "Was it a body? Was it the Dumpster Killer?"

Josh swore under his breath. Those damn reporters! "A body was found in the dumpster, yes. Now, you say you got the license number of the van?"

She nodded. "I gave it to one of the uniformed officers."

"Did you notice the make of the van?"

She shook her head. "I'm not good with that, but it didn't seem to be too new. And it was dark, dark blue, or maybe black. It was hard to tell."

"Did you get a good look at the man?"

She took a deep breath, and reached for the boy's hand. The boy, his eyes on her face, seemed to be listening carefully to every word.

"Yes. I saw him very clearly."

"How did that come about?"

"Well, after the man dumped . . . whatever it was into the dumpster, a little boy carrying a dog, Donnie here, stepped out from behind the dumpster, not six feet from the man. The man was startled. He froze for a minute, and then he started toward the boy. The look on his face, the man's that is . . . It looked like he was going to hurt the boy, so I turned my lights on and hit the horn. The man threw his arm up in front of his face, but I saw him pretty clearly before he did." She shivered.

"He had a round face, young, sort of boyish. When I hit the horn again, he got back into the van, and began backing out. Just as he reached the end of the alley, he turned around, and that's when I saw the license plate. That's about it."

Donnie leaned forward, across Casey's lap. "I think he was a bad man. He looked at me real mean."

"And so you got a good look at his face?" said Josh.

The boy nodded. "Yup. It was just like Casey said. Round, like Charlie Brown's face."

"Young?"

Donnie shrugged. "Not *too* old, I guess. He was a grown-up."

Josh exchanged an amused glance with Casey, and the shared moment felt good. It was an effort to turn his attention back to the boy.

"And what were you doing in the alley, Donnie?"

Donnie shrugged again. "Like Casey said. I was looking for Spot."

"And you found him."

"Yup." The boy squirmed. "Casey told you all that stuff already."

Josh smiled. "That's right, she did. But I have to hear what you have to say in your own words. That's the way we do police work. Do you see?"

The boy nodded earnestly. "Yup. I guess so. So you don't get it wrong. Right?"

"Right. So you tell me in your own words what happened."

"Well, like Casey . . . Well, I saw Spot from our window." He pointed upward. "He was sniffing around that dumpster, so I came down to get him. He'd been gone all afternoon, and I knew he was hungry and thirsty."

"And?"

"Well, he was around back of the dumpster, and I picked him up — he was real glad to see me — and when I came around in front of the dumpster there was this wide man, and he looked at me real mean, and I started to get afraid; but then a horn honked real loud, and the man ran to his car and drove away."

"A wide man?" asked Josh.

The boy nodded. "He wasn't real tall, for a grown-up, but he was sort of . . . sort of square." The boy's eyes went to Casey's face as if for verification.

Casey nodded. "He was squarely built."

Josh reached through the window, and roughed the boy's thick hair. "You did good, Pard. Now, do you remember what kind of clothes he was wearing? How was he dressed?"

The boy took a deep breath and let it out. "He had on a coat. One like spies wear. It was . . . It was sandy colored."

Josh looked at Casey. She smiled. "That's right. He was wearing a beige trench coat."

"No hat?"

Donnie shook his head. "No hat."

"The color of his hair?"

Both Casey and Donnie shook their heads. "The lights were real bright," said Donnie. "It was real short."

"Yes," Casey chimed in. "His hair was cut close to his scalp. But it didn't seem very dark."

"And did you see the car, Donnie?"

Donnie shook his head. "I wasn't looking at it real good. I was looking at the man. But it wasn't a regular car. There wasn't no windows in the back."

"Was it a van?"

The boy looked relieved. "Yup. That was it. A van."

"Anything else you remember?"

The boy thought for a moment, then his face lit up. "Yup. I remember. He had a bad scar. From here to here." With his finger Donnie drew a zig-zag line across his right cheek. "Like in the movies."

Josh grimaced. "Horror movies! Miss Farrel, did you notice the scar?"

Casey shook her head. "No. But then you have to remember that I was much further away than Donnie."

Josh nodded, feeling let down. The kid had seemed to be a good witness, but now they were probably getting into the realm of imagination.

"Either of you remember anything else?"

Both Casey and the boy shook their heads.

Josh stood for a moment, staring at them both. He was very curious as to what this attractive young woman had been doing parked in the alley at this hour; but he didn't want to go into this in front of the boy.

Donnie stirred, making a sound of distress. "Oh, oh. Here they come."

"Who, son?" Josh asked.

Donnie pointed through the windshield to a man and a woman advancing on the car. The woman stumbled once and was caught

27

by the man. Even at this distance it was plain that they were intoxicated.

Josh said, "Who are they? Your parents, Donnie?"

Donnie shook his head vehemently, causing the little dog to look up and whimper. "No! My folks are dead. That's my Aunt Edith and . . . and the man who lives with her."

Josh had no time to comment before the pair was upon him. The man, big, blustery, going to fat, said, "You in charge here?"

Josh said mildly, "You might say that, yes."

The man stooped down to look into the car, then went around to the other side, the woman weaving after him. He jerked the driver's side door open. Through the windshield, Josh could see the boy, Donnie, drawing as close to Casey as he could get. His thin arms clutched the little dog to his chest.

The man staggered, then leaned over to bellow into the car, "You come out of there right now, young man!"

Casey involuntarily reached out to put her arm around the boy's narrow shoulders. My God! Was this what the child had to live with? "You don't have to go, Donnie."

"Yes, I do," the boy said miserably.

"That's right, you do," the man snapped, reaching for Donnie's arm. He turned a bloated, red face to Casey. "And you have

28

no right to meddle in this, lady, whoever you are. He's our responsibility."

Casey felt a quick wave of anger. The man was a pig. Why didn't the cop do something?

She turned to see the detective's reaction, and saw with relief that he was already moving around the car.

Before he could reach the couple, however, the big man had pulled Donnie out of the car.

"Oh, for crissake!" the man said, his voice thick. "That damned dog again. That's why you left the apartment. Well, the dog stays here!" Roughly, he snatched the whimpering animal from the boy's arms.

The detective had reached them now; but Casey, hot with indignation, was already sliding across the seat toward the passenger door.

"No! Spot's my dog. He'll starve out here." Donnie's voice was shrill with pain and anger.

"Don't balk me, boy!" The man was raising his meaty hand.

"Don't hit the boy, sir!" As she slid out the door, Casey heard the cop's voice, calm but authoritative.

Casey watched as the fat man spun around, then stopped short, as he became aware of the tall cop's size and presence. He backed off a step.

"But, dogs ain't allowed in our apartment,"

he said in a whining voice. "We'll lose our lease."

The detective seemed to be making a point of turning a page in his notebook. He said briskly, "May I have your names, please?"

The heavy man eyed the notebook askance. "Brent Karson. And this is . . ." He cleared his throat. "Edith."

The detective glanced up. "Edith Karson?"

"No . . . Uh, we're not married."

"My name's Edith Black," the woman said.

Casey felt stiff and sore. She stretched, watching the detective's face. It was a strong face, with a prominent nose, full lips, and dark, thick brows over intelligent gray eyes — cold now as he questioned the beefy man.

"You live in the apartment building here?"

"Yeah. The one directly behind that gate. Apartment 211."

"And you, Miss Black, you're the boy's legal guardian?"

"Well, not exactly. I took the boy in when my sister and her husband were killed." She sniffed, and her expression turned maudlin. "I'm the only one the poor kid has left."

"But we're going to make it legal, soon as we get married," Brent Karson said quickly. "Just haven't gotten around to it yet."

The detective nodded curtly. "I'll need your telephone number, sir."

Karson blinked. "Why do you need that?"

"Donnie here is a crime witness. I'll need a complete signed statement from him, and, depending on the outcome of the case, he may have to testify in court. But it's late now. He should be in bed. I'll come by tomorrow. Depend on it."

The woman cried, "A boy his age testifying? Donnie's only nine!"

"Doesn't matter, he's a witness," Josh said formally. "But, like I said, right now you'd better get him to bed."

Reaching out a big hand, he ruffled Donnie's hair. Casey found herself smiling for the first time that night. The big cop and the small boy made quite a picture. Norman Rockwell, eat your heart out.

With a grunt, Karson took Donnie's hand, and pulled him roughly away. "All right, young man, come along. But the damned dog stays. Put him down!"

"No!" Donnie pulled back, hugging the dog so tightly that it whined, wriggling.

"How many times do I have to tell you? We can't keep a dog in the apartment; you damned well know that. Now, don't be stubborn." Karson looked at the detective as if appealing for help.

The detective pulled at his nose, said, "I live in my own house, Donnie. How about

31

I keep Spot for you for a few days, just until we can decide what to do about him? You can come and visit him if you want, any time."

Donnie looked from the glowering Karson to the detective and back again. He said reluctantly, "Okay, but you'll take care of him and feed him good?"

"Cross my heart," the detective said solemnly, making a cross with a long forefinger over his heart. "Depend on it."

Obviously still reluctant, Donnie held the dog out. The detective accepted the animal gingerly, reminding Casey of a man holding a baby for the first time.

Karson tugged at Donnie's hand. "Come on, young man."

Donnie, with a quick movement, pulled away. "I got to say good-bye to Casey."

As Karson lunged toward him, he added, "She saved me from the man."

Karson stopped, obviously not happy but unwilling to appear too much the villain.

Casey squatted down as Donnie trotted up, so that she would be on his level. With open spontaneity, Donnie threw his arms around her neck and pressed his smooth, faintly sweaty cheek to hers. Experiencing an advanced case of the Warm Fuzzies, Casey hugged him back.

"Thanks, Casey," he said, then drew his

cheek from hers to look into her eyes. "Will you come see me?"

She pulled him close again. "I sure hope so. I'll do my best."

Satisfied, the boy grinned, and trotted back to his aunt and her boyfriend. As she watched the trio go through the gate, she felt a twinge of conscience. Should she have told the boy that? Already fond of him, she wanted to see him again; but, in her circumstances, would it be possible?

"Shit!" said the man next to her.

Startled, she looked up. "What did you say?"

The detective flushed. "Oh, sorry! I was just wondering why I agreed to this." He lifted the little dog, who looked unhappy. "I don't even like dogs. And one named Spot, of all things."

Casey could not suppress a smile. "Could it be that the big, tough detective has a — excuse the expression — soft *spot* for tow-headed little boys?"

A smile quirked the corners of the big man's very attractive mouth. "The kid is appealing, isn't he? He gets to you; and then to see him with those two . . ."

He shook his head. "It's a damn shame!"

Casey nodded, beginning to feel uneasy now that she and the officer were alone. "Well, is that all you need from me? Can I go now?"

He looked at her, she thought, rather strangely. "There are a few more things I need to know," he said, "like your address. And I'll need a signed copy of your statement, but you can do that tomorrow down at the station."

There was a long pause, as Casey's heart sank to the bottom of her stomach. For a while, caught up in the drama of events, she had felt like a normal person. Now, it was back-to-reality time.

She gave a deep sigh, then looked the tall detective straight in the eye. "I guess you already know my address, don't you?"

He shrugged. "Well, I wouldn't be a very good detective, if I didn't have a pretty good idea. Attractive young women don't usually sit in parked cars in dark alleys at midnight; and they don't usually go around with what looks like all of their personal belongings stashed in their cars. You don't have a place to stay, right?"

His look was not accusing, or judgmental; in fact he looked sympathetic; and Casey felt an unexpected feeling of relief. "Right," she said. "I lost my apartment last week, and I've been sleeping in my car. Is that breaking the law?"

"Nothing that I'll run you in for. Look, it's

already after two. I have a few more things to do here, and then maybe we could have some breakfast. There's an all-night coffee shop a few blocks up the street."

Casey's mouth filled with saliva. She had eaten very little yesterday, hoarding what few dollars she had left. Her hunger warred with her reluctance to accept charity.

As though reading her reservations, Josh said, "Look. No strings attached, and it's not charity. I need to talk to you some more, and I'm sure the coffee shop will be more comfortable than the station. Okay? And maybe until then you could keep the dog with you."

The man was likable, no doubt about it. And she was starving. "That sounds good, Detective."

He threw up his hands. "Josh, please!"

She smiled and reached for Spot. "Okay, Josh, I'll wait for you. There's no place I have to be in a hurry."

CHAPTER THREE

It was three o'clock and still dark when Casey and Josh entered the diner. At that hour there were only a half-dozen people in the place, and they were able to get a relatively isolated booth in the back.

As the waitress handed them menus, Josh told Casey to order whatever she wanted. Throwing delicacy aside, Casey ordered orange juice, coffee, ham, eggs, and a short stack of pancakes. Josh ordered the same.

As they sipped coffee while waiting for their orders, Casey said, "Did you learn anything more?"

"Nothing that will help," he said glumly. "This guy, whoever the hell he is, is one smart bastard. He's left no clues behind at any of the scenes. My big hope is that license number you came up with."

"Then you think the three murders are connected. That the man I saw was the Dumpster Killer?"

Josh grimaced. "That's what the newspapers are calling him, and yes, I think all three murders were committed by the same man. The brass isn't quite ready to agree with me, though after tonight I think they'll have difficulty maintaining that position. The MO is the same, the scene the same. We have a pattern killer on our hands. Depend on it."

"A serial killer, you mean?"

He shrugged. "Whatever. The media is in love with that phrase. Two killings by the same perp and they trumpet serial killer. I prefer pattern killer. This one tonight follows the same pattern as the first two. All women, all killed the same way."

Casey shivered, said softly, "The Soul Eater."

He stared. "What?"

"The Soul Eater. It's something my grandmother used to say."

Josh shook his head. "Catchy. Sounds like the bogeyman. Was she from the old country or something?"

Casey smiled. "Not exactly. She was pure-blooded Hopi, born on the reservation."

He looked at her through narrowed eyes. "Funny, you don't look Hopi," he said, deadpan.

For a moment, she tensed, then seeing that he was teasing, smiled. "Well, this —" she lifted her chin — "is what a half-Hopi looks

37

like. My pop was Irish, which explains the Farrel."

"Good mixture. But what about this Soul Eater?"

"Well, that comes from Hopi legend. In Hopi witchcraft witches or sorcerers are called *powaqa*. There are four classes of *powaqa*, and the fourth class, the most evil of all, live on the lives of others. They must cause the deaths of others, most often relatives, to prolong their own lives. The death of a female gives them four years, the death of a male two years. Grandmother used to call them 'Soul Eaters' in English."

"Well, if that's the case here, our killer has recently added twelve years to his life." He stared at her intently. "Well, now I know where you got those mysterious, dark eyes, Casey Farrel."

She grinned. "Casey N. Farrel, if you please."

"N? I'm almost afraid to ask."

"N for Nesseehongneum, my Hopi name."

"My God, that's a mouthful!"

"Well, if you think that's bad, try the English translation, 'One Who Carries a Flower on the Day of the Ceremony.' "

"It has a very poetic ring to it."

At that moment the waitress came with their food, and Casey turned her full attention to it. It smelled delicious. Josh ate slowly, his brow furrowed, his gaze on his food. Casey was finished long before he was.

When the waitress came with coffee refills, Josh looked up with a start. After she had poured and left, he said, "Sorry. I guess I'm not very good company. I've been thinking about this damned case."

"It's okay. As you can see, I was too busy to notice." She indicated her clean plate.

He smiled sympathetically. "Meals few and far between."

"You might say that. I'm not completely broke, but I'm close enough to it not to make much difference. I've been hanging on to what few dollars I have left, in case of an emergency."

He laughed lightly. "I should think that going hungry could be classified as an emergency."

"Well, it would probably have reached that state in a day or two. Thanks very much for the meal."

"It was my pleasure. And please call me Josh. The name's really Joshua, but no one but my mother has ever called me that."

"Okay, Josh. I like the name Joshua, though. It has such a biblical ring to it."

"Yeah, like the battle of Jericho, I know. My mother says that there has been a Joshua in her family going back a hundred years or more."

He looked at her intently. "Want to tell me what happened to you?"

"It's not really very interesting, or, I suppose, that unusual. I was born and raised in Flagstaff, Arizona, and attended Northern Arizona University there. My mother died when I was fifteen. My father was a pilot. The last few years of his life he flew tourists over the Grand Canyon. My last year at college, his plane crashed into the canyon. He was killed.

"After I graduated, I felt I had to get away, so I went to L.A., Beverly Hills, to be exact. I got a job with a large private investigation agency, and for a while things were fine. Then the owner retired, and his son took over . . ."

She hesitated for a moment, remembering the brief affair with her new boss, her pregnancy, his refusal to accept responsibility, and the miscarriage, which had sent her fleeing back to Arizona.

She gave a start as Josh said, "Were you an investigator?"

"Not really. Oh, I helped on a few cases, but it was mostly secretarial. I might have become an investigator in time, if I had stayed around. I have sort of a flair for it."

"Why didn't you, stay around, that is?"

"The recession hit, business got slow, and

I . . . Well, I didn't get along well with the boss's son, and so I was one of the first to be laid off," she lied. "I couldn't find another job right away, so I came back to Arizona, but to Phoenix, not Flagstaff. Too many sad memories there."

"But surely, if you were good enough to hold down a job with a detective agency in L.A. you should catch on with one here."

She sighed. "You'd think so, wouldn't you? But things are tough here too. All the agencies are laying off, not hiring. Also, the SOB in L.A. not only refused to give me a recommendation, but said that my work wasn't up to par, that I wasn't reliable. And that was my only work experience."

A spark flashed in Josh's gray eyes. "A prime asshole, wasn't he?"

She nodded. "Another thing I soon found out after I was locked out of my apartment here, I couldn't even fill out a job application without a permanent address. General Delivery just doesn't cut it."

"Couldn't you use a friend's address?"

"I haven't been in Phoenix long enough to make friends, and even if I had, I wouldn't want them to know about my situation. It's humiliating!"

He nodded. "Yes, I can see that it would be. Look, I'm not promising anything, so

41

don't get your hopes up, but maybe I can help. The Governor owes me a favor, and he's in the process of forming a new task force with the aim of looking into areas of trouble, including crime. The task force's purpose will be strictly investigative, with no power to prosecute, only to suggest solutions. When crime areas are investigated, all evidence will be turned over to city or state officials to prosecute. One area I know they will be investigating is that of the street people." He smiled faintly. "You should have a leg-up there."

She looked at him curiously. "Why would you do that for someone you just met, Josh? Not that I don't appreciate it, but . . ."

Josh, ignoring her interruption, said briskly, "I think I can swing it for you, but it may take a couple of weeks. Bureaucracy moves at a snail's pace. Meanwhile, I have a temporary solution for you. I have a house on the north edge of Phoenix. It has two bedrooms. You are more than welcome to occupy one of them."

Casey's cheeks reddened. "Wait just a darned minute here. What are you suggesting?"

Josh held his hands up in front of his face. "Goddamn, but you're thorny. Let me finish, before you get indignant. No strings attached. You need a place to stay for a while, and I

42

happen to have an unused bedroom. If you're thinking this is a come-on, disabuse yourself of that thought, lady. The room has a lock you can use."

She looked at him searchingly. "From the size of you, you could break down a door without even trying."

Now it was his turn to huff. "Look, I've never been so hard up that I have to force a woman, any woman. Depend on it. I was just trying to do something nice. I see so much shit. . . . Shit. Forget it, if you aren't interested, you just have to say no."

"Sorry. It's just that I'm a little rattled just now, and this is the first time anybody has offered to do something nice for me in a long time. By the way, is there a Mrs. Whitney?"

"Used to be. She split. The usual cop disease, divorce. I should have known better. She went back east a year ago. She didn't want anything from me, left me the house." Bitterness soured his voice. "Sweet of her, wasn't it?"

"No children?"

"No. Thank God for small favors. Not that I don't like kids, I do; but it would have made it all the harder."

"And so, explain to me why you are offering to do this for me."

"Not because of your bod, be sure."

43

She bristled. "What's wrong with my bod?"

He sighed. "Give me a break, will you? The inconsistency of women! A minute ago you thought that's why I offered to let you stay with me, and you were insulted."

Casey could not hold back a smile. "So, I was wrong about that, maybe. You still haven't given me an answer."

"Out of the goodness of my heart?" He cocked an eyebrow at her. "Believe that?"

"I'm not sure."

He leaned toward her. "Look. You're a witness, maybe a very important one, if and when we catch this guy. I need to know where you are at all times. How could I get in touch with you, no permanent address, sleeping in alleys in your vehicle? This way I'll know where you are."

Casey grinned "Now, that I can believe. Under those conditions, I gratefully accept your kind and generous offer."

Josh blinked, taken aback by her sudden agreement. Then he grinned slowly. "Make your mind up quick when you finally get around to it, don't you? I like that in a woman."

"Thank you, Detective," she said in a dry voice. A sudden buzzing sound caused her to jump. "What was *that?*"

He was reaching into his pocket. "My

beeper. I have to call in." He slid out of the booth. "Don't go away. I'll be right back."

Casey was facing toward the front of the coffee shop where two pay phones were visible. Sipping coffee, she watched as Josh dropped a coin in one of the phones and punched out a number. She wondered if she should have told him the truth about why she had fled Los Angeles. Still, he was little more than a stranger, why bare her soul to him?

His call was brief, and in a few minutes he was striding back toward the booth. There was a spring to his step, and his face was alight, the gray look of fatigue gone.

He looked down at her. "You finished?"

She nodded.

"That was the precinct. They've caught the scumbag you saw driving the van. I have to get downtown. Here . . ." He took a notebook from his pocket, tore out a page, and drew a quick sketch. "This is my address and directions how to get there. You drive on out to the house, and I'll catch a cab downtown. And take care of Donnie's dog, okay? There's some hamburger in the fridge. I'll bring home some dog food."

Casey took the page without looking at it. "You're going to trust me, a complete stranger, to go into your house alone?"

He grinned crookedly. "There's not much

45

of value there to steal. Besides, if I can't trust you alone in my house, how can I trust you as a witness?"

She glanced down at the notebook page. "What time will you be home?"

"That's a question you never ask a cop, Casey." He cleared his throat with a look of embarrassment. "You'll know which bedroom is mine and which is the guest bedroom. My bed isn't made up."

He took a key ring from his pocket, removed one key, and handed it to her. "The fridge is full of beer and TV dinners, in case you get hungry or thirsty. I'll see you later."

CHAPTER FOUR

Josh was closeted with an Assistant DA, Michael Bannerman. It wasn't yet eight o'clock, and Bannerman was grumpy about being rousted out so early. But he was young, ambitious as hell, and a strict letter-of-the-law man — a little too rigid in that respect to suit Josh.

Bannerman peered out at Josh from under a blonde cowlick, narrow green eyes troubled. "I don't know, Detective Whitney. Our case isn't exactly what I'd call ironclad . . ."

"After all the times we've worked together, it's still Detective Whitney?"

Bannerman sighed. "I think that it's better to keep a distance between a prosecutor and the officers working a case, but okay, Josh it is. I'm still not all that happy with the case."

"I don't see it. For starters, we have an eyewitness to the scumbag dumping the body."

"But not to the actual commission of the crime. Besides, you should know what value eyewitnesses have in court. One will say green, the other red. And your other witness, Josh, is a nine-year-old boy! As for your witness seeing this guy dumping a body, he claims it was only a bag of trash he was putting into the dumpster."

"The main witness is an adult, and she gave us the license number which helped us catch this guy."

Bannerman gestured. "One of the homeless, a street person."

Josh had difficulty containing his irritation. From experience, he knew that Bannerman was playing devil's advocate, but still . . .

He said doggedly, "Homeless she may be, but it's only temporary. It really isn't her fault. She's respectable."

"They all say that, Josh. A wino panhandling you for the price of a bottle will swear up, down and sideways that it's no fault of his that he's on the street."

"Well, in this case it happens to be true. And the perp is claiming he was dumping his garbage?" Josh snorted. "Come on, Michael!"

Bannerman shrugged. "That's his story."

"What else is he saying? Where is he?"

"He's being interrogated. And he's saying very little."

"Denying everything, of course."

"Innocent as a babe. Being hassled by the cops. The whole nine yards. There's a shyster with him now. He wouldn't say a word until we got him a lawyer."

"That's par for the course. Find anything on him or in the van that ties him into the killings?"

"Nothing on him and the van is presently being gone over inch by inch. If they've found anything, I haven't been told yet."

"How about the van? Stolen, or is it his?"

"It's registered to him."

"Brazen sonofabitch, isn't he? Doing the killings using his own vehicle."

"If he's the one."

"Oh, he's the one. I have a feeling."

"Unfortunately, Josh," Bannerman said dryly, "a jury doesn't often convict a defendant on the feelings of a cop."

"We'll find enough to nail him, Michael. Depend on it."

"I hope so. I want this guy as badly as you do."

Josh shoved his chair back. "I'll drop down to the interrogation room and see how it's coming."

When Josh got his first look at the suspect through the one-way mirror in the room adjoining the interrogation room, he felt a stab of dismay. There was no scar visible on the suspect's round, baby face. Of course, Donnie could have mistaken a shadow for a scar. Or he could have superimposed a scar on the suspect's face from some horror movie he had seen on the tube. A nine-year-old had an active imagination.

The suspect looked in no way threatening. His skin was as smooth and pink as a baby's bottom, and he wore a look of pure innocence. His eyes were brown, guileless; and his brown hair was cut short. Only his hands gave him away. They were large and powerful. In them he held a tennis ball, transferring it from one hand to the other, squeezing it rhythmically.

Probably a real basket case, a psycho, Josh thought. Probably his attorney would plead him insane, and he'd get off with a few years in a nut house.

But it was his job to nail the scumbag, place him on trial before a judge and jury. Then it would be out of his hands. That was all that was expected of him.

Josh's glance went to the man beside the suspect. He recognized him, Kirk Sanders, a sleazy defense attorney. He was sleek, overweight, with the eyes of a ferret, sweating like a pig. But he was a slick one. Sanders knew every trick in the book, and wasn't above inventing a few of his own. He cared very little for the welfare of his clients. His chief interest in a case revolved around two things — how much he could squeeze out of the poor sucker, and how much notoriety he could gain for himself. Josh concluded that Sanders may have finally found a case that could fatten his reputation if he could win an acquittal, or even a successful insanity plea. The Dumpster Killer was sure-fire, bound to garner reams of juicy publicity.

Josh shook his head and left the room. In the hall, he lightly rapped on the door of the interrogation room with his knuckles. In a moment the door cracked, and the officer who had been questioning the suspect peered out.

"Oh, Josh! Hi!" The officer, Bob Parsons, was one of the detectives assigned to Josh's squad in the hunt for the Dumpster Killer.

"How's it going, Bob?"

Bob Parsons sighed. "Not too good. I didn't have much of a shot at the suspect before that sleazeball Sanders showed. And he clammed up until Sanders came hustling in. Now Sanders keeps butting in almost every time I ask a question."

"What's the perp's name?"

"Raymond Tibbets."

"Is there a sheet on him?"

"Clean as a whistle, not even a traffic ticket."

"You know that we have a witness saw him

dumping the body."

"Tibbets claims he wasn't dumping any body. Says he was dumping a bag of trash into the dumpster."

"I know. Bannerman told me. Where does he live?"

"He has an apartment in Glendale."

Josh laughed harshly. "That's at least five miles away from that particular dumpster! He must have driven past fifty dumpsters to get to that one. It won't wash, Bob."

"I asked him about that. He says he was just out driving around, enjoying the evening, in no hurry to dump the sack of trash."

"If he did drop off a bag of trash, and of course he damned well didn't, then there has to be an item or two in that bag to identify it as his."

"Maybe, maybe not."

"Has the van been gone over yet?"

"They just finished a bit ago."

"Find anything?"

"A pair of those throw-away gloves. They're at the lab now, but I doubt they'll show anything. And a bag of large plastic bags was also found, with several gone. The bag the victim was stuffed in is of the same type, but I don't think there is any way to prove it came from the same box. They're a popular brand. Probably half the city uses them."

"Who arrested him?"

"A uniform on patrol. Nice young guy, Ken Waters. According to his story, he spotted the suspect's van driving forty-five in a thirty-five mile zone. Then the suspect apparently saw the cruiser behind him and slowed down to well under the limit. Waters tailed him for a few blocks, then pulled him over. He questioned him, thought he acted suspicious, and called for backup. When another patrol car arrived they tossed the van."

"For no more reason than probable cause? Waters didn't know at the time that there was an APB out on the van?"

"That's the way I understand it. The APB came in a few minutes later."

Josh shook his head. "Well, the main thing at the moment is that we got him. I'll go in and have a few words with the guy."

"Want me to go in with you? Play good guy, bad guy?"

"No, you must have been at it for a spell. You're probably sick of the guy by now. I'm going to come on to him nice and easy, see what I can get." He gripped Parsons's shoulder. "Go have some breakfast. You probably missed it."

"You're right about that."

Josh opened the door to the interrogation room and went in, careful to lock it after him.

Tibbets and Sanders, who'd had their heads together, looked up with a start.

"When are you going to release my client?" Sanders demanded in a blustery voice.

"All in good time, Counselor," Josh said amiably. "You know the menu. Questions, questions." He showed his badge to Tibbets. "I'm Detective Sergeant Josh Whitney, Ray. I have a few questions."

"I've had it up to here with questions," Tibbets said.

"I'm sure you have, Ray; but there's a routine that has to be followed." Josh took the other hard chair in the room, turned it around, straddled it, and crossed his arms over the back. "I'm a little curious about something, Ray. You told the other officer that the bag you threw into the dumpster contained trash from your place. Why that particular dumpster? It's at least a half-hour drive from your address. Surely you must have passed any number of dumpsters on the way."

"I told the other cop that."

"Suppose you tell me." Josh kept his voice soft, conversational, one friend to another. "You know how it is with cops, questions, questions."

Tibbets shrugged. "I was just out driving around. Then, as I turned back toward home, I suddenly remembered the bag of trash, so

I stopped off to dump it."

"In an alley a block long? How did you even know that there was a dumpster there?"

"Always a dumpster in an alley behind apartment buildings."

"You seem to know an awful lot about dumpsters. You know what the press are calling this killer? The Dumpster Killer."

Sanders leaned forward belligerently. "Detective, you're out of line here!"

Josh waved a hand at him. "Ray, let's go back a little. You said that you were just driving around. Where, exactly? Downtown? Van Buren?"

Tibbets moved the tennis ball from his right hand to his left, squeezing. "I was on Van Buren, sure."

"Looking for hookers, maybe?"

Sanders said quickly, "You don't have to answer that, Ray."

"I don't mind, Mr. Sanders. What if I was? Nothing wrong with that, is there?"

Josh said, "It's a crime if you pick one up and have sex with her. Do you make a habit of that?"

"Maybe. That's what they're there for, ain't it?" His eyes came alive for an instant, daring Josh to make something of his statement.

Josh stared into those eyes, trying to peer into the soul of the man. He saw a certain arrogance there. Years of homicide experience had taught Josh that a man who killed more than once, a pattern killer, had a strong belief in his own cleverness, his invincibility. This was even more true if the man was a sociopath, which Josh believed this one to be.

He said casually, "This Dumpster Killer, whoever he is, is stupid, you know. Depend on it."

A spark of anger flickered in Tibbets's eyes, and Josh felt a pulse of triumph — he had struck a nerve.

Tibbets said, "Seems to me he ain't all that stupid, *whoever* he is. You cops ain't caught him yet."

Sanders stirred uneasily. "Ray . . ."

Both men ignored him.

Josh said, "Maybe, maybe not. Time will tell." Abruptly, he changed direction. "What do you do for a living, Ray?"

"I repair things. TVs, TV satellite dishes, radios, computers, things like that."

"Free-lance?"

"Yeah."

"Make a good living at it?"

"Yeah, a very good living," Tibbets said with a touch of pride. "I've built up a good rep. I get a lot of repeat business."

"Leaves you pretty much on your own, doesn't it? No one looking over your shoulder or telling you what to do."

"I like it that way. Don't like taking orders from some asshole who doesn't know as much as I do."

"I can see how a man might feel that way. Lots of free time, come and go as you please."

"Anything wrong in that?"

"Guess not." Josh changed direction again. "A pair of surgeon's gloves was found in your van. Use them in your business?"

Tibbets again switched the tennis ball, his glance sliding away. "Sometimes. Sometimes I have to get into the guts of whatever I'm working on. Delicate work. Don't want to leave dust or oil inside."

"Right," Josh said dryly. "You always carry a box of plastic bags in your van?"

"Sure. They come in handy."

Josh fixed his gaze on Tibbets's eyes. He had always been confident that he could tell by the eyes if a suspect was lying or not. "Ray, did you kill those women? Did you kill that girl last night, then drop her body into the dumpster?"

As Tibbets started to change the tennis ball to his other hand, Josh reached quickly across the table and plucked it out of the other man's grip. "Well, Ray, did you?"

Sanders said, "Don't answer that, Ray!"

"Why not?" Tibbets waved his hand at his

attorney, his gaze locked with Josh's. "I didn't kill anyone, and you can't prove that I did."

Josh felt a stab of disappointment. Tibbets's eyes were blank again, without any expression whatsoever; and although Josh was convinced that the man was lying, there was nothing in his eyes that gave the lie to his words.

"That trash bag you claim you dumped, Ray, what was in it?"

Tibbets shrugged. "Cans, like coke and beer, frozen dinner cartons, shit like that."

"No old bills, old envelopes with your name and address on them? Nothing like that."

"Nope." Tibbets's grin held a touch of insolence. "I keep things like that for at least a year, sometimes more."

"Commendable, I'm sure," Josh said. He studied the suspect for a bit in silence. Tibbets returned his stare impassively, for a moment, then a crafty look spread over his features. As he watched the change, Josh felt himself becoming annoyed. Somehow the arrogance of this kind of man always got to him. The smug self-satisfaction was a kind of insult.

"Look," said Tibbets, "would it help if I took a lie detector test? I have nothing to hide."

Josh, his eyes narrowed, looked back at Tibbets's arrogant face, and fought back a strong desire to punch it.

"You know that lie detector tests are inadmissible as evidence in court," he said.

Tibbets shrugged. "Yeah, I've heard that. But I thought it might, you know, set your mind at rest. Then you could get back to looking for the *real* killer."

Sanders leaned forward. "I'd strongly advise against it," he said.

Josh didn't respond. He knew that some people, psychopaths in particular, could fool any lie detector invented. He suspected that Tibbets was one of those people. Surely he must have taken such a test before, to be so certain of the results.

He said, "I appreciate the gesture, Tibbets, but since the results are not admissible, such a test would do neither of us any good."

A sneer twisted Tibbets's rather full lips. "You mean it won't do *you* any good, because I would come out clean as a whistle. Well, I *insist* on it."

He turned to Sanders, who was looking worried. "I can do that, can't I?"

Slowly, Sanders nodded. "But I advise against it."

Tibbets shrugged. "I'd feel better if I did. It would show that I'm clean."

Josh sighed. "Okay, I'll set it up." He got to his feet.

Sanders said, "*Then* will you release my client?"

"Release him? Oh, no. I'm booking him for the murder of that young woman," Josh said. "Depend on it, Counselor."

CHAPTER FIVE

Casey found Josh's small house without difficulty. It hung over the edge of a deep wash in northeast Phoenix, a cantilevered, wooden building. She let herself in with his key as Spot hurried in ahead of her, his paws scratching for purchase on the hardwood floor.

The small living room was comfortably furnished. There was a large fireplace against one wall, blackened, showing some use. Another wall was lined with bookcases overflowing with books. The remaining wall was all glass, facing north, providing a spectacular view of the desert, and the mountains brooding in the distance. There were only a few other houses along the street, the nearest a good hundred yards away.

The kitchen, facing east, had a sliding glass door that opened onto a wide, wooden deck. The sun was just coming up as Casey stepped out onto the deck and crossed to the railing. The deck jutted out over the wash, the sloping ground about ten feet below. Already the air was warm. In Phoenix in June the temperature during the day was often close to the hundred degree mark.

Leaning on the railing, Casey looked down into the wash. As she did so, movement caught her eye. A cold chill rippled the flesh along her spine as she saw the large rattlesnake moving sinuously along the bank. Quickly she stepped back. She was absolutely terrified of snakes, even the non-poisonous variety.

Shuddering, she retreated inside, closing the glass doors behind her.

In the small kitchen she opened the refrigerator and rummaged through it. She smiled at the typical bachelor collection of food. The freezer was crammed with TV dinners, but in the meat tray she found odds and ends of leftovers: cold meats; cheeses; a partially eaten pork chop; and the remains of a T-bone steak.

She looked through the dish cupboards for a saucer, put the pork chop and the steak on it, and put it down on the floor for Spot, who wagged his short tail frantically, and set to with a vengeance. Naturally, he had both bones on the floor within a few minutes.

Casey left him to it, and set out to explore the rest of the house. Besides the living room and kitchen, there was a dining nook; and off a short hallway, two bedrooms, with a bathroom in between. A small laundry room completed the layout.

Casey was surprised to find the place so neat. Even Josh's bedroom, with its unmade bed, was reasonably tidy; however, it seemed to her that the linen on the bed was in need of changing. She found fresh linen in a hall closet, stripped the bed, and made it with clean sheets and pillow cases.

While she was doing this, she thought longingly of the bathroom. For the past few weeks she had been forced to make do with hurried sponge baths in service stations and restaurants, where she had always been afraid of interruption.

When she was finished with the bed, she went into the bathroom. There was a tub with a shower. Her first thought was a quick shower, but the temptation of a long soak in the tub was too much. She undressed while she ran a hot tub, locked the door in case Josh should return, and sank into the steaming water with a luxurious sigh.

She remained in the tub until the water was almost cool and Spot began to scratch at the door. Sighing with pleasure, she got out of the tub, dried herself briskly, and put on her bathrobe. She felt better than she had in weeks. She had early on decided that the lack of bathing facilities was the worst feature about being a homeless person, even worse than hunger.

Opening the door, she gazed down into the limpid brown eyes of the dog. "What's the problem, kiddo? Still hungry?"

With the dog following, she returned to the kitchen where she found the steak and chop bones gnawed clean, but Spot didn't seem interested in food. He led her to the front door, where he stood looking back over his shoulder expectantly.

"What is it, boy? Oh . . . You need a walk, right?"

She looked down at her robe and slippers. She didn't want to get dressed again, not now. She recalled that the house was relatively isolated. "Okay, kiddo. But we can't go far, not with me in my robe, so do your business fast, okay?"

She opened the door and the dog scampered out of the house. She followed as far as the front stoop. Belatedly, she thought of some kind of leash. If the dog got away from her, Donnie would be desolated.

She took two steps after the animal, then stopped as she remembered the rattlesnake. There was no way she was going out there.

But she found that she needn't have worried. Spot didn't go far, and after performing his chore he came trotting back to squat at her feet, looking up into her face, tongue out, tail thumping the ground so hard that the dust flew.

Casey shooed him back into the house. He followed her all the way down to the guest bedroom. When she shucked the robe and slippers and got into the bed, Spot jumped up and joined her, snuggling down next to her legs.

"I don't know as Josh will much care for you sleeping on this bed, kiddo."

She scrubbed his ears and he gave a soft grunt of appreciation. He was a cute little creature. She considered chasing him out and closing the door, but the effort involved was too much to contemplate. The feel of a real bed after so long was too delicious to leave it even for a moment. She was asleep the moment that the thought was completed.

She awoke slowly to the aroma of pungent coffee. Without opening her eyes she could feel the heat of the sun warm on her face, and knew that it was late afternoon.

Josh's voice said, "I know that you must have been tired, but are you going to sleep the clock around?"

"I just might, now that you mention it," she said with a smile in her voice.

She opened her eyes to see him looming over

65

her. Again she was struck by just how big a man he was. There was a cup of steaming coffee in his hand, and he wore a smile; yet his face was gray with fatigue and stubbled with whiskers.

She sat up. "Josh . . . Haven't you been to bed yet?"

"Nope."

"You do put in long hours. How about food?"

He cocked his head, a look of almost comical surprise spreading across his features. "Come to think of it, not since we had breakfast together early this morning."

Casey noticed that Spot was now sprawled across the robe where she had tossed it across the foot of the bed. Holding the sheet up to her neck, she reached down to nudge him. "Off, kiddo!" The dog gave her a wounded look, and jumped down. She scooped up the robe.

Josh watched the dog trot out of the room. He grinned lopsidedly. "Looks like you two have become fast friends."

She pulled the robe on over her shoulders, saying defensively, "I hope you don't mind him sleeping on the bed. I didn't have the heart to tell him no."

"I don't mind, if you don't." His grin widened. "I could say that worse have probably slept on that bed."

"I don't think I want to go in to that." She slipped out of bed, belting the robe. "Why don't you take a shower, shave, whatever; and I'll have something to eat ready for you when you're done?"

"You a good cook?"

"Any idiot can cook bacon and eggs, and I noticed that you have those items, along with about every TV dinner under the sun."

"Oh, I stopped off at the market on the way home and picked up a few things. Lots of dog food, plus a couple of humongous steaks, potatoes, things like that."

"I think I can manage to cook a steak."

"There's a barbecue out on the deck. You can use that. You can cook the potatoes in the microwave."

"How do you like your steak?"

"Just singed on the outside." He started out of the room, and then stopped. "Oh, if you want a drink, you'll find the makings in the cabinet above the sink. I have pretty much everything."

"What do you like? I can have it ready for you when you finish in the bathroom." She grinned slyly at him. "Proper little house-wife, aren't I? Drink and dinner waiting for hubby after he comes home from the wars."

"Sounds good." He returned the grin. "I'd

like a very dry martini. Gin. On the rocks."

"A martini!" She stared. "I've never made one. I don't even know *how* to make one."

"I do. It's simple. You just pour a couple of jiggers of gin over ice cubes, add a couple of drops of vermouth, stir well, and stick it into the freezer until I'm ready for it. There are those who insist that martinis should be shaken not stirred, as stirring is supposed to 'bruise the gin'; however, I do not put credence in that theory."

Casey raised her right eyebrow, a trick she had been perfecting since high school. "Well, then stirred it shall be, sir." She saluted smartly, as he gave her a benign nod, and left the room.

As she dressed, she was conscious of feeling *very* well indeed. It had been a long time since she had felt this hopeful and this expectant. She tried to tell herself that it was simply the fact that she was well fed, rested and clean, but she knew that a good portion of her elation came from being around Josh. He was a *very* attractive man. However, she didn't want to dwell on this thought just now. In her present situation, she was in no position to get romantically involved. She would just take it day by day, as she had been doing.

In the kitchen, she found that Josh had put the groceries away, except for the steaks and the potatoes, which were sitting on the counter. Spot had followed her into the kitchen, and now sat looking up at her hopefully, tail thumping the floor.

"Okay, kiddo. First things first, right?"

Opening a can of the dog food, she put half the contents into a bowl and set it down on the kitchen floor. Spot squatted beside the bowl and dug in happily.

Casey scrubbed two of the potatoes, prepared the steaks, and fired up the gas barbecue. While the barbecue was heating, she mixed herself a gin and tonic, made Josh's martini, then put it into the freezer. She found that Josh had bought fresh vegetables for a salad, which she prepared. By that time Spot had finished his food and was curled up in one corner of the kitchen, sound asleep. Casey put the potatoes in the microwave and, carrying the remains of her drink, she went out onto the deck and started the steaks.

As she was turning them, Josh came out with his martini. His tumble of dark hair was still wet from his shower, and was slicked down on his skull. He had put on faded jeans and a T-shirt with the logo "Go, Cardinals" printed across the front. He was barefoot.

He took a sip of the martini. With a pleased smile he nodded and sniffed appreciatively at the odor of cooking meat. "The steak smells wonderful, and the martini is perfect. In my opinion you'd make a great housewife to come home to."

Casey grimaced. "Now, don't go off in that direction, Detective. I'm not planning on becoming a housewife, thank you very much."

"I wasn't going in any particular direction, just trying to pay you a compliment, in my clumsy fashion."

He cocked his head to one side. "But since we're on the subject, why not? Seems to me that marriage might be the solution to your problems." He grinned. "Get you off the streets, anyway."

She flashed him an angry look, then laughed slightly. "You've got a weird sense of humor, you know that?"

He shrugged. "Takes a weird sense of humor to survive as a homicide cop."

"Why don't you do something useful, like setting the table? The steaks are about done, and the potatoes should be, too."

"Right." He saluted her with his glass, finished the drink, and went back inside.

When Casey came in with the steaks on a platter, the table was set for two, and Josh was making himself another martini. "You want a taste?"

She made a face. "No, thanks!"

When they were seated and had begun eating, Casey said, "You know, I saw a rattle-snake from your deck this morning. Are there many of them around?"

"A few. But they won't bother you if you don't bother them."

"I have a horror of snakes, always have had." She shivered, then gave a strained laugh. "It's ironic, I suppose, considering that my family belongs to the Snake Clan."

Josh glanced up from his plate. "You told me that both your parents and grandparents are dead. Do you have any relatives living?"

"Just my uncle, Claude Pentiwa, my mother's brother, and his children. They live on the reservation, but I don't see much of them. Uncle Claude didn't approve of my mother marrying white."

She took a sip of water. "Enough of that. How did it go today? Is this guy they caught the killer?"

Josh finished chewing a bite of steak, nodding. "I'm convinced of it. He'll come up for his bail hearing tomorrow, but I'm sure that under the circumstances, Bannerman — that's the Assistant DA who'll be handling the case — will be able to convince the judge to deny bail."

"Well, I should hope so. A man who kills like that certainly shouldn't be running loose on the streets!"

"A nasty piece of work, a real scumbag." Josh frowned.

"One thing bothers me, though. Donnie said that the man he saw had a jagged scar on his face. This guy has no such scar. You didn't see anything like that?"

Casey shook her head. "No, but then I was too far away to see that clearly. It could have been a shadow across his face, and Donnie just took it for a scar."

"I thought of that. Or it could just be the kid's overactive imagination."

"And you have to remember that we were both under a bit of stress right then."

"There's that," Josh said with a nod.

"I guess now that you've caught the killer, you'll want me to clear out of here."

An expression of surprise crossed Josh's face, and Casey realized that she had caught him unaware.

He hesitated a moment before answering. "Not at all. You'll be needed as a witness at his trial. God knows when that will be. You should stay until that's over. There will be a preliminary hearing shortly, and you'll be needed for that."

He looked at her intently. "In fact, you can stay here as long as you like. How can you find a place to live without money or a job? Stay here until you get your life in order."

Casey was silent for a moment. She was deeply touched by his offer. "No strings?"

"No strings. I thought we had already settled that."

"You're right. We have. It's just that you're my first Good Samaritan, and I guess I just don't know how to react properly."

"I'm not a Good Samaritan," he said gruffly.

She smiled. "No? Well, you'll certainly do until one comes along." She stood and began collecting dishes.

"I just don't want you to get the wrong idea. What I am is a mean-assed cop making sure an important witness is available."

She carried the dishes over to the sink, and began rinsing them before putting them into the dishwasher. Over her shoulder she said, "Of course, what you are really after is someone around to see that the beds are made and the dishes washed."

"There's that." He gave a crooked grin. "But I'll do my share. Depend on it."

As Casey started back toward the table, the phone on the wall rang. She paused to answer it. "Hello?"

There was a brief silence, then a small voice said tentatively, "Is this the policeman's house?"

"Right. Is this Donnie?"

"Yes. I'm calling to see if Spot's okay."

73

"Spot's fine. He's been well-fed, and right now he's snoozing up a storm in the corner."

"Shit!" Josh said from the table. "I forgot all about the kid. I have to go over there and get an official statement from him." He got to his feet. "Give me that."

Into the receiver he said, "Donnie? Sorry that I didn't get back to you. Yes, your dog is fine . . . Look, I know that you would like to see for yourself, and I need your statement. Why don't we do this, if it's all right with your aunt, it's still early. I'll hop over, pick you up, bring you over here and you can visit with your mutt while I take your statement. Is your aunt there? Okay, put her on and let me clear it with her."

As he waited, Josh said to Casey, "She'll probably be delighted to have a free baby sitter for a few hours while she and her squeeze go out and booze it up . . ." He turned back to the phone again: "Ms. Black?"

CHAPTER SIX

Ray Tibbets's preliminary hearing was held two weeks later. It had been Michael Bannerman's decision to try Tibbets for only the last death. "Josh," he had said, "we just don't have anything but the MO to tie him to the other two killings. If we try him for all three, we're going to diffuse our case; and it's not going to be all that easy to get a verdict of guilty on the one."

Josh ignored Bannerman's reservations. Bannerman was a worrier, a perfectionist, and like most prosecutors, in Josh's experience, he wanted every i dotted and every t crossed. The mark of a good prosecutor was the number of convictions on his record.

Josh, however, was less than pleased by the judge they had drawn — His Honor, J.T. Ballard, called "Judge the Bastard" by cops and prosecutors alike. He was a strict interpreter of the law, and if the prosecution presented a weak chain of evidence, or any improper evidence, he always came down on the side of the defense.

Josh didn't want to miss a moment of the hearing. Too much was at stake. He had several weeks of leave built up and he had no other pressing cases on his plate, so he took some of his leave.

The Dumpster Killer case was sensational enough to draw full media coverage, and public interest was high, so the courtroom was filled almost to capacity.

As Josh entered the courthouse, he found Casey and Donnie sitting on a bench outside the courtroom. Donnie's aunt, looking grumpy, sat beside the boy.

Josh had seen a great deal of Donnie over the past two weeks, and had grown quite fond of the boy. Since school was out for the summer, he picked the boy up at the apartment building at least three times a week, and drove him over to visit with Spot. Away from his aunt and her live-in, the boy was relaxed and fun to be with. He was also very bright and aware for a child his age.

Casey, too, was happier now. Josh's connection on the governor's task force had come through. Casey was due to start work next week, and she was on cloud nine.

There was one development, however, that put something of a damper on the general good spirits. An enterprising reporter from one of the newspapers had tracked Casey down, finding her with Donnie in the yard before Josh's house. Angrily, she had refused to be interviewed; however, the photographer accompanying the reporter had snapped their picture. The photo had appeared the next day, identifying Donnie and her as the principal witnesses against the Dumpster Killer.

Josh had told Casey that she had to expect such media attention when involved in a case as newsworthy as this one. "That doesn't mean that I have to like it!" she had snapped back.

Now, taking a seat between Donnie and Casey on the bench in the hall outside the courtroom, Josh said, "You're both here. Good."

"I'm here, but I'm nervous as hell," Casey said.

Josh gave her what he hoped was a reassuring grin. "Now, why should you be nervous? Everything will be fine. Depend on it."

Edith Black said angrily, "I don't know why we have to perch out here on these hard benches."

"Witnesses aren't allowed in the courtroom until after they've given testimony, but you can go in if you like, Ms. Black." Josh glanced pointedly at the cigarette smoldering in her hand. "But you won't be allowed to smoke in there."

"I'll wait out here with Donnie, thank you."

Josh ruffled Donnie's hair. "You okay, sport?"

Donnie nodded seriously. "I'm fine, Josh. Kinda excited, is all."

"Just think of it as an experience you'll always remember."

Josh turned to Casey. "Casey, been thinking about the new job?"

Her face lit up. "I can hardly think of anything else!" She touched his hand. "And I owe it all to you. I don't know how I'll ever repay you, Josh. And don't you dare say what I know is in that evil mind of yours."

He assumed an injured air. "Now how do you know what's in my mind, Ms. Farrel?" He laughed, then sobered, touching her cheek lightly with his fingertips. "Favor for favor, Casey. Help us nail this creep and that will more than repay me. Speaking of which, I'd better get inside."

Although he had been in charge of the investigation, Josh didn't expect to have to testify. He hadn't arrested the perp, and he hadn't personally uncovered any pertinent evidence.

He had just seated himself directly behind Bannerman's table when Tibbets was led into the courtroom by a bailiff. Tibbets was dressed in a new blue suit, white shirt, and a sober tie. He was escorted to the defense table, where he sat down beside Sanders.

Josh experienced a pang of misgiving. With that baby face and innocent look, it might not be easy to convince a jury that Tibbets was the Dumpster Killer.

As though feeling Josh's gaze on him, Tibbets glanced around. For just a moment, his eyes blazed with a maniacal fury. Then Sanders leaned across the table to say something to him, and Tibbets turned to face the bench.

Tibbets had sailed through the lie detector test, which hadn't surprised Josh in the least. It had only confirmed his theory that a psychopath — which he now believed Tibbets to be, without a doubt, could lie to a lie detector without causing a single quiver on the graph. Also, a thorough search of Tibbets's apartment had uncovered nothing damaging. They had to go with what they had.

Since this was a preliminary hearing, and there was no jury to be swayed by the rhetoric, there were no long-winded opening speeches from either side.

Josh was amused at the appearance of the defense attorney. Sanders was attired in a wrinkled, seersucker suit. His shirt billowed out over his pot belly, and his long, graying hair was shaggy. Must be modeling himself after the long-dead Clarence Darrow, Josh reflected dryly.

The first witness for the state was the young officer who had been driving the patrol car that had answered the call. He was followed by other officers and plainclothes people who had later arrived on the scene. Sanders didn't cross-examine a single one. Each time, at the end of Bannerman's examination, Sanders popped up and said, "No questions of this witness, Your Honor."

However, after Bannerman had finished with Ken Waters, the officer who stopped Tibbets for driving over the speed limit, Sanders stood and said, "If I may beg the court's indulgence, Your Honor, the defense has no questions of this witness at this time, but we would like to reserve the right to recall the officer for cross-examination at a later time."

Judge Ballard frowned at the defense attorney over the half-glasses perched on his prominent nose. "I hope you do not intend to make a habit of this, Counselor. Any time a police officer has to be in court to testify, he must necessarily be relieved of his duties. Please remember that this is a preliminary, not a trial."

Sanders said solemnly, "This is the only witness the defense will recall, Your Honor. The reason for this will become abundantly clear at the time."

"Very well. The witness will hold himself subject to recall," Judge Ballard said grumpily. He rapped his gavel. "Call your next witness, Mr. Bannerman."

The next witness was the Assistant Medical Examiner, Dr. John Aikman, a slight man in his fifties, who had served as a medical examiner much of his professional life. In his testimony for the prosecution, he stated that it was his opinion that the victim, one Sandra Shaw, had been strangled, and that her body showed some contusions and bruises that would indicate that she had put up a struggle.

When Bannerman completed his questioning, Sanders arose and slouched toward the witness. Josh leaned forward with interest. This was the first witness Sanders had chosen to question.

"Dr. Aikman, you testified that you found evidence of a struggle, indicating that the victim fought for her life, is that correct?"

"That is correct."

"In your examination did you discover any evidence, any evidence at all, that would indicate the defendant as her killer?"

Dr. Aikman hesitated. "No. I did not."

"You did not." Sanders turned his back on the witness, took a few steps toward the courtroom, then whirled around to re-face the witness. "Dr. Aikman, do you have any knowledge of the profession of the victim, Sandra Shaw?"

Bannerman was on his feet, mouth open to object.

Sanders rushed on, "Was she not a prostitute by profession?"

"Your Honor, I strongly object!" Bannerman shouted. "The profession of the victim has no relevance to these proceedings!"

Judge Ballard scowled. "Mr. Sanders?"

"The profession of the victim is entirely relevant, Your Honor. It is our intent to show that women who prostitute themselves are prone to suffer random violence."

The gavel rapped lightly. "Objection sustained. You know better, Mr. Sanders. I must remind you that you are not performing for the benefit of a jury."

Sanders flipped his hand. "No further questions of this witness."

As Sanders turned back toward the defense table, Josh saw a slight smile on his lips.

"Will the prosecution call its next witness?" Judge Ballard said. "Let's try to move matters along here."

Bannerman stepped forward. "The prosecution calls as its next witness, Donnie Patterson."

A bailiff was sent out into the hall to fetch Donnie. When he came in with the bailiff, his aunt trailing behind him, Donnie looked around apprehensively.

Josh managed to catch his eye, and give him a reassuring smile and a wink. Donnie smiled back, squared his narrow shoulders, and marched up to the witness chair. As he listened to the boy being sworn in, Josh thought, the kid's got guts. He'll make a good witness.

Gingerly, Bannerman led Donnie through the events leading up to his face-to-face confrontation with Ray Tibbets.

Then he said, "Donnie, the man you saw that night, is he in the courtroom?"

"Yes," Donnie said in a voice that shook slightly.

"Would you point him out, please?"

Donnie leveled an accusing finger at Tibbets. The finger trembled, then steadied.

"Let the record show that the witness identified the defendant. Would the accused please stand?"

Tibbets stood, looking straight ahead.

Bannerman said, "Is this the man you saw, Donnie?"

Donnie bobbed his head. "Yes, sir, that's him!"

Bannerman turned away. "No more questions of this witness."

Sanders stood, but did not leave the defense table. "Now, Donnie," he said in a fatherly tone, "is your eyesight good?"

Donnie stared at him in puzzlement. "Yes, sir."

"Had your eyes tested recently?"

"No, sir."

"Suppose we test them now, then." Sanders picked up a square of cardboard from the table. "Donnie, this is a chart like the ones eye doctors use to test vision. Can you read the top line?"

Donnie rattled the letters off without hesitation.

"Good. Now, how about the bottom line?"

Again Donnie read off the letters with no hesitation.

Sanders was smiling. "Very good. I'd say that you have 20/20 vision, about as good as it gets."

Sanders put the cardboard down and picked up several sheets of paper stapled together. He slouched over to the witness stand to take up a position before Donnie. "Now, Donnie, I have here a copy of your statement taken the day after the defendant was arrested. I would like to read . . ."

Bannerman jumped to his feet. "Where did you get that?"

Sanders smiled, all innocence. "That's for me to know and you to find out, Mister Prosecutor."

The gavel rapped. "Gentlemen, please address your remarks to the bench. Now, what is this?"

"Your Honor," Bannerman said hotly, "the statement in counsel's possession has not been entered into evidence, therefore it is improper for him to read from it!"

"But it should have been entered into evidence, Your Honor," said Sanders smoothly. "It is the statement of a witness taken during the investigation, taken by the officer in charge of the investigation, Detective Sergeant Joshua Whitney. As such, it should have been one of the prosecution's exhibits."

"It is the prosecution's call as to what evidence shall or shall not be exhibited at a trial," Bannerman said.

"Mr. Sanders . . ." Judge Ballard frowned down from the bench. "Is this document pertinent to your examination of this witness?"

"Very much so, Your Honor. It has direct bearing on the credibility of this witness."

"Very well. I will allow it."

"Exception, Your Honor," Bannerman said, and sat down.

"Exception noted. Proceed, Mr. Sanders."

"Now, Donnie, I will read from your statement. Question: Donnie, did you notice any distinguishing marks on the man you saw? By that, I mean did you notice any moles, warts or scars on the man you saw? Answer: Yes, sir. He had a zigzag scar across his right cheek, sort of purple-colored."

Sanders looked up. "Now, Donnie, are those your words?"

Donnie shrank back in the witness chair, shooting a glance at Tibbets. "I . . ." He cleared his throat. "Yes, sir."

Sanders faced about. "Would the defendant please stand?"

Tibbets stood.

"Now, Donnie, a moment ago you testified that the defendant is the man you saw at the dumpster on the night in question. Is that not correct?"

Donnie swallowed. "Yes, sir."

"Donnie, I want you to look closely at the defendant. Now, tell me, do you see a scar on his face?"

Donnie's cheeks reddened, and for a moment he lowered his eyes. Finally, he shook his head.

"You'll have to speak up, Donnie. Yes or no?"

"No, sir." To Josh the words sounded defiant. He thought he knew how the kid must feel.

Sanders gestured, turning away. "No further questions of this witness."

Bannerman rose to his feet, started to speak,

then hesitated. Behind him, Josh expelled a sigh, as an insight struck him like a slap in the face. Tibbets had plastered a fake scar on his face as an attempt at a disguise. And he had gotten rid of it some time between the dumpster and the time he had been stopped by Officer Waters. That was the only answer; but it was far too late to do anything about it now.

"Any questions of this witness on re-cross, Mr. Bannerman?"

Bannerman expelled his breath. "No, Your Honor."

"Then you may step down, young man. Call your next witness, Mr. Bannerman."

"The state calls Casey Farrel."

Josh made a thumbs-up gesture at Donnie as the boy passed him, but he saw that the boy wasn't buying it. He shook his head dolefully and trudged on back toward his aunt.

Josh swiveled his head to look back. Edith Black was already standing in the aisle. When Donnie reached her, she grabbed his hand and started out of the courtroom. Donnie pulled his hand out of her grasp, said something to her, and shook his head. She leaned down to talk to him, her face screwed into an expression of displeasure. Donnie shook his head again, then sat down in the seat she had just vacated. The woman glared at him, then stamped her foot and marched out, meeting Casey and a bailiff on their way in.

Casey's gaze sought out Josh at once. He gave her an encouraging smile. He doubted it was very convincing. Already a witness to Sanders at work, Josh knew that she was in for a rough time. She returned his smile and went on down the aisle and into the witness chair.

Bannerman went through much the same routine with her as he had with Donnie, leading her carefully up to her identification of Tibbets as the man she had observed putting the bag into the dumpster.

When it came his turn, Sanders approached the witness with a stern countenance. "Miss Farrel, you have testified, under oath, that you saw a body put into the dumpster in the alley. Are you positive that's what you saw? Could it not have been a bag of trash?"

Casey's head went back. "I know what I saw!"

"Do you indeed? Witnesses are notoriously unreliable as to what they . . ."

Bannerman said wearily, "Objection. Counsel for the defense is lecturing the witness, Your Honor."

"I concur. Mr. Sanders, please confine your remarks to what is pertinent."

"My apologies to the court, Your Honor,"

Sanders said unrepentantly. "Miss Farrel, are you employed?"

Casey looked startled. "Not at present, but I will be going to a new job . . ."

"Yes or no will be sufficient. Were you employed at the time of the incident you claim to have witnessed?"

Casey shot a glance in Josh's direction. "No."

"Please speak up, so we can hear you."

"No, I was not."

"In fact, you had been unemployed for quite some time, had you not?"

"Yes."

"Is it not a fact that you were unable to pay your rent, and were locked out of your . . ."

Bannerman boiled up. "I must object, Your Honor! I fail to see how the unemployment of this witness is relevant!"

"It has to do with the credibility of the witness, Your Honor."

Judge Ballard frowned in deep thought. "I will allow the question. Objection overruled."

Smirking, Sanders turned back to Casey. "That means you must answer the question, Miss Farrel. Due to your lack of employment, you were locked out of your apartment, is that not correct?"

Casey said in a low voice, "Yes."

"And were reduced to sleeping in your car?"

"Yes."

"In essence then, you became one of the homeless, correct?"

"Your Honor!"

"Yes, Mr. Bannerman," Judge Ballard said in a dry voice. "I must caution defense counsel to restrain himself from making sidebar remarks, if at all possible."

"My apologies, Your Honor. So, Miss Farrel, you were sleeping in your automobile in that alley on the night you claim to have seen the defendant. Is that correct?"

"I was, yes."

"And before you saw the defendant, you were asleep, sound asleep."

"I was."

"And what woke you?"

Casey appeared hesitant. "Well, it was a sound of some sort. As soon as I woke up, I saw this dog nosing around the trash barrels, and assumed that it was the rattle of the trash cans that wakened me."

"Light sleeper, are you?"

Casey shrugged. "Sometimes, sometimes not."

"Of course, I should imagine that sleeping in an automobile night after night is uncomfortable, not especially conducive to sleeping."

"Your Honor, is defense counsel asking a

question, or making a comment?"

"Yes, Mr. Sanders, let's move along, shall we?"

"Yes, Your Honor." Sanders wheeled on Casey. "Miss Farrel, I suggest to you that you were still groggy from being awakened so abruptly, at the time you claimed you saw the defendant. I suggest that what you *thought* you saw, was not what actually occurred."

"I was quite awake. I saw what I saw," Casey said doggedly.

"Did you? Did you indeed?" Sanders turned his back on her and crossed halfway to the defense table. He spoke without looking at her. "Where do you currently reside, Miss Farrel?"

Oh, shit, Josh thought, as Casey shot a glance at him, then as quickly looked away.

Sanders wheeled on her. "You are presently living in the home of Sergeant Joshua Whitney, are you not? You, an important witness for the prosecution, are living with the homicide detective in charge of the investigation!" He made two lunging steps toward her, and thundered, "Is that not the truth, Miss Farrel?"

Josh saw that Casey was making a tremendous effort to maintain her composure. She almost succeeded, except for the color that suddenly stained her cheeks.

"I'm not *living* there, not in the sense you mean."

"Oh?" Sanders leered. "I wasn't implying anything beyond the simple question, Miss Farrel, but then perhaps you'd care to explain to the court what *you* mean?"

Casey's color brightened, and Bannerman called out, "Objection, Your Honor."

"Yes, objection sustained. Rephrase your question, Counsel."

"Let me put it this way, Miss Farrel. Are you at the present time residing at the home of Sergeant Whitney?"

"Yes," Casey said in a subdued voice.

The courtroom buzzed. Judge Ballard pounded his gavel.

Sanders turned away. "No further questions of this witness."

"Does the prosecution have any re-direct, Mr. Bannerman?"

Bannerman's voice sounded tired. "No, Your Honor."

"The witness may step down. Call your next witness, Mr. Bannerman."

Sanders whirled about. "Your Honor, earlier I reserved the right to recall one of the prosecution witnesses, Officer Waters. I would like to do so at this time."

Judge Ballard frowned, then sighed. "Very well. Recall Officer Waters to the stand."

When an openly apprehensive Ken Waters was again on the stand, Sanders said, "Officer Waters, you have previously testified that you stopped the defendant's van because he was exceeding the speed limit. Is that correct?"

"Yes. He was driving about ten miles over the speed limit in a residential district."

"And that is the *only* reason you stopped him?"

"I figured that was sufficient reason," Officer Waters said stiffly.

"I'm sure it was, Officer," Sanders said smoothly. "Now, would you again tell the court what transpired after you pulled the van over?"

"Well, since I was alone in the cruiser, I called for backup."

"Any reason for you to do that?"

"I thought it advisable, since the van struck me as suspicious."

"Suspicious? Any reason, aside from the purported traffic violation?"

The officer hesitated. "Well . . . I just had a feeling."

Sanders cocked his head to one side. "A feeling? I see. Please continue, Officer."

"When Carter, my backup, arrived, I proceeded to question the driver of the vehicle, after seeing his driver's license. He struck me as more nervous than he should have been just for being stopped for a traffic violation. So, I proceeded to search his vehicle."

"And did you find anything unusual?"

"No, sir. I did not."

"According to your prior testimony, you did find a pair of thin rubber gloves and a box of plastic trash bags. Is that correct?"

"Yes, sir. I did."

"But there was no indication that these items were linked to a crime, any crime, was there?"

"No, sir. There was not."

"But you did then place the defendant under arrest, did you not? Please explain to the court why you did so."

"Right after I conducted the search I received a call on the radio. There was an APB out on the van and the driver."

Sanders paced for a few moments, head down, then he stopped before the witness again. "Now, Officer, let's get this perfectly clear about the time here. You placed the defendant under arrest *after* you searched his vehicle, not before?"

Officer Waters hesitated, shooting a questioning glance at Bannerman.

Sanders stepped to one side, blocking the line of vision between witness and prosecutor. "Do not look at the prosecutor for signals, Officer."

"Your Honor, I object!"

"Sustained," Judge Ballard said wearily. "Just answer the question, Officer."

"It was after the search, sir."

Sanders flipped a hand. "No further questions of this witness."

As Sanders crossed toward the defense table, Josh leaned forward to speak to Bannerman in a low voice. "Maybe you should put me on the stand, so I can give the reasons why Miss Farrel is staying at my place."

Without looking around, Bannerman said, "No. That would only be opening up the whole can of peas."

"Seems to me that Sanders had already opened it."

"And with you up there, he'd only open it wider. Forget it!" He shook his head. "Forgive me for saying so, Josh, but taking that girl in was one of the stupidest things I've known you to do."

Josh, starting a hot retort, was interrupted by Judge Ballard: "Call your next witness, Mr. Bannerman."

Bannerman stood. "That concludes the prosecution's case, Your Honor."

"Mr. Sanders?"

Sanders bounced up. "The defense calls one last witness, Your Honor." He half-turned toward the prosecution table. With a smirk, he said, "The defense calls Detective Sergeant Joshua Whitney."

Bannerman, halfway back into his seat, froze, gaping at the defense attorney.

"About to raise an objection, Mr. Bannerman?" Sander's smug smile widened. "Why should the prosecution object? Detective Whitney *was* the officer in charge . . ."

The gavel banged. "Mr. Sanders! You are out of order!"

Bannerman sank back down, said weakly, "No objection."

After Josh was sworn in and Sanders had established his credentials, the defense attorney said, "Detective Whitney, was the defendant given a lie detector test before he was charged?"

Josh tensed. "He was."

"And what were the results of that test?"

Bannerman's face went red. "Objection! The results of a lie detector test are not admissible!"

"Defense is well aware of that, Your Honor," Sanders said smoothly. "On the other hand, I believe we should be made aware of the results of that test. After all, this is a preliminary, no jury is seated, and I am certain that Your Honor will not be unduly swayed."

Judge Ballard glowered down at Sanders,

then rubbed his jaw. "The witness may answer the question."

"Detective Whitney?"

"The results were negative," Josh said through tight lips.

"The defendant was asked, during the test, if he killed Sandra Shaw?"

"He was."

"And what was his response?"

"He denied killing her."

"And the graph showed that he was telling the truth, did it not?"

"The graph did not show that he was lying. However, you realize that such results are not conclusive. There are some individuals who are able to . . ."

"Your Honor," Sanders said angrily, "will you please instruct the witness to confine his answers to yes or no."

"The witness is so instructed."

"Detective Whitney, we have heard Miss Farrel testify that she has been residing in your home. Is that correct?"

"Yes."

"Is it the usual procedure for an important witness, *any* witness, to reside at the house of a police officer involved in the investigation of a case in which said witness is also involved?"

"Not usual, no."

"Then why did you depart from procedure this time?"

Josh hesitated.

"Detective Whitney," Sanders prompted. "We are waiting."

Josh slumped back in his chair. "Miss Farrel had no permanent residence. It might have been difficult to contact her when it came time to testify."

"No permanent residence? In fact, she had no residence at all, is that not correct?"

"That's correct," Josh said stiffly.

Sanders, obviously well pleased with himself, stared at Josh for a moment, then said in a soft voice, "Detective Whitney, while Miss Farrel has been residing in your home, have you been intimate with her?"

The courtroom erupted, the gavel banged, and Bannerman sprang to his feet.

As the courtroom grew quiet again, Sanders gestured. "I withdraw the question. I have no further questions of this witness."

Judge Ballard said, "Does the prosecution have any questions of this witness?"

In a strangled voice Bannerman said, "No, Your Honor. No questions."

"The witness may step down."

Sanders moved over in front of the bench. "Your Honor, at this time, I would like to make a motion."

"What is the nature of your motion, Counselor?"

"I move that all charges against the defendant be dropped."

"I object, Your Honor!"

Judge Ballard batted a hand at Bannerman without even looking at him. "On what grounds, Mr. Sanders?"

"On the grounds that the prosecution has failed to present a prima facie case against my client, Your Honor."

"Are you prepared to expand upon that statement, Mr. Sanders?"

"I am indeed, Your Honor. In the first place, there is the testimony of the prosecution's two eyewitnesses. Now I ask you," he sneered openly. "One is a nine-year-old boy who testifies that the man he saw at the dumpster had a vivid scar, while it is painfully obvious that the defendant does not have such a scar. The second witness, a homeless person living in her vehicle, is unemployed and at present living with the police officer in charge of the investigation."

"Your Honor, please!" Bannerman said. "I strongly object to counsel so characterizing Ms. Farrel."

"Yes, Mr. Sanders," the judge said in a dry voice. "As you recently reminded me, this is a preliminary hearing with no jurors to impress, so please make an effort to restrain your . . . eloquence."

"But most important of all," Sanders continued as if he had not been admonished, "is the fact that no physical evidence has been found connecting the defendant to the murder of Sandra Shaw. Even if we accept the evidence of the two so-called eyewitnesses that the defendant was seen at the dumpster, there is nothing to show that he was not, as he has stated, simply there to drop off a bag of household trash. Nothing more, nothing less. The prosecution makes much of the fact that a pair of rubber gloves and a box of plastic trash bags were found in the defendant's van. Is that a crime? The defendant uses the gloves in his work, and the trash bags are common, found in any market. Also, the prosecution has not proved that the bag in which the victim was found came from that particular container."

Sanders took a deep breath. "In addition, the officer who stopped the defendant searched his vehicle without cause, without a warrant. It was an illegal search, made by the officer, by his own admission, before he had knowledge that an APB had been put out on said vehicle, made on the strength of a *feeling* the officer had."

"Yes, yes, Mr. Sanders," Judge Ballard said

irritably. "Is that the extent of your motion?"

"Yes, Your Honor. It would save the state the expense of a jury trial if the bench would rule in favor. I believe it is abundantly clear that the prosecution's case will not stand up before a jury."

Judge Ballard rapped his gavel. "The Court stands in recess for one hour. I will deliver my decision on this motion at that time." He was gone with a swish of robes.

With a sigh, Josh stood, stretching. Bannerman whirled around, glaring at him. "You screwed up, Whitney! Screwed up royally!" Before Josh could frame a rejoinder, the prosecutor stalked up the aisle.

The spectators were filing toward the exits. Josh followed along, feeling depressed and weary. He found Casey and Donnie waiting for him in the hall.

Casey, her face worried, looked up at him. "What does all that mean, Josh?"

"It means that Sanders is trying to get the case against that scumbag thrown out of court."

"Do you think the judge will do that?"

Josh shrugged tiredly. "I wouldn't even try to guess. Judges *and* juries are notoriously unpredictable. It could go either way. Casey, there's a drink machine at the end of the hall. Would you like something cold? Donnie?"

"I'll have a Coke," Donnie said.

"Anything," Casey said.

The three of them moved down to the pop machine, and Josh fed coins into it until they each had a cold drink.

Donnie took a long drink, then said, "My aunt was mad 'cause I wouldn't leave with her. I told her you'd take me home, Josh. Was that okay?"

"Sure thing, sport." Josh ruffled the boy's hair. "In fact, we'll drive by my house, and you can visit with Spot for a while. I have to go downtown, but Casey can drive you home later, if that's all right with her."

"All *right!*"

"So, what's going to happen if this creep is released?" Casey demanded. "And don't you dare say, depend on it!"

"I wasn't going to, Casey," Josh said heavily. "All we can do is wait and see."

Judge Ballard called them back in exactly one hour. When everyone was seated, he looked first at the defense table, then at Bannerman. "I have carefully considered motion by the defense, and I find that much of his argument has merit. Considering the fact that the state's chain of evidence is weak, and that the testimony of the two witnesses identifying the accused is also questionable, this court has no alternative but to dismiss all charges against the defendant." The gavel rapped. "The defendant is hereby remanded from custody."

With a rustle of robes, Judge Ballard disappeared into his chambers. Bannerman snapped his attache case closed, and hurried out without a word to Josh. Josh stood with Casey and Donnie as the courtroom cleared of spectators. He stared balefully at Ray Tibbets.

Casey, her voice tight, said, "So, what now, Detective?"

Without taking his gaze from Tibbets, Josh said, "There's one good thing about this. Since Tibbets hasn't been tried and found innocent, we can still nail him if we find more, stronger evidence, and his defense can't claim double jeopardy . . ."

He broke off as Tibbets swung around to meet his gaze. Tibbets started toward them, brushing Sanders aside as the attorney tried to stop him.

Tibbets planted himself before Josh. Donnie reached out for Josh's hand, crowding close.

Tibbets looked down at the boy. His face wore a seraphic smile, but his eyes were as void of expression as marbles.

"The smallest one first," he said in a soft voice. His gaze came back to Josh and Casey. "The woman next. As the biggest, you'll be last, cop."

CHAPTER SEVEN

Sanders took Tibbets by the elbow, and began urging him toward the door. Tibbets seemed to go along willingly enough; but his dead eyes held Josh's gaze until the door closed behind him.

"Josh . . ." Donnie squeezed Josh's hand. "Does that mean they're letting the bad man go?"

"I'm afraid so, Donnie," Josh said heavily. "He walks, at least for now."

Casey said, "And in the meantime?" She shivered. "That man frightens me, Josh! He threatened Donnie. You heard him. He threatened all of us!"

"Men in his situation often make threats; but they rarely carry through on them. He'd have to be crazy to try anything now!" And yet, Tibbets did hover on the edge of madness. Josh was certain of that.

Casey frowned, eyes flashing, "But what if he *does* try something?"

Josh scrubbed his knuckles across his chin. "I don't think he will; but it's best to be careful. When you're in the house alone, I'll have a prowl car come by. And I have an extra gun in the house. You ever use one?"

"Of course not," she snapped. "Why would I ever have used a gun?"

"I'll teach you."

"Oh, great! That's all I need. Shooting lessons, so that I can protect myself against a madman!" She ran her fingers through her hair, mussing it. "I don't know why I ever got involved in this mess in the first place. I was much better off sleeping in my car."

Josh grinned. "How can you say that, Casey? You've got a place to stay, you've got a job, you get to be around me. What more could you want?"

Casey batted a hand at him, her gaze going to Donnie. "Besides, that weirdo said, 'The smallest one first.' That means he'll be zeroing in on Donnie first. You going to teach *him* how to use a gun?"

"Of course I'm not . . ."

Donnie stood straighter, said stoutly, "I'm not afraid of that man."

Josh managed a smile. "I know you're not, sport, and there's no reason to be. We'll see that he's put away soon, before he can get around to hurting you."

"Oh, yes, Donnie, depend on it," Casey said dryly.

Josh felt himself flush. "I deserve that, I know. But I was sure that we had this guy nailed. Well, you win some, lose some."

"I'd rather that this time you'd won," she retorted. "Well, it's done. No use gnashing my teeth. Now, let's take Donnie home to visit with Spot."

Donnie bounced on his toes. "Yes!"

"Maybe we should call your aunt first."

"She don't care what I do." Donnie looked down at his feet.

"Doesn't," Casey corrected absently. To Josh she muttered, "Some loving aunt she is. Well, come along, Donnie, let's hit the road."

When Josh got home that evening, Casey had dinner cooking — a pot roast and little red potatoes — in the Crock-pot.

Josh sniffed, beaming. "I could get used to this, coming home to a good-looking woman in the kitchen and a roast cooking."

"Don't get too used to it, Detective," she said tartly. "It won't last forever, you know."

"You keep saying that you're not much of a cook, yet this is the third great meal you've whipped up."

"Don't get carried away. You haven't tasted it yet. Besides, what's so hard about putting a roast in the Crock-pot? Even Donnie could probably manage that."

"Did Donnie have a good visit with Spot?" At the sound of his name Spot came trotting in from the deck, tail wagging, tongue lolling. He squatted on his haunches at Josh's feet, looking up hopefully. "Sure didn't take the beast long to learn his name after Donnie christened him, did it?"

"Maybe that was his name already. After all, he *does* have spots."

"Could be," he said with a shrug. "Well, me for a quick shower before dinner."

"I suppose you'd like a martini waiting, Master, when you get out of the shower?"

"That would be nice," he said breezily, going down the hall.

Casey, staring after him, felt like stamping her foot. Then she smiled, laughed aloud. How could you stay mad at the big jerk for long?

She had his martini waiting when he came back, working on a vodka tonic herself. He had put on a garish sport shirt, faded jeans, and sandals.

She pretended to shield her eyes. "A person needs sun glasses around a shirt like that!"

"Glad you like it," he said, tipping the martini glass. "Ah, good, after a hard day at the office."

"And what, besides that miserable hearing, made it so hard?"

"For one thing, I had to rattle a few cages to get the department to continue to investigate Tibbets as the Dumpster Killer. Most of the brass wanted to hold back, said if we couldn't convict him on what we had now, how could we hope to do it at all? But I think it'll move ahead, if halfheartedly. Secondly . . ." He became serious. "I did my damnedest, Casey, to get you and Donnie some kind of protection, but . . ." He shrugged. "The best I could get was the promise that the unit that patrols this area will check the house when they're in the neighborhood."

He took a deep breath. "And, my captain chewed my ass pretty good for having you living in the house here. He threw around phrases like suspension and demotion, but that was only to let me know how pissed he was."

"I'm sorry, Josh."

"No big deal. The captain knew from the beginning that you were staying with me. I wouldn't have done it without telling him. At the time, he thought it was a good way to keep you on tap. None of us figured that Sanders would bring it out at the hearing. The only reason the captain got on my case was because Bannerman told him that having you here contributed to Tibbets being freed. Personally, I doubt it made all that much difference." His glance slid away. "I also got a call from Tod Burns today."

Casey went tense. "Burns? The man who heads the task force?"

Josh nodded. "That's the one. He was unhappy about the publicity."

"So, I'm fired before I even start."

"No, no. I talked him around. I reminded him that I was calling in a favor the governor owes me, and that it's all a tempest in a teapot, anyway. Two weeks from now the papers will be full of some other crime, and nobody will remember your name. Also, I lied a little. I told him that we weren't living in sin."

"We're *not* living in sin, damn you!"

"Wait, wait." He held up his hands in a now-familiar gesture with this prickly woman. "You didn't let me finish. I told him that you were paying me rent."

She stared at him hard, then turned away to check the Crock-pot. "Roast'll be ready to eat shortly. Josh . . ." She faced him. "I'm moving out of here, finding a place of my own, as soon as I get my first pay check."

"Now, why would you want to do that?"

"That's one way to put a stop to any gossip, and because Tibbets now knows that I'm living here. He'll know where to find me. Besides, won't your captain insist that I move out now?"

"Ah. That's behind us. And anyway, what makes you think that Tibbets wouldn't find you at a new address? He may be slightly tilted, but he's far from stupid. No, you're safer living here, Casey, until we learn if he intends to carry out his threat. Besides . . ." A grin slashed across his face. "I like having you here."

"And I like living here, Josh; I admit it," she said in a subdued voice. "But I feel like I'm imposing, and I can't stay here forever. I have to get my own place sooner or later."

"Let's make it later, okay? And you're not imposing, depend on it."

She looked adorable, in a pair of short shorts and a loose blouse. Her full breasts moved seductively under the fabric. He felt certain that she was not wearing a bra, and he felt a rush of desire, lust, whatever; and not for the first time he wondered how she would respond if he put a move on her. But an inner sense warned him that this was not the right time.

"I'll think about it," she said.

"You do that. And now let's eat." He clapped his hands together. "I'm starving."

A week passed, during which nothing unusual happened, and Casey began to relax. As the tension left her, she said nothing more about leaving.

After her job began, she could think of little else. The first few days were spent in orientation courses, but she could see that the work would be interesting and challenging. Happily, no one involved seemed to have an interest in her living arrangements or her past; at least the subject was never mentioned, for which she was grateful.

Josh spent much of the week pushing the investigation on Tibbets, but there was only so much time he could devote to it. Other homicides occurred, and they were fresh, more pressing, so he had to work on them.

He studied the files on the other two kills attributed to the Dumpster Killer, looking for something that had been missed. Zilch, zero. Discouraged, he finally concluded that they would have to wait for another Dumpster kill. It was a fine state of affairs when another person, or persons, had to be killed so that you could solve previous deaths.

Another week passed, and Josh decided that it was possible that Tibbets, despite his defiance, had been spooked by his arrest and was lying low. It would be the sensible thing to do; but then, serial killers were not what most people would call sensible. Since pattern killers operated out of a compulsion to kill, eventually, the Dumpster Killer would strike again.

During these two weeks Josh managed to spend most of his evenings at home, with Casey. He figured that during the day, with dozens of people around her, she was probably fairly safe.

He was also very concerned about Donnie, and warned the boy's aunt to keep a close watch on him, not to let him out alone, and definitely not to leave him alone at night. He checked on the boy as often as he could, and hoped that the woman was doing what he had told her. Unfortunately, he could legally do no more.

But he could look after Casey, and he did so. He found these evenings spent at home very pleasant. Casey was usually doing what he thought of as "homework" associated with her new job, and he would keep busy with paperwork that had to be done anyway. Even though each of them was involved in their own work, it was companionable. Later they would have a drink and watch television. Josh was amused by Casey's habit of making comments and talking back to the set. Many times he found himself wanting to pull her close and kiss her, but something — he wasn't sure what — held him back.

But one evening at the end of the second week after the hearing, Josh was called away. It was about ten o'clock, and a man had been found with his throat cut. The night crew was short handed, and Josh had been called in. He strapped on his gun, cautioned Casey to keep the doors and windows locked, and, with great misgivings, left her alone.

After Josh was gone, Casey puttered about for a while, actually glad to be on her own for an evening. She had yet to make a decision about getting her own place. She found comfort and security in Josh's hulking male presence, and dreaded living alone again. At the same time, she was well aware of why she was procrastinating — she was very attracted to Josh.

Admit the whole truth, girl, she scolded herself; you're falling for the guy!

Yet she wasn't quite ready to set up housekeeping with him. She knew what Josh wanted — it was in his eyes, his touch, in almost everything he said. But he had yet to make a move, which she appreciated but found a little puzzling. The few men she had been close to had never been shy about coming on to her. Why was Josh holding back?

She had slowly come to realize that he was much more sensitive than his tough cop, gruff exterior indicated, but was he *that* sensitive?

She laughed ruefully, chiding herself for being a hopeless romantic. Her experiences over the last year, with the detective agency head, the miscarriage, the dreary stretch as one of the homeless, should have shattered most of her illusions.

Wandering out of the kitchen, she picked up the TV guide. A movie, a golden oldie, *Casablanca,* was on the tube, colorized, but still one of her favorites. She had seen it a number of times, but it was worth seeing again. Clicking on the set, she settled back, smiling to herself. Talk about a hopeless romantic!

Shortly after the movie started, Spot came padding in, hopped onto the couch with her, and settled against her legs.

Absorbed in the movie, Casey scrubbed his ears, sending him into ecstasy. He was asleep, snoring softly, long before the movie was over.

As the credits scrolled across the screen, Casey switched off the set. A glance at her watch told her that it was almost midnight. She wondered when Josh would be home. He'd told her that covering a fresh homicide could take hours.

Getting up from the sofa roused Spot, and, according to Josh's instructions, Casey whistled the dog out onto the deck, and pacified him with bowls of food and water. The deck was high enough above ground so that he wouldn't be tempted to jump off. Josh had been firm about this one thing. "That dog can be in the house when we're up and about, but I don't want him on the beds, or scratching and whining at the bedroom doors during the night. When we go to bed, he goes out onto the deck. Understood?"

So Casey, despite Spot's soulful looks, locked him out on the deck and retired to her own room. By the time she was in bed, it was well after midnight, and she hadn't heard Josh come in.

She drifted in and out of sleep, annoyed that she kept listening for any sound indicating that Josh was back. Finally, full sleep claimed her, but it seemed that she had only been asleep for a moment when an alien sound woke her. She glanced at the glowing numerals of the bedside clock — 1:35. What had awakened her? Josh?

Breathing shallowly, she listened, and heard a strangled yelp from the direction of the deck. Quickly, she sat up and swung her feet to the floor. As she did so, the boards quivered slightly. She held her breath, but heard nothing more. Undecided, she sat for a moment. There were raccoons and coyotes roaming about the area, she knew. Could Spot have seen one? Why was his bark cut off so abruptly?

She shivered, as if from a sudden chill, reached for her robe, and got out of bed, turning on the overhead light. Going down the hallway, she glanced into Josh's bedroom as she passed. It was empty. In the kitchen she fumbled along the wall for the switch to the deck light.

Usually, when she turned on the lights at night, Spot charged the glass door, tongue out, tail wagging. Tonight, there was no sign of him. Cautiously, she slid the door open, calling, "Spot?"

There was no response. Could he have fallen or jumped off the deck?

She stepped outside. His food and water dish were there, but no Spot.

A motion caught her eye — something moving on the deck railing. Cautiously she approached, and saw that it was a length of cord tied to the top rail. Leaning over, she peered down, then recoiled with a muffled scream.

It was Spot! He had been strangled. A piece of cord had been twisted around his neck and tied to the railing, and now he swung jerkily back and forth, like an uncertain pendulum.

CHAPTER EIGHT

When Josh returned home at 2:00 a.m., he found Casey still on the deck, the dead dog cradled in her lap, rocking back and forth.

As he stood over her, she looked up with eyes swimming with tears. "Spot is dead, Josh. What will we say to Donnie?"

He squatted down beside her. "Give him to me, Casey," he said in a gentle voice.

Reluctantly she relinquished the animal. Josh examined the small animal closely, fingering the cord still around its neck. "He was strangled, I see. Any idea how it happened?"

She shook her head. "I heard a noise; it woke me up. I came out onto the deck and found Spot hanging from the top rail, there." She pointed to the spot where the dog had been tied.

"Who would do a vicious thing like that, Josh? Of course!" Her eyes went round with fright. "It was that man, Tibbets, wasn't it?"

"More than likely," he said soberly. He stood, extending a hand to help her up. "Come on back inside. I'll take a look around, and then I'll bury Spot."

She rose to her feet. "But what are we going to tell Donnie?"

"The truth, I suppose. He's going to be heartbroken, but he'll make out okay."

Once Casey was safely inside, the deck door locked again, Josh took his flashlight and looked over the premises thoroughly. He was fairly certain that the killer was long gone, but it was possible that he had left some sign of his presence. Josh found nothing. The ground beneath the deck was spare and rocky, and took no footprints. The only clue left by the killer was the cord that he had used to strangle Spot.

Returning to the house, Josh got a plastic bag from the kitchen, tied the body of the dog up in it, and went out to the garage for a shovel. In the wash behind the house, he dug a hole deep enough to insure that prowling animals would not be able to get to the body, and into it gently placed the plastic-shrouded body.

When he was finished, he leaned on the shovel and said softly, "I'm sorry, Spot. I know I gave you a hard time, but I . . ."

Shaking his head, he broke off and turned away. If he ever caught the bastard who did this . . .

Back inside the house, he made certain that all the doors and windows were locked, and turned out most of the lights. As he made his way down the hall toward his bedroom the door to Casey's room opened.

"Josh!" She looked very vulnerable, but she also looked very desirable in a sheer nightgown, the light behind her outlining her body. "Josh, I don't want to sleep alone tonight."

He hesitated. "You sure about this?"

She bobbed her head. "I've never been more sure about anything. I'm frightened, Josh."

He reached out to run a forefinger across her cheek, his touch lingering on her parted lips. She shivered, and clutched at his hand.

"Let me shower first."

When he returned, wearing a robe, his hair wet, she was in bed, the sheet drawn up to her chin. Her eyes looked enormous. He shucked the robe. Her gaze roamed over him, a muffled sound coming from her at the sight of his erection. Quickly, she reached out and switched off the bedside lamp.

As Josh approached the bed, she threw back the sheet, and he stretched out beside her. As his big hands tenderly touched her breasts, she sighed deeply. Closing her hands around his, she pressed them against her tumescent nipples.

"Josh . . . Don't read too much into this.

I don't know how I'll feel about it tomorrow. Right now, I'm spooked. I need someone . . ."

"Hush, Babe. Forget about tomorrow." He placed a finger across her lips.

He began to make slow love to her with his lips and fingers, caressing the hollows and contours of her body. Casey gave herself up to sensation, her flesh throbbing everywhere he touched. Here, in bed, in her arms, the tough image he projected was put aside. He was a gentle, caring lover, clearly in no rush, waiting for her.

But soon he was roaring ready. With plucking fingers she urged him over her, into her. At the moment he entered her, he captured her mouth, his tongue probing between her parted lips.

As their mutual pleasure broke, Casey rose to meet him, straining, a muted cry wrung from her.

They lay side by side, holding hands, bodies sheathed in perspiration.

"That was good, Josh," she said with heaving breath. She ran the palm of her hand across the matted hairs on his chest. "It's been awhile."

"Yeah, it was okay."

"Okay? Just okay?" At the sound of his muffled laughter, she hit him on the shoulder with her fist. "You're a complete bastard, you know that, Detective?"

"It's what I do best."

She was quiet for a few moments. Then: "Josh, I was thinking about what Tibbets said in court. 'The smallest one first.' At the time I thought he meant Donnie, but he must have meant Spot. That would mean that Donnie is next, wouldn't it?"

Josh sighed heavily. "If Tibbets is the one who killed the dog, yeah."

"Of course he's the one. Who else could it be?" She raised herself to stare down into his face in the dim light. "We have to do something, Josh. I'd never forgive myself, or you, if something happened to that child."

In the dark van, from across the wash, Ray Tibbets stared at the house through night binoculars. He knew that it was risky to linger in the neighborhood; but he could not resist the temptation to watch what happened when the cop and the girl discovered the dead mutt. Tibbets had been watching the house for several nights running, waiting for the cop to leave the girl alone. Tonight it had happened.

After he had seen the cop leave, he had waited until all the lights were out. Then, in his dark clothing and rubber gloves, he had approached the house, walked under the deck

121

at the point where it was nearest to the ground, talked softly to the dog, and thrown a chunk of hamburger up over the deck railing. The stupid mutt was so friendly that he hadn't even barked.

While the mutt swallowed the meat, Tibbets had scaled the deck support, gained the deck, and strangled the dog. A piece of cake for a man with his talents.

He recalled the deed now, with a throb of pleasure. He had killed his first dog — his own pet — at the age of twelve. It had been the first incident of real pleasure he had experienced in his dreary existence. In some way, killing the animal had made him feel stronger, more important. It was almost as if the life force, the energy that the dog had possessed, was now his. His mother had not been able to understand why he hadn't cried over the death of the animal.

After that, over the years, he killed many animals; until he discovered, last year, that he received even more pleasure, and more power, if he killed a human.

The first one had been an accident. Always sexually charged, he had never been good with women. He didn't know what to say to them, how to treat them. He saw other men, often less physically attractive than himself, charm themselves into women's sexual good will; but how they did so remained a mystery to Tibbets. In addition, the need to flatter, charm, and coax women into giving him what he considered his due, made him terribly angry.

So he had tried a prostitute, a busty young blonde he picked up on a street corner, like he had seen it done in the movies.

She had taken him to her cheap room in an even cheaper hotel. The room had been messy and dirty, and the sight of it had made Tibbets's anger surge. He deserved better than this!

Before the girl was completely undressed, he had grabbed her, and felt his anger grow, increased by the sight of her body and her smell. As he pressed his fingers into the soft flesh of her arms he reveled in his own power.

The girl began to struggle, shouting at him, but her struggles only incensed him further. Throwing her onto the unmade bed, he unzipped his jeans and threw himself onto her body.

For an instant he felt pure horror. He had gone soft; he had been unmanned! The violence of his rage and shame moved his hands to her throat. It was so soft, so vulnerable. And as she tried to scream, his hands tightened. The sound stopped, but her body began to thrash wildly beneath his, and as he felt the movement, he felt himself grow hard again, hard and implacable. Hard and powerful.

As her body gave a final spasm, a great surge of pure pleasure surged through him, so powerful that it left him shaking. For a long moment he swooned, tossed by the receding waves of sensation.

When he regained his senses, the girl was still beneath him, and he was amazed to see that he was still erect.

Warm satisfaction filled him. This was the way it should be. He had not lost his power, not spilled his male energy; yet he had received a pleasure greater than any he had ever experienced. He had been chosen to know a great secret. He had been given a great power. He felt strong, clear-headed, and filled with purpose.

He had run across no real problems in disposing of the body. When it was good and late, and the hotel and the street were quiet, he had put a hat and coat on her. Then he put her right arm across his neck, grasped it with his right hand, put his own left arm across her back and around her waist, and walked her down the one flight of stairs and to his car, parked a block away.

If anyone had noticed, they would have seen only a sight not unusual in this area, a man and his drunken date stumbling down the sidewalk.

It didn't take long to drive out to the desert. He always carried a shovel in the van, and he buried her in a hollow some distance from the road. Afterward, he went home and slept like a baby.

So she had been the first, and he had known immediately that she would not be the last. However, he made for himself a few rules. No more cheap rooms. He couldn't take them to his own place, that would be too dangerous; but he would do them in his van, being very careful not to leave any traces of their presence. It would all be very neat and clean, and he would be sure that there was no connection to him.

And that's the way it had gone. Three takings now, and each one as good as the last. And, despite the arrest, they had nothing on him, nothing at all.

Tibbets smiled to himself. Now he was going to take a male, two males, first the boy, and then the man. He had never taken a man before, although he had considered it. It seemed to him that if there was pleasure in taking animals and more pleasure in taking women, there might be even greater pleasure in killing a man; for after all, men were larger and stronger than women and therefore should contain more energy and power. The thought filled him with excitement.

Holding the binoculars in his left hand, Tibbets squeezed the tennis ball in his right. Squeeze and relax. Squeeze and relax. He had very strong hands. The better to throttle you with, my dear. He laughed aloud. After killing the dog, he had considered taking the woman as she sat there crying on the deck, but he had forced himself to wait. The waiting would be delicious. And, he wanted all of them, the boy, the cop, and the woman to fully realize what was in store for them.

CHAPTER NINE

Early the next morning, Josh drove to Donnie's apartment building. Dreading having to tell the boy about his dog, Josh trudged up the stairs to the second floor, and down the hall to the apartment door. He rang the bell and waited what seemed a very long time.

When the door finally opened, it did so on a chain, and Edith Black's bloodshot eyes peered through the crack. "Oh . . . It's you!"

Josh sighed. "I'd like to talk with Donnie, please, Ms. Black."

"What is it now?" Her tone was exasperated. "I thought it was all over. Oh, all right!"

She unchained the door and opened it wide. As Josh entered the cluttered living room, Donnie came in from the direction of his bedroom. His face lit up. "Josh!" One full look at Josh's face, and the smile slid off the boy's face. "What is it, Josh?"

Josh took his hand and led him to the couch. "Let's sit down, Donnie. I have some bad news, I'm afraid."

Donnie clung to his hand, his eyes big. "What is it, Josh?"

Josh swallowed. "I'm afraid it's your pooch, Donnie. Spot is dead."

Donnie didn't seem to understand. "How come? He was okay yesterday. He wasn't sick or nothing."

Josh shook his head. "He wasn't sick, Donnie. He was killed."

"That man! That man killed him!"

Josh was taken aback, astounded that the boy should have grasped the likelihood of what he was saying. "We don't know for certain, Donnie; but yes, it's possible that Tibbets killed him."

Behind them, Edith Black gave vent to a snort of disdain. "That blasted dog! Nothing but trouble."

Josh and Donnie ignored her as Josh said, "And that's not all. You remember the threat that Tibbets made in the courtroom, Donnie?"

Donnie nodded mutely, silent tears running down his cheeks.

"Well, we're afraid that Tibbets may try to . . . hurt all of us, you, Casey, and me." God, Josh thought, this is a hell of a thing to be telling a little kid; but he's got to know. I sure can't count on his aunt to look out for him.

He put his arm around Donnie's shoulder.

"We're afraid that he may come after you next."

Donnie dashed at his tears. "I'm not a-feared of him!"

"But you should be, Donnie . . ."

Edith Black interrupted. "You mean that the killer may be coming *here?*"

Josh looked back over his shoulder at her. "I'm not sure, but it's quite possible."

Her thin lips tightened. "You're the police. We're entitled to protection!"

"Yes, you are, Ms. Black. I'm doing everything I can. But I don't think he'll harm you. It's the boy he's after."

"But if he comes here . . . No!" She backed up, fear stamped across her face. "I won't have it! You have to take Donnie somewhere else, away from here!"

"But he's your nephew, Ms. Black . . ."

"I don't care! I don't care! I want him out of here. I should never have taken him in. He's been nothing but trouble."

Josh stared at her in disgust, then turned to Donnie. "Okay, Donnie, let's pack your things and get the hell out of here."

Donnie's face brightened. "Am I going to stay with you and Casey, Josh?"

"Yeah, I guess so. For the time being, anyway."

Josh scrubbed at his chin. He had no idea

what he was letting himself in for, and he would probably live to regret it, but what else could he do?

Donnie hopped off the couch, taking Josh's hand and leading him toward the bedroom. He looked trustingly up into Josh's face. "I'll like living with you and Casey, Josh. And maybe we can get another dog."

See, Josh thought. It's starting already.

Ray Tibbets had just pulled his van into the curb halfway up the block, on the other side of the street, when he saw the cop coming out of the boy's apartment building. He was carrying a large, battered suitcase, and the kid was with him.

They were heading away from him, and Tibbets wasn't worried about being made. His van now bore the name of a fictitious TV repair service. Tibbets himself was wearing a pair of blue coveralls with the same name stitched across the back, and a blue cap.

He watched as the cop helped the kid into the car, and put the beat-up bag in the rear. So, the big, tough cop had a soft spot for the kid and was rescuing him from that aunt of his. Tibbets had been watching the apartment for several days now, and had seen the boy and the woman together enough times to know that the woman had no love for the boy, and that she treated him badly. He had also seen her live-in boyfriend, another fine specimen. For a moment Tibbets felt something very like sympathy for the boy. Tibbets knew what it was like to be mistreated. Well, it would make the kid tough, or — he amended his thoughts — it would, if the kid wasn't scheduled to be eliminated.

And as far as this change of plans, well, it was all part of the game. A new move from the cop, to keep it interesting. He wondered where the man was taking the kid, to a home of some sort? Or, maybe to his own home. He already had the woman there. Wouldn't that be great, all of them together?

Smiling to himself, he slowly started his engine; and when the car across the street pulled away, he made a U-turn and slowly followed it. One thing was certain — the cop knew what the killing of the dog meant.

Josh drove to the station. Parking the car in the station lot, he said to Donnie, "I have to go inside for a minute. You stay in the car, okay? I'll leave the motor going with the air-conditioning on, but don't touch the keys, okay? I'll only be a few minutes, then I'll take you out to the house. You leave the windows and doors locked until I get back. You read me?"

"How come, Josh?"

"Because I say so, that's why!" He softened his tone. "Look, kid, if you're to stay with me, there are a few ground rules . . . Let's put it this way; when I give an order it's to be obeyed. It's for your own good." He smiled to take the sting out of his words. "Is that understood?"

"Yes, Josh," Donnie said solemnly.

"Okay, kid."

Josh ruffled the boy's hair, and got out of the car. Inside the building, he went directly to his captain's office. His captain, Mike Randall, was a twenty-year veteran of the Phoenix Police, on the verge of retirement. He had been off the street for years, but he still was able to identify with those under his command. He was a tough boss, but fair. Josh had always gotten along well with him.

Captain Randall greeted Josh with a nod, running a big hand through thinning brown hair. "What is it this time, Josh? I thought maybe I wouldn't be seeing you so soon after that ass-chewing I gave you over the Tibbets fiasco." He scowled. "I hope it's not about that case again."

"I'm afraid so, Captain." Josh sprawled in the chair across from Randall's scarred desk. "I want round-the-clock protection for Casey Farrel and Donnie Patterson."

132

Randall shook his head in disbelief. "Josh, we've been all over that. I can't provide protection for those two just on the basis of a threat from some weirdo. I simply don't have the manpower."

"It's more than just a threat now," Josh said tightly. "Something happened last night . . ." Quickly, he related what had happened to Spot. "And when I went by Donnie's apartment a short while ago, to tell him about Spot, his aunt spooked. She refuses to be responsible for him, refuses to even have him in the apartment with her. She's a real piece of work, the aunt."

"The boy's dog was killed? Come on, Josh, how do you know it was Tibbets?" Randall made a face. "Your usual 'gut feeling'?"

"That too. But it's more than that. Who else would bother to climb up onto my deck to kill a dog? It's not an easy climb. It had to be Ray Tibbets. And as for my gut feelings, have I ever been wrong?"

"Well, yes, I can remember a few times. But I will admit that you're more often right than not."

"Captain . . ." Josh leaned forward. "I'm scheduled to go on night shift for at least two weeks. All we really need is a man in an unmarked unit outside my place at night. I'll handle the days. With Donnie staying with

133

me, we'll only need one stakeout, not two. Surely, you can spare one man."

"First the woman, now you're taking the boy in. What is it with you, Josh, a soft spot for strays?"

"We got them involved in this. I think we owe them. How often do we bitch and moan about crime witnesses not wanting to get involved? What can we expect if we can't offer them *some* protection?"

Randall gave one of his theatrical, put-upon sighs. "Okay, Josh, you got it. One officer on stakeout at your house, nights. But I don't know how long we can keep it going, if Tibbets doesn't try anything. And you'd damned well better be right about him being a threat. If this turns out to be a false alarm, I'll really have your ass this time."

"It won't be for too long, Captain. I'm convinced I'll nail Tibbets as the Dumpster Killer."

Randall smiled thinly. "That's what I like about you, Sergeant Whitney. Always the eternal optimist."

Donnie was still sitting where Josh had left him. Climbing into the car, Josh said, "See, I wasn't gone too long, was I? I was arranging for another policeman to guard my house when I'm not there at night."

Donnie turned in the seat. He said eagerly, "Josh, can we get another dog?"

Josh sighed. "No, Donnie, I'm sorry." At the boy's crushed look, he quickly added: "Look, you wouldn't want the same thing to happen, would you? Let's wait a little, until we see what happens, okay?"

Casey wasn't surprised to find Donnie at the house when she got home from work that night. Josh had told her that he was seeing the boy that day, and she had already assessed Edith Black as a cold, uncaring bitch. Still, she couldn't resist needling Josh. "Nothing like putting all of your fragile eggs in one basket, is there, Detective?"

Josh looked sheepish. "Well, his aunt practically threw the kid out. What did you expect me to do, take him to an orphan's home?" They were talking in the kitchen, getting in each other's way as they prepared dinner, and the "kid" was in the living room, camped in front of the TV.

"I still think I'd be better off in a place of my own," Casey grumped. "A motel, even."

"I thought we settled that last night." He kissed the back of her neck.

She squirmed away. "Now, stop that, Josh! Last night settled nothing. Last night

135

was . . . well, last night."

"Seemed like more than that to me," he said with a leer.

"We're sitting ducks here, Josh."

"He'd find you no matter where you moved. At least here you have some protection. The captain agreed to have a man here at night, when I'm not here. And I'll be here days with the kid."

Casey stopped chopping vegetables for salad and stared at him accusingly. "You know what I think? I think you're using us as bait, hoping he'll try for us."

He looked a little sheepish. "Partly, I suppose. But if he does try, we'll nail him. Depend on it."

"Seems to me I've heard those words before."

"Look, you want this guy caught, don't you? You don't want to spend the rest of your life looking over your shoulder, do you?"

"No, of course not," she said with a sigh. "And of course I want this nut-cake put away. I'm just not sure this is the way to do it. I'm scared, Josh!"

"Naturally you are, and you should be." He took her hand. "Let's just hope that it's over soon. I'll get home in time every morning to drive you to work, and I'll pick you up again at night."

She drew away. "I have my own transportation, thank you."

"You shouldn't be driving alone. Who knows where Tibbets will try to hit you?"

She shook her head. "Tibbets said the little ones first. That means he will try for Donnie next. He's the one to guard."

Josh tried to keep the exasperation out of his voice. "He'll be guarded, don't worry. But if Tibbets can't get at Donnie, he may become frustrated and go for you, particularly if he sees you driving alone. He's a loose cannon, Casey, and there's no telling what he will do."

"Okay, okay!" She batted a hand at him and raised her voice, "Donnie, dinner's ready. Come and eat."

"I don't know how I'm going to take to having a kid underfoot all the time," Josh said in a low voice.

To Josh's surprise, he took to having a kid around very well. Donnie was a constant surprise. He was bright, funny, and an ardent football and baseball fan, who, Josh discovered, had never seen a live game.

Josh knew that the Phoenix Cardinals were just starting training in Flagstaff, and he promised Donnie that he would take him up there to watch a practice before training was over.

One afternoon he took the boy to a minor

league baseball game, and stuffed him with hot-dogs and Cokes until the kid sloshed, earning a tart comment from Casey: "You're spoiling him, Josh! And spoiling his dinner as well."

"Seems to me, after living with the Aunt from Hell, that the kid could use some spoiling," Josh said with a grin. "And what good are kids, if you can't spoil them?"

"Oh, you'll make a great father, I can see that."

"You have something in mind, maybe?" he said innocently.

"When I do, I'll tell you."

Josh hadn't been in her bed since the night Spot was killed. Not that he hadn't wanted to be, but he had felt her drawing back, and sensed that she needed time to come to terms with the situation. Well, he could be patient, particularly when something was worth waiting for.

He had noticed that she too seemed to like having Donnie around. More than once Josh had caught her looking at the boy with a fond, speculative expression, and she often prepared special treats for him.

It was hard *not* to indulge the boy, he was so appealing, and he had been through such a rough time.

Josh found himself wanting to give the kid

138

all the things he had missed, and so, as often as he could, he took Donnie to the zoo, or to the movies — whatever he thought a child Donnie's age might be interested in. Of course all this activity cut into Josh's sleeping time; yet he didn't regret it for one instant.

A week passed in this pleasant fashion, and when there was no further move by Tibbets, Josh began to relax a little, almost ready to conclude that the man wasn't going to carry out his threat. Maybe killing Spot had satisfied him.

Meanwhile, Josh pursued the investigation, although he was getting nowhere fast. All the prowl cars had the description and license number of Tibbets's van. Cops will deny to the death that they keep an eye out for the scumbags that the courts let loose, and will equally deny that they harass these people, yet Josh knew that they often did just that, and he really couldn't blame them. When a cop spends weeks on a case, catches the perpetrator red-handed, then sees the court release the perp on some niggling technicality, it can do something to his or her sense of justice.

Tibbets had already been stopped a couple of times for marginal traffic violations, and generally scanned for any suspicious behavior. Nothing had been found. Josh had talked

139

to each of the officers who had stopped him. They all said that Tibbets had been unfailingly polite and had cooperated fully.

It appeared that Tibbets was indeed keeping a low profile. Yet Josh was still convinced of his guilt, and had no intention of giving up the case.

Every evening that week, before they ate dinner, Josh took Casey down into the wash behind the house and instructed her in the use of the extra pistol. She wasn't a very good student. She flinched and closed her eyes every time she fired, and she couldn't hit the side of a barn.

She said, "I'll never be any good with it."

"You've got that right," he said dryly. "Fine investigator you'll make, not being able to handle a piece."

"I hate guns," she said vehemently.

"Well, that may very well be, but it's the unpleasant truth that you may need to use one. At least now you should be able to do so without shooting yourself in the foot . . . Maybe!"

On Josh's night off that week, the phone rang just as they were finishing dinner. Josh took the call on the wall phone in the kitchen. After he hung up, he turned to Casey.

"What is it, Josh?" Her expression was apprehensive.

140

"I've got to go out, Casey. A body was found downtown."

"But this is your night off!"

"I know, but we're short handed. I'll be back as soon as I can."

"Josh," Donnie wailed, "we were going to watch the Dodgers game on TV together!"

"Sorry kid. I'll make it up to you."

Casey leaned forward. "I'll watch the game with you, Donnie."

Donnie made a face. "Girls don't know anything about baseball."

Casey gave a mock scowl. "Whadaya mean 'girls don't know anything about baseball'? I'll have you know that I pitched for my high-school team, and I was darned good too. Come on, I'll make us some popcorn."

Donnie's expression brightened, and Josh gave Casey a grateful glance.

"I've about decided that Tibbets has backed off on his threat; but be damned sure to keep the doors locked, and the pistol close at hand. I told the dispatcher to send a man, and he should be on his way. He'll probably be here by the time I finish backing out of the garage. I'll call and check on things if I get a chance."

Casey, her arms around Donnie's shoulders, looked at Josh over the boy's head. He could see both her fear and her bravery, and his

141

affection for her threatened for a moment to overcome him. Pulling himself together, he gave her a thumbs-up gesture.

CHAPTER TEN

Ray Tibbets sat patiently in the van, across the wash from the cop's house.

Changing the tennis ball from hand to hand, he squeezed rhythmically. This was the third night he had parked here, checking things out. He knew that the cop was working nights this week. Every night he left the house shortly before eight, just after an unmarked squad car parked in front of the house.

Tibbets grinned in the dark. The stakeout didn't worry him. The plainclothes cop got out of the car every hour or so and walked around the house, then spent the rest of the time in the car, napping.

Tibbets watched the light spilling from the windows of the house, warm and golden against the blackness. The dark of the moon. Tibbets had read that someplace, and liked the sound of it. That's why he had picked this particular night. If the woman followed her usual pattern, she would go to bed soon. When all was quiet, about a half hour past the time when the lights went out, he would go in.

He felt his palms tingle with anticipation, and he squeezed the tennis ball so hard that it squirted out of his hand, bouncing against the windshield. He caught it quickly, with a laugh.

It was somewhat later than usual when the house finally went dark, and by then Tibbets was afire with eagerness. He took a deep breath, snapped on a pair of rubber gloves, and got out of the van, closing the door quietly behind him.

He was wearing black sneakers, pants, shirt, and knit cap. His face was blackened with burnt cork, and he knew that in the darkness he would be almost invisible.

Quietly he made his way down into the wash, where he crouched and waited. The cop should be about ready to make his rounds. When he was through, back in the car and relaxed, Tibbets intended to take him.

Tibbets controlled his breathing, taking the air in and out, slowly and steadily. From the dark distance there came a low rumble. It was the beginning of the so-called monsoon season and clouds had been gathering all day. The air was humid and charged with tension. Tibbets hoped that it wouldn't rain while he was in the wash. He had seen what happened to these dry creek beds when flash floods roared down them. Tibbets wasn't afraid of much, but the force of a solid wall of water was something that even he couldn't fight.

He heard the scuffle of feet, then saw the beam of a flashlight as the cop made his way along the embankment beneath the deck overhang. The light blinked as the cop stopped, and Tibbets tensed, wondering if he had been spotted. He relaxed as he heard the splatter of urine as the man relieved himself. It would have been a good time to take him except that by the time Tibbets crossed the wash and scaled the side of the wash, the cop would be zipped up and back in the car.

When the cop moved on, Tibbets made his way across the wash and up the other side. Moving along the west side of the house, he peered around the corner of the garage. He saw a red glow through the car window as the driver lit a cigarette.

Tibbets drew back. It was difficult to wait, but patience was a virtue he had learned to appreciate. Things done in haste often went wrong. Besides, there was an exquisite kind of pain in making yourself wait. It was so much better when it happened, when you got what you wanted.

Breathing slowly, Tibbets gave the cop time to finish the cigarette, and then additional time to fall asleep.

Cicadas were loud in the trees. Tibbets listened to their musical drone without really hearing.

When there was no movement inside the car, when all was dark and quiet, except for the cicadas, Tibbets, crouching low, moved out toward the rear of the cop car. The driver's window was open, the head of the man at the wheel was back against the seat.

Tibbets grinned savagely, and stood erect, his big hands reaching in through the open window. At the last moment the man came awake. His head jerked as he tried to sit up; but Tibbets's hands were already tightening around his throat. The man gagged, and his body thrashed; but despite his strength, Tibbets's strength was greater.

Tibbets felt a surge of pleasure as the man struggled. He had been right. The more strength a victim had, the greater was the pleasure in taking them!

Then, as the cop's flailing hand connected with the horn button, the horn blared.

The sound, obscenely loud in the darkness, distracted Tibbets, and a black anger filled him as he pushed the man back against the seat.

The sound stopped. Now Tibbets placed a hand on each side of the man's jaw and gave

146

the head a vicious twist. There was a wet, popping sound, and the man's body went limp. The stench of fecal matter immediately fouled the air.

Tibbets pulled back from the car window, but there was no outcry. The house was still dark. Moving away from the car, he waited a few minutes. When the house remained dark, he began making his way around the house and under the deck overhang.

Casey had been unable to sleep. She always felt uneasy at night when Josh wasn't in the house. When he was there, she felt warm and protected. She lay on her back, staring up at the ceiling, thinking of Josh . . .

At the sound of a horn out in the street, she sat bolt upright, her heart pounding wildly. Glancing at the bedside clock, she saw that it was one minute after midnight.

Getting out of bed, she went to the window, pushing the drapes aside to peer out. She saw nothing out of the ordinary. The dark sedan parked almost in front of the house was, she knew, the stakeout car. The sight of it reassured her, and she let the drapes fall as she turned back toward the bed.

As she did so, she felt a slight tremor go through the house. Her body froze as she recalled Josh telling her that one problem with cantilevered houses was that they were apt to quiver slightly when somebody walked on the deck . . .

The deck!

Shaking with sudden fear, she stumbled to the nightstand and pulled out the drawer, reaching for the automatic Josh had given her. As she felt the cold weight of it in her hand, she struggled to recall what Josh had taught her: The gun was a double-action automatic. Pull the trigger once to load the chamber, pull it again to fire. Don't try for an arm or a leg, too small a target, aim for the body, the chest.

Despite her feeling about guns, she found that holding it gave her comfort. Holding it with both hands, already slick with cold sweat, she slipped out of the bedroom and down the short hall to the kitchen. She paused just inside the door, all of her senses straining. The only light came from a night light over the stove.

Again she felt the faint tremor. Narrowing her eyes, she stared at the glass doors to the deck. Was that a shadow beyond the glass?

Then the shadow moved. She heard the clink of metal, as the shadow became the silhouette of a man. For an instant she thought that her heart was going to stop beating, taking her life with it, then she steadied. Raising the automatic, she pulled the trigger once as she brought the weapon up, and again as the gun

148

centered on the bulk behind the glass. The sound of the gunshot was terrifyingly loud in the small kitchen. Glass shattered as the figure reeled back toward the railing, shaking the house.

Given strength by a powerful surge of adrenaline, Casey advanced toward the shattered door holding the automatic ready. She had no idea whether she had hit the intruder, but by the time she reached the door and switched on the deck light, the deck was empty.

Taking a deep breath, she nerved herself to go to the railing and peer over, the gun held before her. A movement on the ground to the left of the deck caught her eye, and she turned in that direction just in time to see a scuttling figure disappear into the brush at the bottom of the gully.

The figure looked like that of a man; but she didn't get enough of a look to tell whether it was Ray Tibbets. But whoever he was, one thing seemed certain — if she had hit him, she hadn't slowed him down much; and if he wasn't badly wounded, he might come back.

At a sound behind her she whirled, the automatic coming up. Donnie, in pajamas, stood yawning in the doorway.

"Casey, what is it? Was that a noise I heard?" His eyes widened as he noticed the automatic.

She lowered the gun, said tersely, "Yes, Donnie. I just fired a shot. There was a man on the deck."

All traces of sleep left the boy's face as he said excitedly, "Was it the van man? Did you hit him?"

"I don't know who it was. I don't think I hit him, or, if I did, I must have only wounded him. He could come back. Go get dressed, Donnie."

"How come? Are we leaving?"

"We may, I don't know yet. Just be ready in case we do."

Donnie ran back down the hall and Casey hurried after him, turning on every light until the house blazed like a Christmas tree. If Tibbets had any idea of coming back for a second try, the lights might change his mind.

In her bedroom, Casey quickly threw on a pair of slacks, a shirt, and a pair of flats. As she slipped her feet into the shoes, she remembered the stakeout parked in the street.

Why hadn't the cop come to investigate? Surely he had to have heard the shot, and the glass shattering. The nearest house was a hundred yards away, and it was understandable that no one there had heard the noise. Presumably everyone was in bed, the house closed up tight, with the air conditioning turned on against the heat. But the cop was sitting right out there in the street! Where the hell was he?

She went to the window and looked out. The car was still there, and she could see the outline of the man inside, his head back against the seat. Casey snorted softly. He must be a heavy sleeper. Fat lot of protection he provided.

Going back down the hall, still carrying the automatic, she poked her head into the bedroom where Donnie slept with Josh.

"I'm going outside for just a minute, Donnie. You stay right here. Do you understand?"

Donnie nodded, his eyes wide.

Opening the front door, she looked carefully around the front of the house. There was no one in sight, and seeing that there was no place for anyone to hide, she hurried out to the parked car, calling as she approached, "Officer! Wake up! Didn't you hear all the noise? We both could have been killed in our beds for all the help you were!"

There was no response from the man behind the wheel. Casey peered in through the open window. "How could you possibly sleep through . . ."

As she leaned closer, she felt the tiny hairs along her spine raise. The man's eyes were open and unmoving. Trembling, she reached inside the car and touched the side of his face.

At her touch, his head rolled loosely to one side.

Quickly she jumped back. "Oh, my God!"

For a moment she felt that her legs might give way. She couldn't move. Then she turned and ran awkwardly back toward the house.

In that moment it became clear to her what she must do. It might not be the best for all concerned, it might not even be best for her, but it was the only solution she could find that might allow her to attain peace of mind.

As she entered the house and locked the door after her, she called out, "Donnie!"

Donnie, fully dressed, came running down the hall. "What, Casey?"

Casey put her hands on the boy's shoulder. "We have to get out of here as quickly as possible. It's not safe to stay here any longer. The police can't protect us. Pack some things."

Donnie's small face creased with concern. "But what about Josh? Shouldn't we wait for him?"

Casey's heart ached for the boy. She knew how much he loved Josh, but she kept her voice brisk. "I'm sorry, but we can't wait. He can't protect us either. Look what happened here tonight. We have to go, Donnie. Josh will understand."

Still looking worried, Donnie trudged back

to his room. Casey bit her lower lip. Was she doing the right thing? Well, she had to do something.

Hurrying into her own room, she tossed the automatic on the unmade bad, then hastily threw some things into a bag. She was grateful now that, thinking she might be moving out any day, she had left some of her things in a trunk in the T-bird.

Carrying the bag, she went down the hall. "Ready, Donnie?" she called out.

"In a minute."

"I'll be in the kitchen."

In the kitchen, she picked up the note pad that Josh kept to take telephone messages, and began to write. When she was finished, she attached the note to the refrigerator with one of the magnets grouped there. She then went to the phone and punched out 911. When a voice answered, she said hurriedly, "A police officer has been killed. He's in a car parked in front of . . ."

The body that Josh had been called out for was found in an alley, but there was no further resemblance to the Dumpster Murders. Male, not female. Throat cut from ear to ear, not strangled. And the body was found propped up against the alley wall, not in a dumpster.

The body, obviously that of a wino, was

missing its shoes. The poor bastard had probably been killed for what little money he might have had on him, and for the shoes. Definitely not the Dumpster Killer.

Even so, the routine had to be run through, and it was well after midnight before Josh could finally head for home.

As he started toward his car parked at the end of the alley, a uniform legged it toward him. The officer said breathlessly, "Sergeant, a call just came in. An officer has been killed, and if I'm not mistaken, it happened in front of your house."

Josh felt as if the man had punched him in the gut. "Oh, Christ. Casey and Donnie!"

He took off at a dead lope. Ramming his car out of the alley, he reached out to fasten the siren on the roof. The sound of its raucous wail seemed to give voice to the emotion that was clogging his throat and chest. Casey and Donnie! If anything had happened to them he would never be able to forgive himself!

As he turned onto his street, Josh saw light blazing from the house. A half-dozen squad cars were pulled up in front, doors open, red lights flashing.

He brought his car to a screeching halt, and was out of it almost before it stopped rolling. As he ran toward the house, he noticed that the garage door was open, and Casey's Thunderbird was gone.

Inside, the house was crawling with uniforms, and it took only a moment to find out that the house was otherwise empty. Casey and Donnie were gone. He let the officer in charge show him the broken window, but his mind was churning with the cross-currents of fear and relief. There were no bodies. Casey and Donnie were, presumably, not dead. But, who was driving Casey's car? Had she and Donnie gotten away? Or did Tibbets have them?

Outside, a number of uniforms were gathered around the unmarked car at the curb. Slowly, feeling his gut clench, Josh walked toward them. They stood aside to let him see into the car; and bile rose in his throat as he saw the angle of Thomas's head.

One of the officers said, "He's dead, Sergeant. Neck's been snapped like a twig!"

Josh straightened up, swallowing. "It was Tibbets. Depend on it. Has the area been searched?"

"Some of the guys are at it now. So far, nothing."

"How about the house? Was it empty when you got here?"

The officer nodded. "Yeah. But the front door was open, and clothes were strewn around the bedrooms. It looks like somebody left in a hurry. Also, the glass doors to the deck are smashed. It looks like someone broke in, or was trying to break in . . .

Josh nodded. "Thanks. I saw. Let me know if your boys find anything."

Turning, he went back into the house, and into the kitchen. This time he paid attention to what he saw. Most of the broken glass was on the deck, so the window must have been broken from the inside.

As he stood looking at the deck, a young uniform touched his shoulder. "Sergeant. I think this was left for you."

He held out toward Josh a sheet of paper. "We found it on the refrigerator."

Full of apprehension, Josh took the paper and read:

"Dear Josh, I'm leaving, and taking Donnie with me. Someone, I'm sure it was Tibbets, tried to break in. As you can see, I shot at him; but I don't think I hit him, and I'm afraid that he will come back. The officer out front is dead, and I am very afraid. I just can't take any more of this, and I no longer want Donnie and me to be sitting ducks. I know that you won't agree with what I am doing, but it seems to me to be the only sensible thing to do. I don't know where we are going, and I don't want you to try and find us.

"I am very grateful for all you have done

for me, and as for Donnie, well, you know that he loves you. This will be rough on him, but not as rough as getting killed. I will be watching the Phoenix newspapers, and if and when Tibbets is caught and sent away for good, we'll be back. Depend on it!"

CHAPTER ELEVEN

Tibbets had not expected the woman to have a gun. The shattering glass, and the bark of the shot, shocked and startled him. He reacted instinctively; leaping across the deck and vaulting over the low railing in a matter of seconds.

Hitting the ground in a roll, which should have brought him to his feet unhurt, he felt his shoulder hit a rock, which threw him off balance. As he came out of the roll and onto his feet, he felt his ankle twist, sending a sharp lance of pain up his leg.

Cursing under his breath, he limped into the cover of the brush at the bottom of the gully. It wasn't until he was in his car, reaching for his keys, that he discovered something worse than his twisted ankle; the rubber glove on his right hand was torn, ripped across the fingers. As he stared at the blood oozing from the shallow cuts on his middle and ring fingers, a cold rage filled him. If the tear had happened when the door exploded, which he suspected it had, his fingerprints could be on the deck rail.

Cursing, he pounded the steering wheel. He knew that he should get away from here, the cops would be coming soon, but he didn't move. He stared across the gully at the house, lit up now like a stage. Damn the woman anyway! He should have realized that she might have a gun, or that there would be one in the house. After all, her boyfriend was a cop! It was a weakness perhaps that he, Ray, didn't think in terms of guns. But to him guns implied a weakness. Resorting to a gun meant that a man wasn't strong enough to kill on his own; he needed help. Also, where was the pleasure in killing from a distance? A man should feel the flesh of his victims, the warmth, the life! In a perfect world, Ray would have dispensed with the thin rubber gloves and taken his victims flesh to flesh; but this wasn't that kind of world, and he had to take precautions. It was like wearing condoms when you had sex, a matter of protection. Still, he performed the act himself, with no other weapon than his own hands. He was a purist.

Still, he should have thought about the possibility of the woman using a gun. He had been lax. She was spooked now, and the second try would be more difficult.

As he stared at the house with narrow eyes, he saw the garage door open, and the Thunderbird nose slowly out. The lights from the house were so bright that he could see the silhouettes of the woman and the boy in the car.

A cold misgiving began to cramp his belly. She was running away, and taking the kid with her. He knew it as surely as if she had told him; and he didn't have a chance of tailing her. By the time he drove the two miles back to the bridge across the wash, she would be long gone.

Frustration and anger overcame him. He tried to choke it back. Now was no time to lose his cool. He would find her. There would be a way. There always was a way, if you kept your head. And the first thing he had to do was get away from here.

Turning on the ignition, he forced himself to step gently on the gas pedal. As the van steadied and gained speed, so did his thoughts. He had killed a cop, and, possibly left fingerprints on the deck. His lips lifted in a grim smile. It was almost funny. You could kill as many whores as you wanted, and there wouldn't be half the fuss that was made if you killed a cop. The bastards just couldn't stand it when one of their own went down. It was pretty strange, really. After all, taking a chance on getting killed was part of a cop's job. A calculated risk, sort of; it went with the territory. That wasn't true in the case of civilians. It just showed what wussies the cops really were.

But to the matter at hand: if he had left prints, and if they were found, the cops would be on his case like ticks on a dog. There was only one sensible thing to do. He turned the van toward Glendale, where he had a small, furnished apartment.

When the big cop had asked Tibbets how he earned a living, Tibbets had not told the whole truth. He made most of his money by installing TV satellite control boxes with the illegal "monkey chips" which allowed the satellite owners to pick up scrambled signals. He always received cash in payment, two thousand in most cases. That way there was no record of monies paid or received, all free and clear of taxes.

And he was careful to be prepared to move at a moment's notice. There was very little in the apartment that belonged to him — a few clothes, toilet articles, sleeping bag, a cache of non-perishable food, and a stash of money, almost five thousand dollars he kept hidden behind the baseboard in his closet. His tools were usually kept locked in his van.

Once inside the apartment, he looked at his ankle. It was an ugly red, and swollen to more than twice its normal size. He didn't take his shoe off, as he knew that he would never get it back on again; and settled for the present for wrapping the ankle above his work shoe with an Ace bandage.

Because of the ankle, his packing took him longer than he wished; still, he was in and out of the apartment in less than twenty minutes. Fifteen minutes later he was at the gates of a wrecking yard. It was now nearly two in the morning. The wrecking yard was in an industrial section, and the streets were deserted.

Tibbets parked his van around the corner from the gate; took his flashlight and a pair of wire cutters from his tool box, and limped down the side street. His ankle hurt like hell, and he moved with only a fraction of his usual speed. It took several minutes for him to get into the lot, and a little longer to find a vehicle with a commercial license plate.

Back at the van, he switched the stolen plate with the one on his van. He knew that the usual procedure was for yards of this sort to report the plates of wrecked vehicles to the ADOT as being out of service; but sometimes this wasn't done right away. Still, he would have to be careful that he wasn't stopped for a traffic violation. At any rate, cops on the lookout for a black van with his old plate number wouldn't stop him, and that should buy him some time.

A few blocks away from the wrecking yard he pulled up by a storm drain and tossed down the old plate.

Then he went looking for a respectable motel with an inside parking lot, where a passing cop car wouldn't spot the van from the street. He could have dumped the van and taken the first plane out of Phoenix, but he had dismissed that idea almost as soon as he had entertained it. He could not turn away from what he had set out to do, and if he left Phoenix, there would be no chance of finding the woman and the kid. Also, people at the airport might remember a limping man. No, what he needed now was a place to hole up for a few days until his ankle got better, a quiet spot where he could work out a plan to find the woman and the boy.

Josh, still staring down at Casey's note, heard a voice behind him. "Sergeant?"

He turned to face one of the forensics team, holding an automatic sealed in a plastic evidence bag. "We found this in one of the bedrooms, lying on an unmade bed."

Josh took the bag. "I recognize it. It's the

piece I gave Miss Farrel for protection. Has it been fired?"

"Twice." The man indicated the shattered glass door. "At a guess, I'd say a bullet is probably what broke the door."

Josh nodded. "Have they found the casing or the slug?"

"I'll check with the others."

Josh stood staring down at the gun in the clear envelope. Casey had evidently fired at the intruder. Had she hit him? But more important, why hadn't she taken the pistol with her? Wherever she was going, it would have been protection . . .

He looked up as the young forensics man came trotting back. His eager face made Josh feel very old and tired. "They found the casing in the kitchen, but no slug. If she missed the perp, it's probably somewhere out there in the brush. But they found a trace of blood on some of the shards from the glass door, and two fresh, bloody fingerprints on the top of the deck railing."

Josh felt his fatigue melt away, replaced by a surge of excitement. "By damn, we may have him. Get those prints down to the station and run a match. If they belong to Tibbets, we've got the bastard this time."

By the time the two police cruisers ghosted

to a stop in front of Tibbets's apartment building, a faint line of light was showing on the horizon.

The building was constructed around an inner patio into which all the apartments opened. There was only one entrance in front of which the cruisers were now parked. Josh recalled from his previous investigation that Tibbets's apartment was on the ground floor on the west side.

Silently the four policemen went through the gate into the patio. All the apartments were dark except three, and Josh breathed a sigh of relief when he saw that one of the three was Tibbets's. He motioned to the other officers and pointed to the lighted window. When they had all moved into position, Josh, gun drawn, sidled quietly along the wall until he reached the door. To his surprise, he saw that the door was open a few inches, and a dark foreboding filled him. Tibbets was gone. He knew it in his gut. Still, he had to go through the motions.

Drawing a deep breath, he kicked the door violently open. As the door banged against the inside wall he went in, moving quickly to one side, his gun sweeping the lighted room. It was as he had suspected. Nothing.

As the others came in, he let his anger and frustration sweep over him. Damn it. Tibbets was ahead of them again!

A fast sweep of the place confirmed this. The apartment was unbelievably neat, but there wasn't a personal item to be found. Tibbets evidently was not intending to return.

Cursing under his breath in a furious monotone, Josh paced the small confines of the apartment. Tibbets had at least a two hour lead on them. He could be anywhere by now, out of Phoenix, even out of the state, down into Mexico. An APB was out on him, and the van, but Tibbets was no fool. He could have gotten rid of the van, or changed the plates.

On the other hand, maybe he hadn't gone far at all. The man was mad, obsessed; and Josh had a gut feeling that he would still try to carry out his threats. It would be a matter of honor with him — if you could use such a term in speaking of something so twisted. It was quite possible that Tibbets was holed up somewhere nearby, until he could get another chance to take his revenge. Josh hoped that Casey and the boy were long gone, out of Tibbets's reach. Perhaps she had done the wise thing in fleeing, after all. Still, he was going to have to put out an APB on Casey and the boy. He hated to do it, but he had no choice. She was an important witness in an officer's death. Also, there existed the distinct possibility that Edith Black, when she learned that Donnie was gone, would lodge a charge of kidnapping against Casey. She was the kind of woman to do that.

It was the third day he had been holed up in the hotel room, but Ray Tibbets thought he was handling the isolation well. After all, he was used to being alone, used to being disciplined. That's what it all came down to. Mental discipline. You trained your mind just like you trained your hands, your body. Everything grew stronger with training.

The condition of his ankle, which he had attended to as soon as he was able, had improved markedly. While it had been mending, he had been preparing for the hunt. Now, he sat propped up on the bed, studying the newspaper pictures of the woman and the boy. He didn't really need the pictures to see their faces. He could close his eyes and conjure their images onto the screen of his mind in perfect detail. Each time he did so, he let the visualization go a step further, until he saw them screaming for mercy, gasping for breath. The thought brought a smile to his lips, and his eyes closed for a moment to savor the moment.

Opening his eyes again, he stared at the pictures. The camera had caught the woman with her head turned, her mouth partly open, her eyes wide, as if she had seen something frightening.

Tibbets smiled, again, a rictus without humor. When next she saw his face, she would truly register fear.

Lowering his eyes to the article below the pictures he read it again, certain phrases seeming to leap from the page: important witness . . . half Hopi . . . recently from Los Angeles.

There were three main highways leading out of Phoenix: I-10, heading west into California; I-17, going north to Flagstaff; and the other branch of I-10, heading south to Tucson and east into New Mexico. From Tucson, one could also go down Highway 89 into Old Mexico.

There were, of course, other, lesser roads; but Tibbets felt certain that a woman fleeing in fear would select a main artery where she wouldn't have to worry so much about speed limits.

The question was, which one? He was confident that she wouldn't drive east, nor would she go into Mexico; there was too much chance of being spotted at the border, and a woman would have to be a fool to drive alone in Mexico.

No, the two most likely possibilities were that she was headed either toward California, or had gone north on I-17. Would she head back to where she had come from or head for new territory? It seemed to him that a woman would head for the familiar. He would try I-10 first.

It was going to be a long, tedious process, unless he got lucky at once. But he had the time, as long as he could avoid the cops, and he should be able to manage that. He'd fooled them so far, hadn't he?

Also he had one thing going for him. The chances were that anyone fleeing without prior planning would have less than a full tank of gas. Somewhere within the first hundred miles out of Phoenix, the woman would have to stop for gas. And, wherever she stopped, the chances were good that someone would notice them, a good-looking woman like that, with a small boy.

He was now ready to leave at any time. Yesterday, he had had the van painted blue at an auto paint shop up the block. However, he intended to wait until the same hour that the woman had left the cop's house. That way he would be travelling along her route at roughly the same time she had been travelling, and thus could eliminate all the service stations not open at that hour.

Carefully he tore out the newspaper photos, and folded them neatly so that he could put them into his jacket pocket. Then, relaxing back against the pillows, he picked up his tennis ball and began squeezing it to an inner rhythm as a dreamy smile settled across his lips.

"I'm coming, woman," he said aloud. "Look back over your shoulder, and you'll see me right on your tail."

CHAPTER TWELVE

When Casey sped away from Josh's house with Donnie, she had no definite destination in mind. Her paramount concern was to get away from the house, from Phoenix, and from any proximity to Ray Tibbets.

For a time her mind was in such chaos that she was operating on automatic pilot. It was only when Donnie asked her: "Where are we going, Casey?" that she looked around her and saw that she was approaching the entrance to the I-17 freeway. Well, it was as good a route as any.

Turning onto the ramp, she tried to make her voice calm and comforting. "I'm not sure, Donnie. I guess that you'll have to help me decide. We want to get far away from that Tibbets man, so he can't find us."

"Are you going to take me back to Aunt Edith?" he asked in a small voice.

Reaching over with her right hand, she patted his knee. "No, sweetheart. No. That wouldn't be safe."

She risked a quick glance at him. "Unless you *want* to go back."

He seemed to huddle within himself. "I don't wanta go there. No way! I wanta go with you, Casey."

"Good!"

Casey felt herself relax. "You know, I'm really glad you're with me. I'd be frightened if I was alone. With you here I feel a lot safer."

She gave him another quick glance, and saw him drawing his little body up. She could swear that he had grown two inches.

He gave her a glowing smile. "Since Josh ain't here, I guess I'm the man of the family, huh? Well, I'll look after you, Casey."

He put his small hand on her arm, and she was amazed by the comfort it gave her. He really was a brave little fellow.

She gave him an answering smile. "Isn't," she said firmly.

"But we'll have to call your aunt," she said. "When she finds out that we're gone, she'll worry about you."

He shook his head. "Nah. She'll probably be glad I'm gone so she and Brent can go out all the time."

"Well, just the same, we have to call her. It's the right thing to do, and . . ."

Donnie gave a bounce in his seat. "We always want to try to do the right thing," he finished, repeating what Casey had previously taught him.

They both laughed, and Casey, looking ahead at the almost empty freeway, wondered at the resiliency of youth.

There were signs over the next intersection: I-17 going north toward Flagstaff and south toward downtown Phoenix, and the junction with I-10 going west into California.

Casey immediately rejected California and the Los Angeles area. She had suffered too much heartbreak in L.A. As the northbound on-ramp came up on her right, she turned onto it without hesitation.

To the north and east was Second Mesa, where her uncle and cousins lived. Her uncle, and at least some of her cousins, would welcome her, and would probably be willing to take them in. She might be safe there. On the other hand, she might be putting what was left of her family in danger . . .

"How come we're going this way, Casey? Where are we going? Do you want me to help you decide now?"

Casey forced a smile for him. "Not just yet, Donnie. I think we'll just drive in this direction for a while. We'll stop somewhere in a little bit, and you can help me decide then. Okay? Why don't you curl up and take a nap now? It's been a busy night."

173

Donnie yawned. "Okay, Casey," he said docilely, and leaning his head against the door, was asleep almost at once.

Casey felt a pang of guilt. He was so trusting. He had put his faith in her without question. He had, in effect, put his life into her hands. What if that trust was misplaced? What if, by running and taking him with her, she had placed him in even greater danger? She knew that she could never forgive herself if anything happened to him.

Still, she just couldn't leave him to the mercy of Tibbets. It still seemed to her that in Phoenix they didn't stand a chance against the madman. At least out here, away from Phoenix, they wouldn't be so easy to find. As far as Tibbets knew, they could have taken any route, be anywhere. They might even have driven to the airport and taken a plane. How could he know?

Feeling a little better, she glanced down at the fuel gauge. During the confusion of her departure, she had given no thought to how much gas was in the T-bird's tank. Now she saw that she had only a quarter of a tank left.

A sign flashed by, Black Canyon City. She tried to remember the name of, and the distance to, the next town. Cordes Junction was a fair sized town. Surely there would be a gas

174

station there; and she had just about enough gas to make it.

There was little traffic at this hour of the morning, and she let herself relax, mulling over possible destinations.

By the time she came upon the sign denoting the Cordes Junction turn-off, she had made up her mind.

As she slowed for the off-ramp, Donnie stirred. He sat up, knuckling the sleep from his eyes. He mumbled, "How come we're getting off here, Casey?"

"We have to get gas."

"Where are we?"

"Cordes Junction. And Donnie, I think I have an idea of where we can go. That is, if you think it's a good idea."

He took a deep breath. "Yeah. Sure. What's your idea?"

"Well, I thought that we could head for Laughlin, Nevada. It's just over the state line. I don't have much money with me, and I think I could get a job there. They have a lot of hotels and casinos, and they must need a lot of help. What do you say?"

"What's a casino?"

She braked for a stop sign at the top of the ramp. "It's a big hotel, where people, grown-ups, gamble."

She waited for the next question, "What's

175

gamble, Casey," but it didn't come.

"Oh," said Donnie wisely. Casey smiled to herself. Did he know what the word meant, or was he pretending wisdom?

As she left the stop, Casey could see several service stations. One was brightly lit, and she turned toward it with relief.

Pulling in at the self-service pump, she turned to Donnie.

"Do you want a Coke or something?"

"Yeah!"

"Okay. Buy me a cup of coffee while you're at it." She opened her purse to dig out some change.

"I have some money, Casey." He waved a hand at her. "Let me buy."

"You don't have to do that . . ."

He was already out of the car, heading toward the small convenience store. Casey stared after him with a fond smile. He was a good kid. She got out of the car and stretched, suddenly aware of her deep fatigue. Trying to will herself into feeling energetic, she began pumping gas into the T-bird.

Inside the store, Donnie got a Coke out of the refrigerated cabinet, and coffee from the machine, and took them over to the cash register. As he dug out his money, a single five-dollar bill, he noticed a rack of maps by the register. He plucked out a map of Nevada,

176

and paid for his purchases.

Despite the fact that they had had to leave Josh behind, he was feeling sort of excited. This was an adventure they were having. He knew that they were in real danger, it wasn't pretend, but he figured that they would get out of it because they were the good guys, and good guys always won. It had felt real good when Casey had said that she was glad he was along. He knew she was counting on him, and he sure wouldn't let her down.

Walking past the narrow counter, he stopped before the large plate glass window and glanced out. Casey was still putting gas in the T-bird.

He took a swallow of the Coke, then set the Coke and the coffee containers on the end of the counter, and opened the map. Remembering that Casey had said that Laughlin was just over the Arizona state line, he traced his finger along the line and found Laughlin — far down in the southeastern corner of the state.

Glancing up again, he saw Casey coming toward the building. Digging into his pocket, he came up with the stub of a pencil, and quickly drew a circle around Laughlin. In all of his nine years he had never been out of Arizona, and he wanted to keep the map as a reminder of his first trip out of state. He re-folded the map, stuck it in his back pocket, picked up the two containers, and met Casey at the door.

He held out the coffee container. "Here's your coffee, Casey."

"Thanks, honey." She accepted the coffee. "You go on out to the car. Be with you as soon as I pay for the gas."

Inside the T-bird, Donnie looked for a place to put the map, and finally stuck it into the side-pocket on the door. Casey came back out and started the car. As they drove toward the on-ramp she said, "Getting hungry, Donnie?"

He nodded. "Yeah. I guess I should've gotten a candy bar back there."

Casey smiled. "Well, it's better that you didn't. We'll be in Flagstaff in about an hour, and I'll buy you a nice big healthy breakfast. We're going to have to wait for the used car lots to open, anyway."

"How come?"

"Two very good reasons. First of all I only have about thirty dollars left after paying for the gas, and we'll need more to get to Laughlin. Second, the police in Phoenix may have put our license number and our descriptions out over the air. That means that other policemen everywhere will be looking for us."

Donnie sat up. "Will they arrest us?"

Casey sighed. "I don't really know; but they

would very probably take you back to your aunt."

Donnie slumped back. "Yeah. Well, we don't want that, do we?"

She shook her head. "No, we don't want that. That's why I'm going to sell the Thunderbird, and buy a cheaper car."

"With a different license plate!"

"That's right!"

"And we won't let the cops, or Ray Tibbets catch us, will we?"

"You're darn right we won't." She patted his knee, and Donnie relaxed and flashed her a cocky grin.

Half to herself, Casey said: "Yeah, we're a regular Bonnie and Clyde Jr., we are."

"Who're Bonnie and Clyde?" Donnie asked.

It was after daybreak when they reached Flagstaff. At an altitude of over seven thousand feet, Flagstaff was at least twenty degrees cooler than Phoenix, which was a great relief, as was the sight of the tall pine and aspen forests, and the fresh smell of growing things. Only a few hours from Phoenix, Casey thought, and yet it was a different world.

Although Casey had no really close friends in Flag, she had made some acquaintances, and now fervently hoped that she would not run into any of them.

Although I-40, which ran east and west, was busy with heavy trucks, the streets of the town, at this hour, were still relatively empty of traffic.

In the quiet of early morning, the town exuded a feeling of peace. Despite the beauty of the setting, Casey had never thought the town itself particularly attractive. Flagstaff wasn't an old-fashioned picture-book sort of town like Prescott, nestled in the pines at a lower altitude, or a resort town like Sedona, surrounded by red-rock wind sculptures. Flagstaff more or less sprawled, caught up in a flurry of recent and not always well-planned growth. Despite the difference in climate, the buildings reminded Casey a little of Bakersfield, or Mojave, in California, towns that had not been planned, but had grown up along the highways and railroad tracks. Still, despite first impressions, it was a town with a lot to offer, a college town, with all the cultural advantages that implied. And, in winter, there was the skiing. A wave of sadness moved her. Would she be able to come here this winter, or would this be the last time she would see the town?

Pushing away the thought, she found a restaurant open for breakfast, and pulled the T-bird into the lot. As they got out and she locked the car, she was overcome again by melancholy. She was going to miss The Bird; it was the first automobile she had ever owned, and she had grown fond of it.

She and Donnie both ate a large breakfast, and then lingered until the waitress began to look at them askance. At eight-thirty, Casey paid the bill and they left the restaurant.

A few minutes later they were cruising along the main street, which had once been old Highway 66, made famous by story and the TV series. Since the opening of I-40, it was no longer the heavy traffic artery it had been in the old days. As she drove, she kept an eye out for just the right used car lot. She wasn't looking for a big lot. She wanted one that looked slightly shady, where she wouldn't be scrutinized too carefully. She knew that the state law required that the sale or purchase of a used vehicle be reported to the Department of Transportation within fifteen days; and she wanted a lot where the owner might be lax about reporting, taking the full two weeks, or even longer. The more time she had before the sale was reported, the more time she would have before the authorities would learn that she was driving a different vehicle.

Finally, she came across what she was looking for. It was a small lot, with perhaps two dozen used cars for sale, located well away from the new car agencies. A banner strung over the lot proclaimed: "Cowpuncher Bob! Come in and let me punch out an honest deal for you!"

Casey turned the T-bird into the lot. The office was little more than a shack, surrounded by the cars. It struck Casey as being a one-man operation, which was perfect for her purpose. Although it was still short of nine, the office door stood open. A tall man wearing cowboy boots, a Stetson hat slanted down over his eyes, was seated by the door in a metal chair tilted back against the wall.

As Casey stopped the T-bird a few yards away, the man came alive, uncoiling a tall, lanky frame. Donnie whispered, "Casey, are you sure this is the place you want? That man doesn't look honest."

Casey had to suppress a smile. The kid had good instincts.

"I know, Donnie; but I have a reason. Just trust me, okay?"

"Okay," he whispered, but his expression remained dubious.

As Casey stepped out of the car, the tall man approached. He swept off his sweat-stained Stetson, revealing a shock of theatrically white hair and a face creased and burned to the color of old leather.

"Howdy, little lady," he said in a deep voice.

"Anything I can do for you?"

Casey choked back a laugh. He was a little too much to swallow, the perfect stereotype of a shifty used car salesman.

Attempting to look feminine and not too bright, Casey smiled up at him. "I want to trade my car in, trade down for a cheaper model."

Cowboy Bob fingered his chin while his sharp eyes evaluated the T-bird. "Well, I don't know. I've got quite a bit of stock on hand as it is."

As he spoke, he walked around the T-bird. Casey felt Donnie take her hand. She looked down at him and saw that he was eyeing Cowpuncher Bob with deep suspicion.

After he had circled the car, Cowboy Bob returned to stand by Donnie. "Howdy, son. This your boy, ma'am?"

"My nephew," Casey said without hesitation.

"Fine looking boy," said Bob, patting Donnie's head. Casey gave Donnie a frown as he jerked away, but the man appeared to take no offense.

Casey found herself being studied by pale blue eyes. "The T-bird paid for, or do you owe on her?"

"It's paid for. The papers are in the glove compartment."

The man looked again at the car. "She's only about two years old. Shame you have to get rid of her."

Casey gave a shot at looking pitiful. "I know. I hate to do it, but I need the money."

The blue eyes appeared to be adding up numbers. "So that's the way of it, huh? Just what kind of car you hoping to drive out with?"

"Something that's in reasonably good condition."

"Got a couple of dozen here." He gestured to the lot. "All in good shape. Always have a good mechanic check them over, fix anything wrong, before I put them up for sale. Why don't you look around, see if anything catches your eye?"

He winked. "You look around on your own. I don't put any high pressure on my customers."

I'll just bet you don't, you big phony, Casey thought as she turned away.

Donnie joined her as she worked her way through the lot, studying the cars. Many of them were too far gone to interest her; and about half of them were pick-ups or four-by-fours, and she wasn't interested in that category.

Finally, she came across a four-year-old Chevy that looked to be in fair shape. She got the key from Cowpuncher Bob, went back to the car and started it up. The engine sounded a little rough, but it smoothed out after a moment. The asking price was a little over five thousand, about the price range she was looking for.

As she got out of the car, Donnie reached in and pulled the hood release. She watched in surprise as he buried his head in the engine compartment. After a moment, he backed out.

"We don't want this one, Casey," he said.

"Why not?"

"Look under here."

Casey moved over next to Donnie and looked into the engine compartment. "What? Donnie, what I know about car engines you could put in an acorn cup."

Donnie pushed out his small chest and straightened his shoulders. "Look how dirty the engine is. It should have been steam cleaned."

He leaned over. "And there are oil spots. It leaks oil. I'll bet it needs a lot of work."

Casey realized that her mouth hung open, and closed it. "How do you know all that?"

Donnie gave her a sly grin. "My aunt's boyfriend, Brent, is a used car salesman . . ."

"That doesn't surprise me in the least," she muttered.

"When he was trying to get in good with

my aunt, he used to take me around his lot and show me what to look for when I get old enough to have my own car."

Casey rubbed her knuckles gently over his hair. He needed a good trim. "You constantly amaze me, young man. Well, let's look some more."

Casey, with Donnie's help, finally settled on a four-year-old Mustang that seemed in fair condition — at least Donnie pronounced it the best one they had looked at.

The price on the Mustang was four thousand, nine hundred and ninety-nine dollars. As if that was supposed to convince the buyer that the car was a deal at less than five thousand. Really!

They returned to Cowpuncher Bob, who had resumed his seat before the small office.

"We've decided on one," she announced.

He pushed his hat back, his eyes glinting. "Which one?"

"The Mustang over there." She pointed.

"Good choice, little lady. I can see you know your cars."

Casey and Donnie exchanged glances, and Donnie grinned.

"Yeah, that little Mustang runs like a fine watch. Good price on her, too."

"The question is, how much will you give me for my car?"

Cowpuncher Bob pushed his Stetson further back on his head, and rubbed his chin thoughtfully, his gaze going to the T-bird.

"Well, like I said, I'm pretty well stocked right now, and I can't offer near the blue-book price."

Casey looked at him coolly. "Your stock won't be increased if I drive out in the Mustang."

He gave a cackle of laughter. "Pretty good bargainer, ain't you, little lady?"

Cowpuncher Bob put on a pretense of deep thought, squinting off into the distance. "Tell you what, ma'am. Take the Mustang, and I'll give you an even two thousand difference."

Casey could feel her face growing hot. She had expected to get ripped off, but not by this amount.

"I paid seventeen thousand for the Bird when I bought it, and, as you pointed out, it's only two years old."

He shrugged. "Well, you know that a new car depreciates two grand or more the day you drive it off the lot. And, I have to be truthful, the used car business is terrible this year. When I do sell the T-bird I'll be lucky to break even."

Right, Casey thought angrily; you'll make out like the bandit you are.

"Course," he said piously, "you might want

to try some other lots. There's a Ford agency a mile or so up the road."

Casey bit back her anger. He had her pegged, all right. He knew she was running from *something* and didn't want to risk a more reputable agency. And the two thousand would see them through, hopefully, until she landed a job.

She hesitated for a moment, and decided to call his bluff. If it didn't work, she would take the two thousand.

Nodding, she said: "Yes, maybe that's a good idea. The other lots should be open by now."

With great pleasure she saw a look of doubt cross his face.

"Come on, Donnie." she took the boy's hand and began to turn away.

"Well, wait now, ma'am." Cowpuncher Bob, moving quickly for such a big man, moved around in front of them. "Don't be in such an all-fired hurry. I looked your car over while you were on the lot, and seeing as how it's in pretty good condition, maybe I can give you a bit more. I guess I could come up with maybe another five hundred dollars. But that's my best offer."

Casey turned back, concealing her smile, pretending to consider. "All right. We are in kind of a hurry. It's a deal."

The paperwork took only about a half hour, and Casey was pleasantly surprised when Cowpuncher Bob opened an ancient safe behind his desk in the small office and counted out twenty-five hundred dollars in cash. She had been nervous about going into a bank to cash a check.

After she had folded the money into her purse, Cowpuncher Bob extended a huge paw. Casey took it gingerly.

"Pleasure doing business with you, little lady," he boomed. "You-all come back again some time, you hear?"

He stood in the doorway, watching, as Casey and Donnie cleaned out the T-bird, transferring everything into the Mustang. He waved languidly as they drove off the lot.

Just before they reached the freeway, Casey pulled into the parking lot of a supermarket and stopped in front of a newspaper vending machine. She bought a copy of the *Arizona Republic*, and quickly leafed through it, hoping to find a mention of what had happened last night. Maybe, if they were very lucky, it would say that Ray Tibbets had been captured. But there was nothing.

Her heart sank, then she remembered that the *Republic* went to bed early. If there was something, it wouldn't appear until tomorrow. Feeling vaguely depressed, she got back into

189

the Mustang and headed for I-40 West.

As they drove away from the supermarket lot, she flicked on the radio, searching for a news station. They were about two miles along I-40 when she found a newscast.

"In Phoenix early this morning, a police officer was found dead in an unmarked police car. A spokesman for the Phoenix Police Department would not go into details, saying only that the man had been murdered, and that the police are investigating a suspect. Meanwhile, in Tucson . . ."

Casey snapped off the radio, glancing over at Donnie. His small face was very serious. "Was that policeman the one who was watching us?"

Casey, unable to speak, nodded.

Donnie lapsed into silence, his head down. For a while they drove in silence.

Suddenly Donnie raised his head. His map! His Nevada map. He had forgotten and left it in the side pocket of the Thunderbird on the used car lot. He opened his mouth to ask Casey if they could go back for it, but she looked so worried he decided not to bother her. After all, he could always buy another one along the way.

CHAPTER THIRTEEN

Josh was growing increasingly frustrated; a week had passed and there was still no sign of Casey and Donnie, or Tibbets.

He had been working around the clock, sometimes sleeping at the station. Nothing. It would appear that they had simply vanished. He could easily understand that Tibbets would be hard to find. If he was still in the Phoenix area he would be stealing license plates and switching. Or, he might have gotten rid of the van, although Josh had a very strong hunch that he had not. The man seemed attached to the thing. Maybe it was because he had committed his crimes in it; or maybe it was that as the only stable element in Tibbets's disgusting life, it represented security to him. Whatever. At any rate, if he remained cautious and did not commit any traffic violations, he could move about fairly freely, and if he left the state, he might remain free for months or years. The thing that Josh was counting on was Tibbets's threats. Josh had the impression that carrying out his boasts was a point of honor with Tibbets, and that the man would not rest until he had made good on them. Which had to mean that he had to show up eventually.

The thing that worried Josh the most was the possibility that Tibbets was trailing Casey and Donnie, or that he had — even worse — found them. But he didn't even want to think about that. Now that Casey was gone, he realized just how much he cared about her, how much he missed her. And Donnie, as well. He was fond of the damned kid.

The only good thing about this mess was, that at least so far, he had received little flack from Captain Randall, or anyone else in the department. Of course, he knew what was in the captain's mind, as well as the minds of all others with knowledge of the case. If they had pursued Tibbets more diligently, a police officer might not now be dead.

At the end of the week, Josh received a phone call from Tod Burns. "Where is Casey Farrel, Sergeant? She hasn't reported for work all this week, and the only way I know to get in touch with her is through you."

Josh, not certain what he should tell Burns, hesitated before answering. "She had to leave town suddenly, Tod."

Tod, whose temper was uncertain at the best

of times, grunted angrily. "Without notifying me? Without a word to anyone? The woman's only been on the job two weeks. What the hell's going on?"

Josh sighed heavily. "I know, Tod; but there's a good reason. It was unavoidable."

Tod grunted again, and Josh could picture his face growing red as it always did when he was upset. "Well, may I know why? Or is this privileged information?"

Josh sighed again. "Look, I'll tell you why she had to leave, but I'm asking you to keep it under your hat. You know that case she was involved in, the Dumpster Killer business?"

"Yes. But that was thrown out, wasn't it? It's all over, right?"

"Not exactly. After Tibbets, the scumbag, was released, he made some threats against Casey, the boy, and me. About a week ago he tried to make good on his threat. He didn't get the boy or Casey; but he did get a good cop who got in the way."

"You mean the stakeout? I didn't make the association."

"No reason you should have. Anyway, Casey evidently freaked out, got into her car and drove off. Took the boy with her. I don't think it was the wisest thing to do; but I can see her reasoning. After all, if we couldn't protect them . . . Well, you get the idea. We've put out an APB on them, but so far, nothing."

There was silence at the other end of the line. When Tod spoke again, his voice was quieter, but still expressed a degree of annoyance. "Well, that puts a little different light on things; but I still don't see how I can hold Casey's job for her. I can understand that she was, is, frightened; but damn it, as a member of my task force she's supposed to be a law enforcement officer herself; and being threatened is simply part of the job. I'm afraid that as of this moment, Casey is out. If she contacts you, please inform her of that fact."

Josh had to struggle to control his own temper. "I'll be sure to do that, Tod," he said in a dry voice, but Burns had already hung up.

Josh slammed down the receiver, saying aloud, "I hardly think that her job is the most pressing thing on her mind just now, asshole!"

Yet, he really couldn't fault the man's reaction. If Casey had been a long-time employee, Burns might have given her some leeway; but with an untested employee of only two weeks . . .

With a sigh, he went back to the desk work interrupted by the call. There were several reports of possible sightings of Tibbets's van and Casey's T-bird from various cops in cities throughout Arizona, but all were too nebulous to really get his hopes up.

He scrubbed his chin pensively, staring at the phone on his desk. There was one thing he hadn't done, something he probably should have done.

Casey had mentioned an uncle on the Hopi Reservation, Claude Pentiwa. It was just possible that she could have gone to him. Of course Casey had said that the old man and she hadn't been in close communication because of the bad feeling Pentiwa still had for his sister, Casey's mother. Still, he was family, and when people were in trouble that's where they usually turned. What was that saying, something about a family, or maybe it was home, being the place that when you had to go there, they had to take you in? In Josh's experience that was just about the truth. At any rate, it was worth investigation.

It took him a few minutes to get the telephone number of the Hopi BIA Law Enforcement Services, on the reservation; and as he punched out the number, he found that his hopes were rising. Cautioning himself against unwarranted optimism, he heard the number ring.

When he got through, he identified himself, gave the woman who answered the phone a simplified version of his reasons for making the call, and was transferred to the Criminal Investigator's office.

The Criminal Investigator introduced himself as John Pela. He proved to be intelligent, efficient, helpful, and he knew Claude Pentiwa. He was also kindly; for when Josh asked for Pentiwa's phone number, he did not laugh; although his voice made it clear that he found the question amusing.

"Claude has no phone in his home, Sergeant. Like many of our people, he chooses to live mainly in the old way. His house is in Shungopavi, on Second Mesa. He operates a small roadside gallery there where he sells locally crafted silver work and Kachinas. That is, he operates the place when he feels like it. He does have a phone in his shop, but sometimes it's closed for days at a time. Things move a little slower up here."

Josh cleared his throat. It was embarrassingly clear that he was dealing with a different world, one about which he knew very little, and the thought made him vaguely uneasy.

"I badly need to talk to him. Is there any way of getting a message to him?"

A note of caution entered Pela's voice. "Just what is this in reference to, Sergeant? Is he involved in a crime?"

"No, not at all," Josh said quickly. "It con-

196

cerns a crime, true, but he is no way involved. Depend on it."

There was a brief silence on the line. "I can do this; I have to go in to Shungopavi this afternoon; and I'll stop by his place and ask him to call you. I can't promise that he will. Claude is . . . well, I guess you might say he's a bit cantankerous. Likes to do things his own way, and in his own time. What's your number there?"

"I'm just about to leave for the day, so I'll give you my home phone number also . . ."

Josh had gone back on days after Casey disappeared so that he could stay on top of the investigation. After talking to the Hopi investigator, he left the station and drove home. As always when he came home now, he felt his heartbeat accelerate, hoping that Casey and Donnie would be there, waiting for him; but the house was empty in a way it never had been before he had taken in his two roommates. The two of them had brought life and activity to the house, and now, without them, the place seemed to be pining.

Feeling listless and drained, Josh showered and fixed himself a pitcher of martinis, which he took out to the deck. He left the door open behind him so that he could hear the phone.

He pulled up a deck chair, propped his feet on the railing, and began working on the martinis. Overhead, thunderclouds were gathering, huge piles of dark and light gray, and the air began to smell of rain. The moving clouds were hypnotic, and Josh thought, very beautiful.

Lightning flashed between the clouds like the flashbulb of a giant camera, and thunder cracked and rumbled noisily. As it did so, the wind came up, and within seconds it was raining heavily, large, fat drops that slanted into the deck with so much force that they sounded solid.

Josh grabbed the martini pitcher, but before he could get into the house the drops of water had become lumps of ice big as marbles.

Josh scuttled through the door, swearing as the hailstones stung his face and shoulders. Those suckers could hurt! As he set the pitcher down on the counter top, the telephone rang.

Wiping off his face and head with a dishtowel held in one hand, he grabbed the receiver off the wall with the other.

"Hello!"

"Sergeant Whitney?"

"Speaking."

"I have Claude Pentiwa for you."

"Great. Thank you."

A pause, and then a deep, resonant voice said, "Yes?"

"Mr. Pentiwa, this is Sergeant Josh Whitney, with the Phoenix Police."

Josh heard a deep grunt. "What police want with me?"

Josh was a bit taken aback. Pela had said that Pentiwa was an old time Hopi, but this man sounded like Tonto in the old radio show, The Lone Ranger. A bit much.

"I believe that you have a niece by the name of Casey Farrel," Josh said cautiously.

Another pause. "Have not seen niece in many moons. Has she committed crime?"

Josh held the receiver away to stare at it. Was this a put on? Frowning, he put the receiver back to his ear, feeling distinctly uneasy. "No. I just need to get in touch with her. Is she with you?"

This time the grammar was impeccable, and the voice somewhat higher, with a distinct British accent. "No. Why should you think she is?"

Tired of whatever game Pentiwa was playing, Josh let his exasperation show in his voice. "Look," he said, "I don't really have time for games. Your niece is an important witness in a murder case, and this has put her in some danger. She has left the area with another witness in the case, and I . . . we, the police here, are very worried about her. We want to know where she is so that we can protect her."

This time the voice sounded Irish: "My niece always was impetuous, much like her mother."

Josh, attempting to curb his impatience, took a deep breath. "Look, Mr. Pentiwa, I'm serious about Casey being in danger. The man who committed the crime she witnessed is a psychotic killer. If he finds her before we do . . . Well, you can guess what will happen to her. Now you are the only person I know who is related to Casey. All I want from you is a straight answer. Is it possible that she might come to you?"

The voice was now deep, but without obvious eccentricities: "It is doubtful. There is bad blood between us. But, if by some chance she does come to me for protection, I shall not turn her away."

Josh stifled a sigh. Talking with this man was like walking a maze. He never seemed to answer directly, not to mention in the same voice.

"I appreciate that, sir, but this man is not only dangerous but shrewd. If Casey does come to you, I ask that you get in touch with me immediately, otherwise your whole family could be put in danger. Will you do that?"

There was a brief silence, then the deep voice said slowly, "If I deem it in her best interests, Sergeant. That is as much as I can promise. Can you give me a description of this man?"

Josh gave him Tibbets's physical description, and his own phone numbers at work and at home. As he hung up, he felt vaguely dissatisfied. The conversation had not gone quite as he hoped — what kind of a joker *was* this Pentiwa, anyway — but he would have to settle for what he could get.

As he turned away from the phone, it rang again. He snatched up the receiver. "Casey?"

The line hummed silently for a moment, then he heard low laughter. "Hello, Josh. Is this Casey a man or one of your many girlfriends?"

The voice struck a familiar chord, yet he couldn't quite place it. "Who is this?"

Rich, vibrant laughter rang in his ear. "My, my. How soon they forget!"

"Janice!" He laughed with her. "Well, it has been a long time, you must admit."

Janice Cartwright was a professional fund raiser. She flitted about the country giving her expert advice and assistance to those raising funds for worthy causes; "and sometimes, not so worthy causes," she had once told Josh, "but it pays."

It did indeed pay, Josh knew, and very well. Josh had met Janice shortly after his divorce, and they usually got together whenever she was in town. She was a very attractive woman, fun to be with, and she wasn't seeking a permanent relationship.

"Sure, all of five months," she said.

"That's a long time in the life of a busy man."

"Solved any good crimes lately?"

He grunted. "Don't ask. Just don't ask. How long are you in town for?"

"A few weeks. One of the local amateur theaters has fallen on hard times and they want me to organize a fund drive."

"That seems like penny-ante stuff for you, Janice."

"Well, I had some free time, and some of the people involved in the theater are good friends of mine. Which brings me to the reason I called, one of these friends is also involved in a dinner theater, and he offered a free show and dinner tonight for a companion and myself. You're one of my favorite companions, so how about it?"

Josh hesitated. The prospect of an evening out, with nothing on his mind but a good time, was tempting. But what if Casey called when he was out? What if Ray Tibbets was captured?

Janice said, "It's a mystery play, by the way, and the audience participates. Maybe, with your expertise, you can help unveil the murderer."

"The way things are going with me right now, I couldn't catch a murderer if he confessed right in front of me."

"On a hard case, Josh?"

"The hardest."

"Then you need some relaxation."

"You're right, I do. Okay, I accept."

The food at the dinner theater was mediocre, but the play was great fun. A comedy mystery, it was played broadly, and Josh thoroughly enjoyed it; he even guessed the murderer.

The fact that Janice was with him no doubt had a great deal to do with his enjoyment. She was a tall, slim blonde, with cool green eyes, and a sophistication that had always struck Josh as a little too artful. To the casual observer she was apt to give the impression that she was an ice maiden; but Josh knew from experience that this was a false impression. She was quite warm-blooded, active and uninhibited in bed.

They lingered over a drink after the play. Josh said, "Where are you staying, Janice?"

"The Arizona Biltmore."

"Going high class, huh?"

"I always do," she said with a shrug. "Besides, it's deductible. You still live out in the tullies?"

"Yeah." He swirled the brandy in the balloon glass, gazing down into it.

"So, your place or mine?" she said brightly.

"Janice," he said hesitantly, "I'm seeing someone. At least I was . . ."

"Was?" She tilted her head, green eyes intent. "So? That must mean it's over."

"Not exactly. You see, it's all part of this case I'm working on. She is an important witness, the perp made threats, and so I had her staying in my house. For her protection."

"Protection? Now that's a new wrinkle." She started to laugh, then stopped when she saw the expression on his face.

"I'm sorry, Josh. Want to tell me about it?"

"There's not that much to tell."

Making it as brief as possible he told her what had happened. When he was finished, Janice studied him intently for a few moments. "Tell me something, Josh. Do you want her back because she's in danger, a witness, or because *you* want her back?"

Josh felt his face flush. "All three, I'd say."

Janice nodded thoughtfully. "And I'd say that you have it bad, my friend. And I'd also say good for you. I have often wondered when, if ever, you'd find someone; since we both know that I'll never settle down, and certainly not with a cop."

She reached out to touch his hand, a caressing touch that turned into a pat. Then, as she sat back, said briskly, "At least we both came in our own cars, so we won't have to suffer through awkward good nights at the door."

"I'm sorry, Janice."

"No need to be, big guy. In fact, I find it kind of touching that there is still a man around who can be faithful. It's refreshing, sort of like finding out that there really is a Santa Claus."

Driving home, Josh felt both angry and glad. Glad he hadn't compromised his relationship with Casey, angry because he had turned away from a healthy tumble in bed with a handsome, willing woman.

He pulled the car into the garage, closed the door, and started for the front door. He heard the phone ringing inside before he had his key out. He missed the keyhole in his haste, and had to try again.

Inside the house he thundered across the living room into the kitchen, grabbed the receiver off the wall, and heard the idiotic buzz of an empty line.

CHAPTER FOURTEEN

Casey let the phone ring ten times, counting.

Then, as a warning light flashed in her mind, she realized what she was doing. If Josh answered, the police might be able to find out from the telephone company what city the call had come from. Because it was a pay phone, they wouldn't be able to get more than the name of the city, but that would be enough. The local police would swarm like locusts, and they would locate her eventually.

It was a stupid move on her part, and now she was glad that he had not been home to answer. It was just that she had wanted to hear his voice, wanted to let him know that she and Donnie were all right. Also, she wanted to know if any progress had been made in catching Ray Tibbets. She had checked the *Arizona Republic* every day during the week she had been here, but there had been nothing on Tibbets.

Walking the three blocks up the street to the motel where she was staying with Donnie, she could see across the Colorado River to the bright lights of the casinos of Laughlin lining the far bank.

She liked Laughlin much better than the more glitzy Las Vegas. Despite the casinos, it was cleaner and less crowded, with something of a small town flavor. She particularly liked the river-front walk along the length of Casino Row, where people strolled, and stopped to lean on the railings to watch the passing river traffic and the hypnotic movement of the water.

Only a few years ago, both Laughlin and Bullhead City, across the river in Arizona, had been only small huddles of buildings, small towns sleeping in the blazing desert sun. Now, with the addition of the big casinos in Laughlin, both towns had exploded with growth, and housing was at a premium. Many of the people employed in the casinos lived in Bullhead City, and although rents here were a little cheaper than in Laughlin, they were still high. Casey was glad that she had the two thousand cushion from the car swap to keep them going until she got a job. She had an appointment in the morning that looked promising.

As she approached the motel room, she could hear the TV going. Poor Donnie, he was probably bored out of his skull. At least the motel had a pool. She had bought him some swim trunks, and he spent part of each day in the water, practicing his dog-paddle. He was such a good kid. Each day he assured her that she didn't need to worry about him. Of course, living with that aunt of his, he was probably used to being alone. When Casey wasn't job hunting, she tried to pay him a lot of attention.

She keyed the door open and went in. Donnie bounced up eagerly. "Did you talk to Josh?"

She shook her head. "No, honey, Josh wasn't home. I'll probably reach him later." No point in telling him that she had realized the risk involved, and wouldn't be calling again.

She dropped her purse on the bed and sat down beside him, her glance going to the TV screen. A baseball game was on.

Donnie looked up at her. His expression was worried. "You didn't call my aunt, did you?"

Casey shook her head. She felt guilty about that, but the same reasoning applied. The police were certain to keep checking with the woman to find out if she had heard from Donnie or Casey. She simply couldn't risk it.

Casey put her arm around the boy, pulling him against her. "Now, why don't you bring me up to date on the game?"

His little face lit up as he began to relate every detail of what had transpired while she had been gone. She listened with only half her mind; the other half kept circling, like a cat not able to settle down.

Casey's appointment the next morning was at the town's newest casino, the Thunderstar. When she had first gone there, two days ago, she had met with a bit of unexpected luck in the form of a second cousin, Simon Morgan, from Flagstaff.

Simon was only one quarter Hopi, and could, in his words, "sneak past as all white." He had been working as a floor guard at the Thunderstar for almost a year.

Casey, delighted to see a familiar face, told him that she was looking for a job, and Simon had promised to put in a good word with the casino's assistant manager.

The next morning Casey dressed with care, and appeared for her appointment promptly at ten o'clock. The assistant manager, Carl Manning, was a harried looking man of indeterminate age. He was also impatient, squirming in his desk chair as if there was a hot plate implanted in the seat.

"Ever worked for a casino before, Miss Farrel?"

"No, sir, I haven't."

"We only have two openings at the moment,

a change girl and a cocktail waitress, both on the floor. Have you ever worked as a waitress?"

It occurred to Casey that a lie might be in order here. After all, she doubted he would check. But she said, "No, sir, not as a cocktail waitress, but I have waited tables in a restaurant." She decided that she wouldn't mention that she had been fired for awkwardness. Truthfulness could be carried too far, and she needed this job.

His tired eyes surveyed her carefully. "There isn't all that much difference. Would you please stand up, Miss Farrel?"

Casey stood, holding in her belly. Hiring for this kind of job, she knew, depended heavily on the appearance of the applicant. Sad, but all too true; and she could not afford to be touchy about it.

He nodded. "Nice figure. I suppose you noticed that our waitresses wear rather skimpy costumes, Old West motif."

She said dryly, "I noticed."

"Some women object to that. Do you have any such objections?"

"I need the job," she said simply.

"Then you have it. You start tomorrow, five to midnight shift. Stop by our wardrobe room for a costume fitting after you leave here. It will be ready when your shift starts tomorrow.

On your way out, Mrs. Thornton, my secretary, will have you fill out an employment form. The pay is two hundred a week for five days, but you can make much more than that in tips, which, of course, are yours to keep. We pay for the costumes. We'll see you tomorrow then."

After the fitting for the costume and the filling out of the employment forms, Casey drove back across the river in high spirits. At least she was employed. She was well aware that she couldn't stay for long — a month at the most. After working for the P.I. agency, she knew that there were ways of obtaining a false Social Security number, but they took time to implement; and time was something she did not have. There had been no choice but to use her real number. It would take about a month for the records of her employment to trickle into the system, and her whereabouts would become known. Hopefully, Ray Tibbets would be in custody by then, and her worries would be over.

She burst into the motel room, throwing her arms wide. "I got the job, Donnie! Congratulations are in order, young man!"

Donnie bounded up from the chair where he'd been watching television. "Yea!"

He ran at her and she hugged him to her, kissing the top of his head.

"Tell you what we're gonna do, kiddo! To celebrate, we're going to take a river cruise this afternoon. Would you like that?"

"Yeah!" He looked up at her with shining eyes. "That would be neat, Casey!"

Ray Tibbets was getting impatient. He had spent five days and nights on I-10, cruising all the way to Indio, showing the pictures of the woman and the kid to all service stations that were open. All to no avail. Each time Tibbets had passed himself off as a husband whose wife had left him, taking his son with her.

He called a halt to the search at Indio. She couldn't have driven beyond that point without gassing up; so he returned to Phoenix, spending the night at a motel just off I-10. The question was: In which direction should he search next?

He decided to try north. After a good twenty-four hour rest, he started out again, at one o'clock in the morning, stopping and showing his pictures at every service station that was open.

He struck pay dirt at an all-night station and convenience store at Cordes Junction. When he showed the pictures to the woman behind the cash register, she studied them for a moment, then looked up at him with a frown.

"Why do you want to know about these two? Are you a cop?"

He shook his head. "No, I'm a husband. That's my wife and son. She, my wife, has run off with the boy. She's been unstable lately, since she lost the baby; and I'm real worried about her and my boy."

The woman looked at him suspiciously. "I don't know whether or not I should tell you anything. Maybe you're one of those abusive husbands I've been reading about."

Tibbets felt a surge of elation. She had already given him the information he sought; but perhaps she could tell him more. Putting on a wounded look, he shook his head. "Ma'am, I know what you're saying; but you couldn't be more wrong. I love that girl like my life, and as for the boy, well, you must know how a man feels about his only son. Please, ma'am, if you know anything, tell me. I've got to find them. The police are doing next to nothing, and it's not safe out there on the highways for a woman and a boy with all the crazies running around these days."

The woman gave a sigh, and her expression softened. "Well, you're right enough about that. Just last week some nut came in here and stuck a gun in my face. He only got a few dollars, because we don't keep over fifty bucks in the register, and did that piss him off! I don't know what he would've done, except that a car drove up to the pumps just then, and he hightailed it."

Tibbets listened patiently, an appreciative smile lingering on his lips. "Then they were here?"

"The woman and the boy, you mean." She peered closely at him. "Well, you don't look like the kind of bastard that would beat his wife and kid. Yeah, they stopped here last week, about three in the morning. The boy came inside while his mother got gas. I always watch the kids pretty close. A lot of them are great for stealing candy. But your boy seemed like a nice kid. He bought himself a drink, even bought coffee for his mother — I remember thinking that was nice — and a road map."

Tibbets restrained his eagerness. "The road map, was it an Arizona map, or for some other state?"

The woman shrugged. "Afraid I don't remember that."

Tibbets nodded. That would have been almost too much to hope for. Still, he had gotten what he really needed.

"I want you to know how much I appreciate your help," he said earnestly, looking at her gratefully.

Her hard face brightened for a moment.

"No need. Glad to be of help."

"I'll certainly tell my wife about you when I find her."

Just as he reached the door, she called out, "Hey! What did your wife and kid do to get into the newspaper?"

He looked back at her. "We were selected as the family of the year by the *Arizona Republic*."

"How nice. Well, I hope that you find them soon."

"I know I will. Thank you again for your help."

Tibbets was still smiling broadly as he left the building. Outside, he burst into laughter.

He drove at a leisurely pace up to Flagstaff, no longer pushed by a sense of urgency. Now, it was only a matter of time.

In Flagstaff, however, he was faced with another decision. Interstate 40 ran east and west out of Flagstaff, and there was another highway going north. Which way had she gone from here?

He stopped at a restaurant, ordered some breakfast, and considered the options. He had researched Casey Farrel as thoroughly as he could. Everything he had learned led him to believe that she was an intelligent woman — or at least as intelligent as a woman *could* be. So, she must know that the T-bird was not exactly low profile. Being a woman, she probably wasn't up to stealing and changing plates, or stealing another car. Also, chances were that she would need some money. Would she think about trading the T-bird? He thought that was entirely possible. If she was, or if she had, Flagstaff would be a good place to do it. It wouldn't hurt to check.

Finishing his breakfast, he cruised along old Highway 66, looking in all the used car lots. He was about to decide that this hunch was a bad one, when there it was, the T-bird, polished and shining, in the front row of a tacky-looking lot — Cowpuncher Bob's. A cardboard sign was propped on the windshield. "Like New! $9,999.00!"

Tibbets, grinning with glee, drove on slowly until he could turn around and return to the lot. It looked like a one-man operation, which was all to the good. Turning in to the potholed driveway, he came to a stop. The man sitting in a metal chair leaning against the wall by the door of the small office building rocked the chair forward and stood up, tilting back a large Stetson hat.

As Tibbets got out of the car, the man ambled toward him. He was much taller than Tibbets, but also much older and lighter; his face showed the effects of years of sun and mileage.

"Howdy, son," he said, holding out a large, well-manicured hand. "If you're looking to deal, I'm your man."

Tibbets never liked to shake hands, but he took the extended paw.

"You thinking to trade that van in? Have to tell you right off that vans are hard to move."

Tibbets made his voice pleasant and light. His habit was to sum up each person he met as he might an opponent, and in the comparison he seldom came up wanting. In this case, he decided that he could break this out-of-condition old hulk in two in seconds. This thought, and the fact of his finding the T-bird, made him feel genial despite the old fart's obvious dishonesty.

"No, I'm keeping the van," he said. "I'm looking for a good transportation car for my wife to drive."

The older man beamed. "Now that I have. Every car on this lot is in tip-top condition."

Tibbets nodded and said seriously, "Yes, I can see that. What about that Thunderbird in the first row?"

Cowpuncher Bob nodded his head. "I can see that you have an eye for fine cars. You couldn't go wrong with that one. Only had one owner, an older lady here in Flag who was moving east to New York, and didn't figure that she would need a car there. It's in tip-top condition, friend. Tip-top!"

Tibbets controlled an urge to smirk. The man was a fool — the worst kind — one of those who thought everyone else was stupid. He turned his back on the salesman, and walked over to the T-bird. Cowpuncher Bob was right on his heels. Tibbets circled the car, wearing a studious expression.

"Why don't you get in, friend?" Cowpuncher Bob said eagerly. "Start her up. Runs like a clock, you'll see."

Tibbets, wondering how much the old con-man had given Farrel for the car — no doubt far beneath what it was worth — complied.

As he started the car, and revved the engine, he looked around the interior of the car, trying to spot anything that might give him a clue as to where the woman and the boy had gone. There was nothing visible. The interior, obviously, had been cleaned and vacuumed. He ached to examine the glove compartment and the door pockets, but that would have to wait.

Cowpuncher Bob smiled ingratiatingly through the open window on the driver's side. "Want to take her for a little drive?"

Tibbets shut off the motor. "That won't be necessary. Sounds to me like it's in pretty good shape."

He opened the door and got out. "Why

218

don't we step into your office and see what kind of a deal we can strike?"

An expression of surprise flickered across the lot owner's face, to be driven quickly away by greed. "Sure thing, friend. I can make you a good deal on her."

Tibbets followed Cowpuncher Bob into the small office, quietly closing and locking the door behind him. The lot owner, heading toward a battered file cabinet in the back of the room, did not notice. "Now, just let me pull the file on that little beauty . . ."

As Cowpuncher Bob pulled out the file drawer, Tibbets drew the powdered rubber gloves out of his pocket and slipped them on.

"Yessir. Here it is. Now . . ."

As Bob lifted a manila folder out of the drawer, and began to turn, Tibbets leapt in front of him and grasped his throat.

The man's eyes widened in shock and surprise. Tibbets, looking into those eyes, smiled, and began to tighten his grasp.

Cowpuncher Bob, eyes now wide with panic, began to struggle. There was more strength in the old man's thin body than Tibbets would have thought possible, and he also had the advantage of Tibbets in height. It was taking too long.

Suddenly releasing Bob's throat, Tibbets quickly spun him around and moved his hands up to place them on each side of the other man's head. Jamming a knee into the taller man's back, he gave his head one quick, brutal twist. The lot owner's body convulsed, a stench filled the air, and the man collapsed.

Tibbets, dizzy with the feeling of in-rushing strength, let the carcass drop. He stood for a few minutes breathing deeply, letting the feeling of power grow in him until it began to wane. Then, leaning over, he felt for a pulse in the neck. There was none.

Feeling relaxed and in perfect control, Tibbets moved to the window and looked out. No one in sight. Reaching for the cardboard Open sign, he reversed it to Closed, and put it in the window; then returned to the body and pulled it behind the desk, out of the line of sight from the windows.

After picking up the scattered papers from the file folder, he went to the desk, seated himself in Cowpuncher Bob's chair, and began to go through the papers.

Slowly, he began to smile. Everything he needed was here, including a description of the newly purchased car, and the bill of sale and registration for the Thunderbird. This last meant that Cowpuncher Bob hadn't gotten around to sending in the details of the transaction to the state. Tibbets's smile widened. Good old Cowpuncher Bob! Picking up the papers, he folded them and stuffed them into his pocket.

Rising from the desk, he looked carefully around the office to see if he had left anything that might incriminate him. The cops might hook him up with this killing — that is if they traced the woman and the boy here — but without hard evidence it would only be circumstantial.

He checked at the window again — still no one in sight — and exited the building, locking the door behind him.

As he walked through the lot, he considered exchanging his van for one of the cars, and then discarded the notion. The only thing on the lot worth stealing was Farrel's car, and he couldn't take that. Any one of the rest of them would probably collapse within a few miles of the lot. The van, on the other hand, was in great condition. He would pick up another license plate on the edge of town. But he did want to search the T-bird's pockets and glove compartment.

Opening the car door on the passenger's side, he first went through the glove compartment; nothing but the manual. Slamming the door, he shoved his hand into the right door pocket, and touched folded paper. Excited now, he pulled it out. A Nevada road map.

Unfolding it, he held it up to the light, and

saw the circle drawn around Laughlin. He laughed aloud. This was just what he had been looking for. He had her now!

Still laughing, he climbed into the van and headed back down Old 66 until he came to the entrance ramp to Interstate 40, where he turned west, toward Nevada.

CHAPTER FIFTEEN

Josh received the call shortly before noon: "Sergeant Whitney?"

"That's me."

"This is Detective Ned Costin, Flagstaff Police. I assume you're still on the hunt for the Dumpster Killer?"

Josh sat forward. "We sure as hell are! Don't tell me you have him?"

The detective laughed. "Don't I wish! But we did have a murder here this morning, and the MO fits your killer."

"A woman? A hooker?"

"No, a man, the owner of a used car lot. There are finger marks on his neck, as if an attempt at strangulation was made; but the man's neck was snapped. And there's more. You have an APB out on a Thunderbird, registered to a Casey Farrel?"

"Yes. Did you find it?"

"It's on the lot, for sale."

"I'll leave within the next hour."

The Flagstaff officer chuckled. "I figured

you would. You won't have any trouble finding the lot. When you hit the center of town, turn right on Old 66. The place is called 'Cowpuncher Bob's,' and there will still be police units on the lot. Can't miss it."

Ordinarily, the drive from Phoenix to Flagstaff took about two and a half hours. Josh, using the siren judiciously, made it in well under two hours.

When he pulled into the lot, a short, slender man in plainclothes emerged from the small office building, and came forward to meet him, hand extended. "Ned Costin, the guy who called."

Josh shook hands. "Sergeant Joshua Whitney. Call me Josh."

"Welcome to Flag, Josh."

"Any developments since we talked?"

"A couple. I don't know if they mean a whole hell of a lot. We had to take the body to the morgue. Come on into the office; there's a man in here you'll want to talk to."

"First, have you learned if the Farrel vehicle was traded in on another vehicle? If so, do you have the license number on it?"

Costin shook his head. "We don't know. One of the drawers in the file cabinet was open, and we found an empty folder on the desk. It was labeled 'Farrel, C.' We figure that the perp must have taken the papers."

"Well, how about ADOT, shouldn't they have the records by now? The time limit for filing is supposed to be fifteen days."

Costin shrugged. "Should have, but Bob Jenkins was a bit lax with his paperwork. Face it, he was a shoddy character. We've had complaints lodged against him in the past by unhappy customers. None of them stuck, but he always skated close to the edge. I called ADOT, and they told me that he was often late in reporting sales and purchases to the department. They have nothing on file from him regarding the purchase of Farrel's vehicle, or any record of her buying a vehicle from him."

Josh scrubbed a hand over his face. "So Tibbets has the papers; and that means that he has a description of the car Casey Farrel is driving. Damn!"

Costin looked at him questioningly. "That's assuming that this Tibbets is the perp."

"I think it's a reasonable assumption. Who else would be interested in that particular car and sale? It's him. Depend on it."

"You may be right, but there's no physical evidence."

Josh sighed. "Yeah. He's real careful. Now, what about this man that I'm going to want to talk to? He a witness?"

"I think that you should talk to him before

I say anything."

Josh followed the other detective into the rickety office building. Inside, a short, dumpy man of about fifty, wearing grease-stained coveralls, was sitting in a metal chair before a scarred desk. He was chewing on an unlit cigar.

Costin said, "Josh, this is Carl Marston. Carl, this is Detective Sergeant Whitney, of the Phoenix Police."

Marston quickly extended a stubby hand, the creases of which were black with oil and grease. Josh reluctantly took it.

"Carl owns the gas station diagonally across the street."

"Were you a witness to what happened here, Mr. Marston?"

"I didn't actually *see* Bob killed, if that's what you mean."

Costin said, "Carl found the body."

"How did that come about?"

Marston hitched his chair forward. "Well, you see, when Bob is open . . . or was open. . . . Anyway, when he was open, and not busy with a customer, he always used to sit outside in that old chair there, tilted back against the wall by the door." He gestured toward the door.

"Today he opened about the usual time, nine; and I saw him sitting out there and waved to him. Then I got busy on the car

I had to service. I have a kid works for me, watches the pumps and such-like. Well, for a while I wasn't paying attention to anything but the car; but a little later, when I stood up to stretch, I saw a van pull into Bob's lot."

Josh felt a surge of adrenaline. "What color was the van, Mr. Marston?"

"Uh, blue, I think. Sort of a dark blue."

"Not black?"

Marston shook his head vehemently. "Nope. My eyes ain't what they once was, but I ain't color blind."

Could Tibbets have painted the van, Josh wondered? If he had kept it, it would have been the logical thing to do.

"Did you see the driver?"

"Not sure. A bit later I looked over there and saw Bob with a feller looking at one of the cars. I supposed it was the same feller, but I didn't see him get out of the van, so I can't be absolutely sure. I wasn't paying much attention, but I remember that he was a youngish feller, shorter than Bob, but big through the shoulders, sort of stocky."

"I don't suppose you noticed the license number of the van."

Marston shrugged. "Nope. Had no reason to."

"Then what happened?"

"Well, like I said, when Bob didn't have

a customer on the lot, he was usually sitting in that chair. When I finished with the car I was working on, I happened to look over there again, and saw that the van was gone, and Bob's office door was closed. I didn't think about it much. Thought maybe he had gone in to go to the john or to get a cup of coffee; but when I looked over again, about a half hour later, the door was still closed, and Bob was nowhere in sight.

"It wasn't near lunchtime, and Bob keeps, kept, a coffee pot perking in the office all day, so I couldn't figure him being off the lot that long. It just wasn't like him. So, I ambled over to see if everything was all right. You know, Bob ain't as young as he used to be, and I thought maybe he'd fallen or something . . ."

Marston paused, blinking.

Josh prompted, "What happened then, Mr. Marston?"

Marston sighed heavily. "When I got to the door, I could see the 'Closed' sign was up. I tried the door, and it was locked. That didn't strike me as right, not near the middle of the day. I went around looking through the windows. Couldn't see nothing till I went around to the right side. When I looked through that one, I saw a boot sticking out from behind the desk, and I knew for certain that something was wrong, maybe a heart attack or something. So I kicked the door open."

Marston shook his head and stared down at his prominent belly. "I tell you, Officer, when I saw him behind that desk, I almost threw up my breakfast. His head was all twisted to one side, and his eyes . . . Well, it was plain he was dead, but I called 911 anyways. Didn't know what else to do."

"Mr. Marston, going back a little, can you remember anything more about the van, or the man you saw, that might help us?"

Marston shook his head. "Nope. Wish I could, but I can't."

Josh motioned toward the door. "Come on outside for a moment, Mr. Marston."

Marston followed him outside, and Josh indicated the Thunderbird. "That T-bird, is that the car Cowpuncher Bob and the customer were looking at?"

Marston pulled off his cap and scratched his thinning thatch of hair. "Could be, but I'm not all that certain. Like I said, I wasn't really paying attention. But I do remember that the car was in the front row."

Josh sighed. "Okay, Mr. Marston. That's all the questions I have."

Costin stepped forward. "Thanks, Mr. Marston. We appreciate your cooperation. You can go now."

Josh and Costin stood side by side, watching

the station owner leave the lot.

Costin said, "So, what do you think?"

"His description of the man talking to Bob fits Tibbets to the ground; and Tibbets drives a van, it was black, but those fast paint places can change the color in a few hours. It may not stand up in court, but I know in my gut that the man was Tibbets. Everything fits. And now the son of a bitch has the plate number and a description of the car Casey is driving, and we don't have shit!"

"We will have, after we check out Bob's inventory list and see what's missing."

Josh snorted. "If he kept a list. If he didn't, we'll have to go through state channels."

"That's going to take a while."

"And Casey and Donnie could be dead by then. Tibbets tracked them this far — which is a hell of a lot better than we did — and he's going to be right on their tail. The only break we have is that we now know that Tibbets probably changed the color of his van to blue. Which reminds me, I have to call Phoenix and change the description on the APB. Can I use the phone in the shack?"

"No reason why not. The place has already been dusted for prints."

"You won't find any of Tibbets's prints," Josh said disgustedly. "He wears rubber gloves. A real careful type."

★ ★ ★

In the office, Josh called Phoenix and after adding the possible change of the color of the van on the APB, he asked to be transferred through to Captain Randall's office.

"Captain, this is Josh. I'm up in Flagstaff."

The captain's voice sounded tired. "Any good news for me? I could use some about now."

"We found Casey Farrel's vehicle in a used car lot up here. There is also a body, the owner of the lot. He has a broken neck, just like the stakeout."

"Tibbets?"

"It has to be."

"Any hard evidence this time?"

"No, but the service station owner across the street got a look at him. Unfortunately, he wasn't paying much attention; however, what he did notice fits Tibbets. The man was driving a blue van. I figure that Tibbets had it painted."

"No sign of Farrel and the boy?"

"Long gone. The files in the office were rifled, and all papers pertaining to whatever transactions she had with the dead man are missing. I'm sure that she traded in her vehicle for another; but with the papers gone, we have no description. . . ."

He paused. "Unfortunately, I have to assume that Tibbets now does."

Randall swore briefly but violently. "Sure doesn't say much for us, does it? A shit like Tibbets can find where the woman sold her car, while all of the law enforcement personnel in the state come up empty handed!"

"Tell me about it," Josh said with a sigh. "Bob Jenkins, the lot owner, was notoriously lax with his paperwork, according to the police here in Flag. If he'd been on the ball, and sent in the paperwork on his transactions with Casey, we would have some kind of a line on her."

"I don't suppose that you've come up with any idea of where Farrel and the boy might be going?"

"Not the slightest."

"So, what next?"

"I thought that, on my way home, I'd swing up to the Hopi reservation. Casey told me about an uncle she has there. I talked to him on the phone a couple of days ago, thinking that she might have gone to ground there; but he says not. The thing is, this uncle is evidently some sort of odd-ball; and it's possible that he wasn't telling me the truth. Or, maybe he was telling the truth at the time, but she might be there now. Anyway, I think that it's worth investigating. I can also talk with the reservation police; ask them to keep an eye out for her, as well as for Tibbets."

"I agree. But don't take too long. I want you back in Phoenix tomorrow afternoon at the latest."

"Will do, Captain, even if I have to drive all night."

"Ha!" Captain Randall said, and hung up.

Josh swung around to find Costin grinning at him through smoke spiraling up from the cigarette in his mouth. "Boss give you a hard time, did he?"

"No more than usual," Josh said with an answering grin. "You heard my side of the conversation?"

"I heard you mention a trip to the Hopi reservation. Why on earth do you want to go haring off up there?"

"One of the missing witnesses, Casey Farrel, is part Hopi. She has relatives there."

"Be sure you get out with your scalp, Josh. They're not too crazy about white cops, even the Feds, nosing around in their bailiwick."

Josh shook his head, "Come on, Costin, even I know that the Hopis didn't take scalps. The worst they would probably do is to stake me out on an ant hill."

At Winslow, Josh stopped and called John Pela at Hopi Law Enforcement Services, telling the investigator that he was on his way to the reservation.

John Pela said, "I wasn't expecting to hear from you again so soon, Sergeant. I have to be at Second Mesa most of the day. Why don't we meet at the Hopi Cultural Center for a late lunch? I'll wait for you in the lobby. You should make it there by around two."

Once off Interstate 40, the drive up to Second Mesa was monotonous, for it cut through miles of high desert with very little vegetation, and almost no habitation, except for a few scattered Navajo ranches. The air temperature was about a hundred degrees, but the air conditioner in the car was good, and Josh sat in comparative comfort, looking out at the gentle rise and fall of the dry landscape.

Since Casey had told him she was Hopi, he had been doing some reading on the subject, and, to his surprise, had found it fascinating.

He had learned that the Hopis, unlike many Native Americans, still occupied their original lands. The mesa village of Oraibi, on Third Mesa, was said to be the oldest continually inhabited city in North America, going back at least a thousand years. That, he thought, was a hell of a long time, and it sure beat the occupation record of the white man; or for that matter of other tribes, like the Navajo, who came into this territory after the Hopi. But, according to archeological evidence, even the Hopi were not the first. It was difficult to read such history without taking the side of the original settlers; yet, what was history but a record of exploration and conquest? It was the same all over the world, a record of movement, conquest, and change. It seemed that man, from his first beginnings, must have started wandering, looking for the good spots; and, if he found such a spot already occupied, he tried to take it away from the present occupants so that *his* tribe, *his* clan, *his genes*, would be the ones to carry on. The remnants of that philosophy still could be seen, tragically, in places like Israel and Ireland. Well, enough philosophizing, Josh thought, bringing his attention back to his surroundings.

He was about two-thirds of the way to the reservation now, topping a small rise, and in the distance, like a sudden mirage, First, Second, and Third Mesa reared their heads above the treeless terrain. Hovering above Second Mesa, loomed a large thundercloud, its lower belly black with the promise of rain. As Josh watched, thunder rolled, and the grey mist of distant rain connected the cloud with the mesa top. Flash floods were a common occurrence here, Josh knew, and he fervently hoped that he didn't get caught in one. In moments an automobile could be swept down a deep wash that had been dry as a bone a moment before. Also, the road to the top of the mesa was steep and twisting.

But the rain, as it so often did, lasted only a few minutes, leaving the air clean and fresh smelling. By the time Josh reached the Hopi Cultural Center, the ground was dry, as if it had never known the touch of water.

John Pela was, as he had promised, waiting in the rather run-down lobby of the Cultural Center. The investigator looked to be in his mid-thirties, a slender, dark, quick-moving man with intelligent eyes.

His hand-clasp was firm. "Sergeant Whitney, happy to meet you. As I said on the phone, I'm surprised to see you up here so soon. Has there been some new development?"

"In a way, yes." He looked over Pela's shoulder.

"Is that a restaurant I see there? I'm starving."

Pela nodded. "Sure, I could use something myself."

They were met at the entrance by an attractive young Hopi woman in contemporary dress, who showed them to a carved and ornamented booth. Josh looked around. The dining room, at this hour, was almost empty.

236

It was, he saw, neat and clean.

A large, serious, light-skinned young man handed them menus. Josh looked it over.

"Is this any good, this lamb stew with fry bread? It says it's a Hopi specialty."

Pela smiled. "If you're really hungry, I suggest something else. It's more of a soup, really, a very small dish, and I guess you could say it's an acquired taste. It's like mixing hominy, little chunks of lamb, and water, with little or no seasoning. I've seen many tourists order it, but not many of them seem to like it. They like the fry bread though."

Josh nodded. "Thanks for the tip. I think I'll have a hamburger. Do they make good hamburgers?"

Pela smiled and nodded. "The hamburgers are good."

While they were waiting for their orders, Josh looked across the table at the investigator. "Mr. Pela, you asked if . . ."

Pela waved a hand. "John, please."

"Okay, John. You asked if there had been any developments. Well, there have been." Quickly, he told Pela what had happened in Flagstaff.

"And you believe that Claude's niece might come here?"

"I think it's a definite possibility, and it seems that our perp may be right behind her.

That's why I drove up here, to warn you and her uncle. This man is extremely dangerous."

Pela nodded. "Well, I'll keep an eye peeled, Sergeant. I just hope that it doesn't happen next week."

"Why? What happens next week?"

"One of our important ceremonies, the Snake Dance. Aside from a gathering of the Hopi from all points of the reservation, tourists will be pouring in here by the hundreds." He grimaced. "Not exactly the best time for a murderous madman to be loose on the reservation."

Josh whistled. "Well, all we can do is hope that she, and Tibbets, don't arrive during next week."

Pela nodded. "Whatever happens we'll do the best we can."

"I'm certain of that."

Their food had arrived, and Josh took several bites of the hamburger before saying, "Tell me about Claude Pentiwa, Casey's uncle."

Pela grinned. "Claude is one of a kind, an eccentric in every sense of the word. As I hinted to you on the phone, he pretty much goes his own way, and to hell with the rest of the world."

Josh wiped his mouth with his napkin. It was cloth, which he appreciated. "I sort of got that impression myself when I talked with him. One minute he was making like Tonto, the next he was doing a British Lord. It was weird!"

Pela laughed. "He was putting you on, Sergeant."

"I figured that much," said Josh ruefully. "Does he do that to most people?"

"Most white men, yes. You see, Claude spent a number of years away from the reservation. Some of that time he spent in Hollywood, acting in movies. At one point — I was never too clear on just how it happened — he ended up in Italy making some of those spaghetti westerns, playing an Indian, of course. The cast was large and mostly European, and Claude is an excellent mimic. Now, when he wants to upset the white folks, he does what he did to you. He doesn't like you *Bahanas*."

"*Bahanas?*"

"Anglos. White people. He hates all you white people, so you had better watch yourself with him."

Josh shook his head and grimaced. "Great. Just what I need. You said that he now sells Hopi craft work?"

"Yes. Mostly silver. He's also a fine silversmith himself."

"Do you know if he's in his shop today?"

239

Pela nodded. "When you called, I figured you'd want to talk with him, so I stopped by there earlier; but I didn't tell him you were coming. I thought he might take off if I did."

Josh shook his head. "Well, thanks for the warning. I'll approach him with caution."

From the voice on the phone it had been hard to imagine the man, and Claude Pentiwa proved to be something of a surprise. Taller than most of the Hopis that Josh had seen, Pentiwa was broad-shouldered and trim-waisted, with rather long legs. His head was large and his features strong, with prominent cheekbones. His hair, worn shoulder length, was streaked with grey, and held back by a colorful head-band. He was a striking and handsome man, with very cold eyes.

He looked up from a work table behind the counter, as the bell heralded Josh's entrance to the shop.

"Mr. Pentiwa," Josh said, "I'm Sergeant Josh Whitney of the Phoenix Police. I spoke to you on the phone a few days ago about your niece, Casey Farrel."

Slowly, Pentiwa put down the piece of silver on which he had evidently been working, and stood up to face Josh. The dark eyes showed no friendliness.

"Yes. I remember. Why are you here? I told

you that I have not seen my niece in several years." Pentiwa's voice was deep and resonant, an actor's voice.

Josh weighed his words, determined to be as calm and as cool as the man opposite him. "I know that, sir, but there have been some new developments in the case, and I thought that you, and the reservation police, should be made aware of them."

Josh thought he saw the slightest hint of curiosity in the black eyes. The man nodded. "All right then, tell me what you have come to say."

Josh returned the nod. "As I told you, there is a man after her, and the boy who is traveling with her, a psychopath who has already killed several people. This morning he killed again, a used car lot owner in Flagstaff."

Pentiwa frowned. "What has this got to do with my niece?"

"Casey's car was found in the lot. It appears that she traded her car for another. The papers on the sale were missing from the files in the office. It seems clear that the killer took these papers. That means that he knows what kind of a car Casey is now driving, and its license number."

"I still don't understand why you are telling this to me."

Josh stifled a sigh. "Because, I still think

that she may eventually come here; and that man will be right on her tail. If she does come here, so will he; and he is a very dangerous man. He is also very smart."

Pentiwa grunted. "Thank you for your concern. However, I do not believe that my niece will come here. Like her mother, she has, so far, shown little interest in her heritage. She has taken the pencil. She has lived her life as a white woman, and as such, she would no doubt feel uncomfortable here."

Josh felt himself growing annoyed with Pentiwa, but tried not to show it. "But you told me on the phone that if she did come to you, you wouldn't turn her away."

Pentiwa nodded. "That is true."

"Then can I count on you to notify me, if she *should*, by some remote chance, call you, or turn up here?"

"Yes, Sergeant. I can do that."

"But *will* you do it?"

Pentiwa gave an exaggerated sigh. "Yes, Sergeant, I *will* do it, if such a situation arises."

Josh, gritting his teeth to keep from saying something that would alienate the older man, nodded and left the shop, thinking that Casey's uncle was an extremely irritating man.

Engrossed in his thoughts, Josh did not see Pentiwa follow him out of the store to stand staring after him. When the white policeman's car had disappeared from sight, Pentiwa turned his head and spat over his shoulder, to the west.

CHAPTER SIXTEEN

Casey felt proud of herself. She had made it through her first five days working at the casino and had only dropped one tray of drinks. And that hadn't really been her fault; a casino patron, having lost heavily on the slots, had barged into her on his way out, and knocked her on her butt, charging on without so much as an apology.

As a newcomer to the job, she had been assigned to work the aisles between the slot machines. There was a lot of ground to cover, and the tips were smaller than they were at the tables; but Casey didn't mind. She found the study of the winners and losers among the slots players endlessly fascinating. She couldn't believe some of the things she saw. It wasn't at all unusual to see a player, who had been playing a particular machine at the end of Casey's shift, still working the same machine when Casey reported to work the next day. Many players worked two or three slots at a time, jealously guarding their machines. Casey had even seen one man pull a gun to ward off a perceived intruder.

On the other hand, some slot players dropped only a coin or two in one machine, then moved on to the next. And some stood behind other players, coin-filled paper cups in their hand, until the current player moved on to another machine.

"All gamblers are weird, Casey," Simon had told her, "but slot players are the weirdest."

This was an assessment that Casey had to agree with, and one which was reinforced as she watched the players feed coins into the slots. Many of them played until they were gray and slumped with fatigue, their hands black from handling the coins. Time stood still in this lighted world without clocks, where there was no night or day. The murmur of human voices was drowned out by the sound of the machines: the thump and click of the slots; the clang of bells and sirens when the machines paid off to the accompaniment of flashing, varicolored lights. It was, to Casey, like some strange limbo, a world apart.

Simon had told her, "Watch for the winners, Casey. Gravitate to the jackpot bells with your tray. A winner always likes to celebrate with a drink, and they're in a mood to tip heavily."

Casey found this, like all of Simon's advice, to be on the mark, and she was soon making good tips. Even the losers sometimes tipped well, begging her to wish them good luck, which she always did.

So, things were going as well as could be expected, even the problem of what to do with Donnie while she worked. She knew that the boy was used to being on his own; yet she hated to leave him alone night after night. At Simon's suggestion she often brought him with her. The casino had a video game room, where the parents could dump the kids while they gambled, and several nights a week, Donnie settled in at one of the machines and played happily for hours, using the free slugs that Simon provided.

Every day, after arising late in the morning, Casey bought a *Phoenix Republic* at the vending machine in the motel office, and read it carefully. Every day she was disappointed; there was nothing about Tibbets.

By the end of her second week at the casino, her uneasiness began to grow. Another week or two, at the very most, and she and Donnie would have to move on. Even staying that long was risky; any day now the record of her employment could become available to Josh, and he would come charging after her. Could he arrest her if she refused to return to Phoenix with him? Probably. Technically, she supposed, she could be considered a kidnapper.

She had even crossed state lines with the boy.

Once or twice she thought of confiding in Simon. He was family — although she didn't really know him that well — but what good would it do?

She knew that he was curious about Donnie; it was only natural that he should be. She had told him that Donnie was the son of a good friend who was having trouble with her husband, and that she, Casey, was helping by taking care of the boy for a few weeks. Simon had apparently accepted her lie, yet she could see the skepticism in his eyes.

On this evening, Donnie had stayed behind at the motel to watch one of his favorite programs, so, when Casey's break came up, she found a seat in one of the fast-food areas of the casino, and ordered a cup of coffee and a sandwich.

"Eating alone tonight, I see," said a smooth voice.

She glanced up into the handsome face of Cliff Thornton. Cliff was a blackjack dealer. He was tall and dark, with deep-set black eyes and a pencil-line mustache. Conforming to the casino's Old West motif, he was attired in fawn-colored trousers, a black frock coat, a ruffled white shirt, and a black string tie. He looked every inch the river-boat gambler.

She said, smiling up at him, "Donnie decided to stay home tonight, TV."

"Let me get something to drink, and I'll join you. If that's all right."

Casey nodded. She watched him walk over to the counter. She'd met Cliff her first night here. Without being obvious about it, he had made it known that he was attracted to her. Since then, he had, several times, asked her to have dinner with him, and she had always refused. He was an attractive man; but she had too much on her plate already, and she knew that, in her present situation, it was unwise to get too close to anyone.

Cliff came back with a glass of cola and a sandwich, and sat down opposite her. "Simon tells me that you're staying at a motel in town. Are you looking for an apartment?"

Casey looked down into her cup, mentally berating Simon for his friendliness. Still, it wasn't his fault. As far as he knew Casey was on the up and up. And, Cliff, being interested in her, had probably asked about her.

"Not yet."

"Why not? I know apartments are expensive and hard to find, but they can't be as expensive as a motel."

Casey toyed with her cup handle. "Well, I'm not certain how long I'll be here."

He peered at her closely. "Don't you like the job?"

Casey shrugged. "The job's okay, for what it is; but I may have to put Donnie in school come September, and I don't know if this is the place for it."

Cliff frowned. "Simon told me that you are just keeping the kid until his mother gets her life straightened out."

Inwardly, Casey sighed. That was the trouble with living a lie; once you started, you had to keep building, and in time the structure became so unwieldly that it collapsed.

"I may have him longer than I anticipated. If I do, I'll probably need to find a daytime job someplace where they have good schools."

"Well, I think that it's a fine thing you're doing. Not everyone would take on such a responsibility for a friend."

His smile was warm and kind, and Casey experienced a pang of guilt. What would he think of her when she packed and left Laughlin, without a word to him? It was something she would have to do soon.

He took a few bites of his sandwich, while Casey finished her coffee. Then he looked directly at her and said, "How about taking you to lunch tomorrow, Casey?"

"We'd have to take Donnie along. I don't like to leave him alone any more than necessary."

He smiled wryly. "I guess I more or less expected that, but I also guess that I can live with it."

She had been certain that telling him that Donnie would have to go along would discourage him. Now, she had no alternative but to say, "Okay, then."

His smile softened. "I'll pick you up at your motel at twelve sharp, tomorrow. What motel is it?"

She gave him the name, feeling paranoid.

Cliff took them to another casino for lunch. The dining room was attractive, and overlooked the river. It was also quite elegant — enough so that Donnie seemed a bit intimidated. Casey tried to put him at ease.

The menu offered a wide selection of choices. Casey chose a chicken stir-fry; Cliff ordered a steak, and, although Casey tried to tempt Donnie to choose something different, he ordered his usual hamburger. Kids, Casey thought, must live on hamburgers, peanut-butter and jelly sandwiches, and cold cereal. Had she been like that?

When the food arrived, Casey found it well-prepared and tasty. With the good food and the fine view of the river, it should have been an enjoyable luncheon, but it was not. It had taken Casey only a few minutes to realize that Cliff was not at ease around children, and

Donnie, evidently sensing this, was sullen and uncooperative.

Shortly after they had begun their meal, Cliff looked at Casey pleadingly, and she renewed her efforts to get the two males into a conversation. "Donnie is an ardent sports fan," she said to Cliff, brightly.

Cliff looked relieved. "Which are your favorite teams, Donnie?"

Donnie perked up. "Baseball, I like the Dodgers. Football, the Phoenix Cardinals. But the Cardinals, they ain't been doing too good. Not last season, anyway."

"Aren't, Donnie," Casey said automatically.

Cliff said, "I have to admit that I don't follow any one team in particular. When you're betting the spread, you can't root for any certain team. If you do, you get emotionally involved, and you can't afford that."

"The spread?" Donnie said blankly.

"Sure, kid, that's when . . ."

"Cliff," Casey said warningly.

"Huh?" Cliff looked at her, then held up his hands. "I'm sorry, Donnie."

Donnie leaned forward. "Why can't you tell me what you mean?"

Cliff, his expression uncomfortable, shrugged his shoulders. "It's pretty complicated, kid, and nothing you need to know about. What I should have said is that when you are betting on a particular team, loyalty to that team doesn't figure into the equation. Do you see what I mean?"

Donnie's dark look answered that he didn't. He returned his attention to his hamburger, and for the rest of the meal, he pointedly ignored Cliff.

When they had finished eating, Cliff drove them back to the motel. Donnie asked for the key, and was out of the car and into the room without even saying good-bye to Cliff.

Cliff looked at Casey with a grimace. "Doesn't look like I made a big hit with the kid. Is it something I said?"

Casey shrugged. "Usually he's open and friendly with everyone."

Cliff ducked his head. "Thanks a lot."

Casey, realizing how what she had said must have sounded, laughed and put her hand on Cliff's arm. "Don't let it worry you. Kids are funny, and Donnie's been through a lot lately."

Cliff put his hand on top of hers. Her instinct was to draw her hand away, but she was afraid that would seem unfriendly. She let it stay.

"Could he be jealous? I mean, even little boys sometimes get crushes on grown women. Or, are you seeing someone else, someone the boy likes, and so he resents me?"

Casey now pulled her hand away, gently,

and lifted it to push her hair behind her ear. This man was all too astute.

She hesitated, then spoke. "It's true that I was seeing someone, a man with whom Donnie grew very close. Donnie still misses him."

Cliff's dark eyes were probing. "And you, do you miss him too?"

Casey lifted her chin. "Yes. I do. He's a good man, and a good friend."

Cliff's eyes narrowed. "Then why aren't you with him? Or, is that any of my business?"

Casey shook her head, but smiled to take the sting out of her words. "No, Cliff, it isn't. There is a good reason, but it's much too long and complicated a story to tell."

Cliff lifted his palms in a sign of surrender, and assumed his usual, cocky smile. "Okay, Casey. I'll try not to poke my nose in where it doesn't belong. But I'd still like to see you again. How about dinner some night, alone? I'm off Monday, and I believe you are too, correct?"

She sighed. "I'll think about it and let you know, okay? And thanks for the lunch."

Inside the motel room, Donnie was slumped in a chair, staring glumly at the silent TV screen. Casey wanted to take him into her arms, but perhaps that wasn't the best way to deal with this. Sitting down opposite him, she said calmly, "Donnie, you weren't very nice to Cliff. Would you tell me why?"

He looked up at her, frowning. "That man gambles, Casey."

Casey suppressed a smile. "Well, of course. That's what he does for a living."

Donnie shook his head. "No, I mean he bets on *ball* games! He doesn't even care about the games, or the teams. He even said so!"

Again Casey fought to keep back a smile. "I know, dear; but he is a professional gambler, and that's what they do. I know that it must be hard for you to under . . ."

"I'll bet Josh doesn't bet on ball games," Donnie broke in.

"We don't know that for sure, Donnie. Maybe he does sometimes."

"Well, if he does, I'll bet he bets on his favorite team, and I'll bet it's because he thinks his team is the best. I wish Josh was here, Casey."

This time Casey did reach for the boy, pulling him off the chair and into her arms. She felt close to tears. "We both do. We both do."

"Josh don't treat me like a kid," Donnie said.

"Doesn't," Casey said.

"Doesn't," Donnie said dutifully.

Casey pulled away and looked down into

his unhappy little face. "Do I treat you like a kid, Donnie?"

Donnie lowered his head. "Well, no. But you're a girl."

"Oh," Casey said, pulling him close again.

Donnie's voice, muffled against her shoulder, sounded higher than usual. "Casey, how come we can't go back to Phoenix, and Josh. How come?"

Casey bit her lip. "You know why, Donnie. I know it's hard on you; but it is on me too. Just be patient a little longer. They should catch Tibbets any day now. Then we can go back."

She stood, leaning down to cup his face between her hands. She kissed him on the forehead. "I have to get ready to go to work, Donnie. Do you want to go with me?"

"Nah." He twisted away from her. "There's a ball game on tonight that I want to watch."

Ray Tibbets had been in Laughlin for three days now, and he was growing increasingly frustrated. He had cruised the streets and the casino parking lots, looking for the Mustang, but so far had not found it. Had that Nevada map with Laughlin circled been left in the Thunderbird to mislead him? No, she couldn't be that clever.

And then, shortly after eight on the third

255

night, he spotted the car in an employee parking lot at one of the casinos. Elation surged through him like a powerful drug. He parked the van nearby, so that he could keep the Mustang under observation, and settled down to wait, squeezing his tennis ball, switching it from hand to hand.

Normally, Tibbets had the patience of an experienced hunter; but tonight he felt impatient and restless. He had been hunting these two for so long, and now they were so close. Since she was parked in the employee parking area, the woman must have taken a job at the casino — thank Cowpuncher Bob for that. If the old shit had paid her the proper difference between the cars, she wouldn't have had to look for work, and she might have been harder to find.

Since the car was parked here at this hour, it was probable that the woman was working the swing shift, and that meant that she wouldn't be getting off work until midnight. Would he be able to wait that long?

Tibbets attempted to calm himself, concentrating on the tennis ball, going over what he would do to the woman when he took her.

After what seemed like a great deal of time had passed, he looked at his watch. One hour. He began to fidget. Perhaps he should go into the casino and look for her, see if she was really there. It was possible that she had gotten rid of this car, too. Maybe someone else was driving it. If that was the case, he shouldn't be wasting his time here.

Convinced that what he was doing was sensible, Tibbets got out of the van. The casino floor would probably be packed at this hour, but that was all to the good. It would enable him to spot her, without her spotting him. Once he knew that she was really there, he would come back out and wait until she came out. He would then follow her to wherever she and the boy were staying, and do them both. The prospect was so delicious that he paused for a moment to savor it, then strode toward the casino, feeling every inch of himself come alive with anticipation.

Since it was Friday night, Casey was already exhausted, and she was only halfway into her shift. But the tips had been good — her best night yet — and at the end of her shift tonight, she would receive her pay check.

The thought of that pleasant prospect gave her renewed energy, and she finished serving drinks to three women and one man on one row of slots, and approached a second man with the one drink left on her tray.

As she stopped beside the man, he motioned to her. "Just a sec, babe. Wait until I feed the monster here. Maybe you'll bring me luck. I sure as hell need some."

Casey watched, smiling, as he fed three quarters into the machine, and pushed the button. She jumped as lights flashed, bells rang, and quarters cascaded noisily down into the coin catch basin.

The player jumped up from his stool, his hands held high in a victory salute. "Goddamn it, I did it. You brought me luck, babe."

He spun around, arms wide as if to embrace her. Prepared, Casey took a step backward, her tray carefully held between them. "Congratulations, sir," she said primly.

Leaning down, he scooped a double handful of quarters out of the catch basin and dumped them onto her tray. "That's for the drink, and the rest is for you. And you can bring me another drink, soon as you get the chance."

"Thank you, sir."

She turned away, scooping up the quarters and stuffing them into the bag at her waist — a nice tip — then went up and down the aisles that were her responsibility until she had orders for enough drinks to make a trip to the service bar worthwhile.

When the drinks were prepared, she carefully placed them on her tray and started back to her section. As she turned the corner around the change booth she almost ran into a man coming from the opposite direction. Looking up, she found herself staring into the startled eyes of Ray Tibbets.

The feeling of shock was so great, and so unexpected, that she actually feared she might die. Frozen, she watched recognition dawning. From somewhere she drew the strength to throw the tray, drinks and all, into his face. Tibbets fell back a step, a grunt of pain escaping him as he pawed at his alcohol-blinded eyes.

Casey, panicked to her core, turned and fled, bumping into people, pushing them out of her way.

Suddenly, she was halted, as strong arms grasped her and a deep voice said, "Casey! Whoa, what is it?"

She looked up into the face of her cousin, Simon. Her mind moved with frightened speed. She turned and pointed. "Simon, that man," she pointed at Tibbets who was still rubbing at his eyes, "he tried to attack me."

"Did he now?" Simon released her, giving her shoulder a reassuring squeeze. "You stay right here. I'll have a little talk with that sucker."

Giving his belt a hitch, Simon started down the aisle toward Tibbets.

Casey didn't wait to see what happened.

Hopefully Simon would delay Tibbets long enough for her to get away. Running to the service bar, she ducked under the door, scooped up her purse, and ran to the exit nearest the employee parking lot.

There was no one in the parking lot, and with trembling hands, she managed to get the Mustang unlocked and started. As she drove out of the lot, she looked in the rear-view mirror, but no one was behind her.

Taking a deep breath, she tried to think logically. She was paid up at the motel. All she would have to do was get Donnie, throw their things into the car, and head out of town. Damn it, why hadn't she told Simon who Tibbets was; but there hadn't been time for explanations.

And her pay check, she could have used that; but maybe it would pay for her costume, which, she suddenly realized, she was still wearing. Well, no use crying over what could not be changed. She had gotten away, for the moment, and she must make the moment count.

CHAPTER SEVENTEEN

When Ray Tibbets finally got the liquor out of his eyes, he found himself confronted by a huge hulk of a man.

The man's broad face was cold. He stood, hands on his hips, his stance threatening. "The cocktail waitress just told me that you tried to attack her, mister. What's the story here?"

Tibbets's vision was still blurred, and he blinked back the tears stinging his eyes. He kept his expression open and innocent, his manner and voice as polite as a well-disciplined child. "I have no idea what you mean, sir. I tried to attack no one."

The big man frowned. "That's not the way she tells it." He looked down at the broken glass and the tray on the floor. "And if nothing happened, why did she throw drinks in your face?"

He nudged the drink tray with the toe of his boot.

Tibbets spread his hands, still blinking away tears. "I have no idea, sir. It just came out of nowhere, for no reason that I can think of."

The big man shook his head. His expression was skeptical. "Do you know her?"

Tibbets shook his head. "I never saw her before in my life," he said blandly.

"Well, I'd like you to come along to my office. I'm Simon Morgan, casino security." He pointed to the patch on the arm of his uniform. "I think we should have a chat."

The guard took Tibbets's arm, not roughly, and steered him toward the back of the casino. Only an iron discipline enabled Tibbets to maintain his facade of calm. By acting too hastily, by not waiting until the woman had gotten off work, and following her home, he had blown it. By the time he extricated himself from this man, she and the boy would be long gone.

Momentarily, he toyed with the idea of attempting to break free. Tibbets thought he could take the guard — the man was big, but like many big men he probably thought that his size made him unassailable — and he would probably not be prepared for a direct, fierce, attack. However, there was no way to tell how many other security men were on the floor, and Tibbets did not want to take another foolish risk. One mistake a night was enough. At any rate, he had found the woman once; he could do it again.

Inside the small office, Morgan closed the door and turned, holding out his hand. "Could I see some I.D. please?"

Tibbets had prepared himself for just such a contingency before he had left Phoenix. Politely, he opened his wallet and removed the fake driver's license.

The guard scanned the license before looking up. "James Foster. Any other identification, Mr. Foster?"

"Sure thing." From his wallet Tibbets took out a Social Security card, well-aged and worn. He smiled disarmingly. "No credit cards. I always pay cash."

Simon examined the Social Security card. "You're from Tucson, I see. And what do you do for a living, Mr. Foster?"

"I have my own business. I repair TVs, radios, stereos, that kind of thing."

"Been to Laughlin before, Mr. Foster?"

"Nope. That's why I'm here now. Haven't taken a vacation in over a year. I've been reading about Laughlin, and thought I'd come up and check it out. Maybe lose a few bucks."

Simon returned the license and card, then leaned back against the desk, his keen gaze on Tibbets. "I'm still puzzled as to why Miss Farrel would throw the drinks in your face, and then tell me that you tried to attack her."

Tibbets shrugged. "I have no idea. Why don't you ask her?"

"I think I'll do just that."

Tibbets felt himself tense as the guard picked up the phone on the desk and punched out a number. What if he was wrong? What if the woman hadn't fled?

He watched as the man spoke into the receiver, then waited, blunt fingers drumming on the desk top. Several seconds passed, and the guard grew ever more impatient. Then he straightened up, turning his back to Tibbets, and spoke in a low voice.

After the brief conversation, he hung up slowly, turning again towards Tibbets. "That's strange. Miss Farrel has evidently left the casino."

Feeling a surge of relief, Tibbets assumed an expression of confusion.

Again, the guard turned his back, and punched out a number on the phone. He spoke a few words, too low for Tibbets to hear, then waited for several seconds before hanging up again.

He faced Tibbets, his face puzzled. "And she doesn't answer the telephone in her room."

Tibbets's mind raced. He had been right. She had taken off.

The guard spoke again. "I just don't understand this at all. It's damned strange."

Tibbets said, "Maybe she mistook me for somebody else. Or maybe . . ." He laughed with a twist of contempt. "Maybe it's the wrong time of the month for her," regretting the words the second they were out.

The guard scowled blackly at the remark, then gestured sharply. "I still think there is something going on here, but I have no grounds to hold you. You're free to go, Mr. Foster, but don't come back. Understood?"

Tibbets nodded. "Understood. Thank you, Mr. Morgan."

Simon scowled at the closed door long after Foster had left. Something wasn't right about this whole incident; he could feel it in his gut. He knew Casey well enough to know that there had to be a reason for what she did. Was she in some kind of trouble? She had been acting mysterious ever since she had arrived in town. But if she was in trouble, why hadn't she told him? It was damn confusing.

Simon knew that he had nothing that warranted calling in the police; you can't arrest a man for having drinks thrown in his face. But he decided that there was one thing he could do; he could go to Casey's motel and ask her what the hell was going on. ⊙

Safely inside his van, Tibbets vented his

rage, pounding on the steering wheel and cursing vilely in a low monotone.

When his hand began to throb painfully, he started the van and drove across the river into Bullhead City, in search of a motel where he could spend the night and plan his next move. What little sleep he had gotten in his three nights and days in Laughlin had been in the van; and there was always the chance that a prowling cop might spot him and decide to hassle him. He didn't want that tonight.

He found a motel room and locked himself inside with all the material he had on the woman and the boy. He went through it all again, carefully, line by line. While re-reading the article in the *Arizona Republic,* one word leaped out at him — Hopi!

The woman had seen him now; knew definitely that he was on her trail. She must be desperate — the thought made him smile — so where would she go? Very possibly the reservation might seem to her a safe haven.

He squeezed the tennis ball in his right hand, letting the tension and frustration flow down his arm and out through the contracting and expanding ball. He made his decision. He would try the reservation, and if she was there, she would soon learn that there was no haven, no place of safety, while he was alive.

★ ★ ★

When Casey left the casino, she had driven directly to the motel and parked in front of their unit, leaving the motor running. It took her two tries to fit the key into the lock.

Donnie, startled, jumped up from the chair in front of the TV. "Casey! It's not time for you to be home. How come?"

Casey tried to keep her voice calm. "Gather up your things, Donnie, quickly. We're getting out of here right now."

He stared at her in bewilderment. "How come?"

"Donnie, just do as I say!" She took a deep breath, spoke in a calmer tone: "Ray Tibbets is here in town, Donnie. He came to the casino. He may be right behind me. Now get your things together."

She was in the motel room less than fifteen minutes. With two quick trips, they had everything in the car. Just as they started out for the last time, the telephone rang. Donnie started for it.

"No!" Casey shouted. "Don't answer that!"

Donnie turned a troubled face to her. "But it might be Josh, Casey."

"I don't care if it's God himself. Look, it can't be Josh, Donnie; he doesn't know where we are. Whoever it is, it can only be bad news. Now let's get out of here."

They had been driving for about fifteen

minutes when Donnie said, "Where are we going, Casey?"

"To Second Mesa, the Hopi Reservation. My uncle lives there."

"How come there?"

"Because it's the one place that Tibbets might not think of looking for us. I'm hoping that my people will take us in."

My people, she thought. It felt strange, saying that. Was she even entitled to say it, considering the few times she had visited the mesa. Yet, when her grandmother had been alive she had felt that they were that, her people. She had been proud to be Hopi. It had seemed romantic and mysterious.

Donnie was staring at her curiously. "Are you an Indian, Casey? You never told me that you were an Indian."

Casey smiled. "Well, I'm half Indian. Why? Does that bother you?"

Slowly, he shook his head. "You don't look very Indian. Maybe a little. Is it fun, being an Indian?"

Casey could see the questions piling up behind his eyes.

"I don't have time to go into that just now, Donnie. We'll talk about it later, okay?"

He thought a minute, then nodded. "Okay."

Donnie was quiet for all of ten minutes, then, "How come you didn't change out of your costume, Casey?"

Casey sighed. "Because I couldn't take the time, that's why. I'll stop at a gas station restroom somewhere along the way and change."

As she drove, Casey kept glancing up into the rear-view mirror, looking for a black van on her tail. There was very little traffic this time of night. Whenever headlights appeared in the mirror she felt the cold surge of fear. Since she dared not drive over the speed limit, most of the vehicles eventually passed them. There were no black vans.

It wasn't until they reached Kingman and turned east on Interstate 40, that her panic began to subside, and she could begin to think rationally. Again, she berated herself for not telling Simon who Tibbets was; but at the time she could think of nothing but the necessity of getting away. Some cool-headed crime investigator she was going to make. But there was something so terrifying about Tibbets, wearing that innocent, baby face, yet harboring such implacable evil. He was relentless; he just kept coming. Like the monsters in horror films, it seemed that nothing could stop him.

Slowly, anger began to replace the fear. She was weary of running, sick of living in fear. There had to be some way to stop him, something she could do. She ached to fight back.

But right now she needed a safe place, a place where she could regain her equilibrium, and get her act together.

Donnie said, "How did that man find us, Casey?"

She glanced at his troubled face in the dash-light. "I have no idea, kiddo, and believe me I've thought about it."

They rode along for a few miles in silence. Then Donnie said in a small voice, "I've been thinking, too. It was my fault, Casey."

She gave him a startled glance. "What do you mean? How could it be your fault?"

"When you bought the car in Flagstaff, I had a map of Nevada, and I circled Laughlin with my pen. I forgot, and left the map in the Thunderbird. Mr. Tibbets must have found it."

Casey felt a surge of anger, and resisted a momentary impulse to reach across the seat and slap the boy across the face; but as fast as the impulse came, it was gone. She forced a smile, said, "What the heck, kiddo. That may be the way he found us, or it may not. He would probably have found us anyway. The so-and-so just never gives up."

Donnie brightened. "Then you're not mad at me?"

"No, kiddo." She reached over to ruffle his hair. "We're in this together. I've done some

270

stupid things myself since this whole mess started."

They stopped for breakfast in Flagstaff at eight o'clock in the morning. While Donnie finished off his meal, Casey got a handful of quarters from the cashier, and, going over to the pay phone, punched out Simon's number in Laughlin.

"Casey!" Simon's voice quickened. "Where the devil are you? And why did you take off like that? I went to your motel, but you'd already packed up and gone."

"It's not important where I am, Simon. What happened to Ray Tibbets?"

"Ray Tibbets? Who's Ray Tibbets?"

"The man who tried to attack me in the casino."

"That was a man named James Foster. At least that was what his I.D. said."

"That I.D. was faked, Simon. His real name is Ray Tibbets. You've read about the Dumpster Killer down in Phoenix. Well, that's him."

"The Dumpster Killer? Casey, don't you think it's time you told me what's going on?"

"Not now, Simon. I don't have the time. Call the Phoenix Police, talk to a Sergeant Josh Whitney. Tell him that Tibbets was in Laughlin. Josh will tell you what it's all about."

"Don't you think *you* should call him?"

"No! I don't want him to know where I am. Just do it, please, Simon. I'm sorry that I got you involved in all this."

Simon laughed shortly. "I don't even know what you're talking about, but what are relatives for?"

"Well, I want you to know how much I appreciate it. And tell your boss that he can hold my pay check, and I'll see to it that the costume is returned eventually. I'm hanging up now, Simon. Good-bye."

As Casey approached the booth again, she saw the middle-aged waitress talking to Donnie. As Casey slid into the booth, the waitress said, "Your son here tells me that you're from out of town, just passing through, but didn't I see you two in here a couple of weeks ago?"

Casey shot Donnie a look. He was her *son* now? Donnie's glance slid away. Feeling apprehensive, Casey debated lying, but finally decided that there was no reason to do so. "Yes," she said. "That's right, we were. You have a good memory."

The woman smiled, and winked at Donnie. "Well, I never forget a good looking man. Besides, that was the week we had the murder." The waitress shuddered. "Terrible thing, everybody's been talking about it. We don't have that many murders here in Flag."

Casey's feeling of apprehension grew. "What murder? I guess I didn't read about it."

The waitress leaned forward, hands on the table. "Man up the road a piece. Fellow name of Cowpuncher Bob. Owned a used car lot."

Casey felt her body tense with shock. She stole a look at Donnie, and saw that the boy's face had gone white. She hoped the waitress would not notice. "What happened?"

"The papers say that the man's neck was broken . . ."

Casey tuned out for a moment. The killer had to be Ray Tibbets; Donnie was right! But why hadn't she read about the murder in the *Arizona Republic?* Of course, she had only been looking for something on Ray Tibbets . . .

She tuned back in to hear the waitress saying: "I just don't know what kind of world it's getting to be. It seems a person isn't safe anywhere anymore. Now you two be careful on the road. Don't go picking up any hitchhikers, or anything."

Casey answered the woman's smile, and put down a generous tip. "Don't worry," she said, as she took Donnie's hand. "We'll be careful."

Trying to control the shaking of her hands, Casey led Donnie to the car. Thank God she had called Simon. Maybe, if they were very lucky, the police would catch up to Tibbets before he found them. Maybe, if they were very *very* lucky, Tibbets would look for them in the wrong direction, the wrong place. The thing was, it seemed to her that it was Tibbets who was having all the luck.

Josh found Simon Morgan waiting for him when he got off the small plane from Phoenix. The security guard was as big as a pro line-backer, with a square face, and intelligent brown eyes. His handshake was crushing.

"Heard anything more from Casey?"

"Not since she called yesterday. My car's right outside, Sergeant."

As they walked to the car, Josh said, "And you have no idea where she was calling from, or where she was headed?"

Simon shook his head. "She wouldn't say."

Josh sighed. "Well, we'll check out your incoming calls; that will tell us where the call came from, but it sure won't help with where she's going. You have any thoughts? Even a guess would do."

Simon drove for a bit in silence. "Not really. You have to understand something, Sergeant. I don't really know Casey all that well. She's only a distant cousin; and the only times I saw her, before this, was when she came to Second Mesa to visit her grandmother. That

274

wasn't very often, and the visits stopped after the old woman passed on. I hadn't seen Casey in years, until she popped up out of the blue, here in Laughlin. I don't get back to the reservation much since my mother died. I've only been back a few times in the past ten years."

"Do you know Casey's uncle, Claude Pentiwa?"

Simon nodded. "Sure, although we're not close. He's not an easy man to get along with."

"Yes, I've met Mr. Pentiwa," Josh said wryly.

"Then you understand what I mean," Simon said. "He's something, isn't he? Like Casey, I'm something pretty much *persona non grata* since I left the reservation to live among the *Bahanas*. Which is pretty funny, once you consider that Claude spent years away from the reservation, making movies. But, of course, there's no worse fanatic than a recent convert. You would think he invented 'Native American Culture' the way he carries on."

"I'm curious, why do you use the last name, Morgan?"

Simon shrugged. "I find it easiest, when living among white people, to blend in. That's one reason Claude is pissed, that I would change my name and pass myself off as a non-Hopi. Actually, I never deny my Native American blood, I just don't mention it. I'm pretty light-skinned, and I can pass for one of the darker-skinned Anglos. It's just a matter of convenience."

"Do you think that Pentiwa will take Casey in, if she should come to him for help?"

"I can't answer that. He may, or he may not, depending on his mood. But I doubt very much that she will go there; she hasn't seen Claude in five or six years."

He gave Josh a sideways glance. "Isn't it about time that you tell me what this is all about, Sergeant? Casey promised that you would fill me in."

Josh gave him a sketchy account of what had happened, not finishing until they were in the casino where Simon worked, having lunch.

When Josh was finished, Simon shook his head. "She really got herself into a fix, didn't she? It might have helped if she had told me. I could have held this Tibbets."

"That reminds me." Josh took a blow-up of the picture of Tibbets from his briefcase. "Is this the guy who was here?"

One look, and Simon nodded. "That's the guy. No doubt about it. He sure doesn't look like a killer."

"Well, he is. Depend on it. Tell me all you can remember from the driver's license and Social Security card he showed you."

Simon gave him what information he could, as Josh wrote it down. "I'll get this on the radio, but I doubt he'll use that identification again. When he bought the forged papers, he probably bought several sets. He may be a nut-cake, but he possesses all the street smarts."

Simon said, "Wouldn't Casey have been better off staying in Phoenix, where she had police protection?"

"I think so, but evidently Casey doesn't. That night when Tibbets came to the house and killed the stakeout, that really spooked her. It must have seemed to her that our protection was worthless, and running the only answer."

"What are your chances of catching this guy?"

"Not a whole lot better than they were yesterday, or last week. We just have to keep plugging away, hoping for a break, hoping that he doesn't catch up to Casey and Donnie before we catch up to him."

"Well, good luck, Sergeant."

"Thanks, Simon. I could use some about now. And thanks for your help. Also, if Casey should call you again, try to get her to turn herself in at the nearest police station, then call me at once, you hear?"

* * *

Josh spent the next eight hours in Bullhead and Laughlin, showing the pictures of Casey, Donnie, and Tibbets, at every gas station, convenience store, and fast-food restaurant in town, but no one would admit having seen them.

By the time he finished it was late afternoon, and he was exhausted, but he had one more stop to make before he rested and got something to eat and drink — the motel where Casey and Donnie had been staying.

The owner of the motel was manning the desk. Josh flashed his badge. "Sergeant Josh Whitney, Phoenix Police, Homicide. You had a Casey Farrel staying here, Room 118?"

"I did, yeah. She checked out some time last night, without a word to anybody." The man's watery blue eyes squinted at Josh. "She involved in a homicide?"

"A witness," Josh said curtly. "I'd like to check out the room, please."

"Sure, but I don't think you'll find anything. She didn't leave anything behind, and the unit has already been cleaned."

"I'd like a look anyway." Suddenly, Josh felt weary and heavy with discouragement. He said, "Is the room rented for the night?"

"Nope, not yet."

"Then, I'll take it."

"Glad to oblige, Sergeant."

He gave Josh a registration card. Josh signed and handed over his credit card. Then he accepted the key to 118 and moved the rental car down the line to park before the room.

He had no idea of what he expected to find. It was a typical motel room: two double beds separated by a bed stand supporting a telephone; TV set; dressing table and chest of drawers; two chairs; and a round table with a reading lamp suspended overhead. The bathroom was small, but clean, and the closet roomy.

Josh opened all the drawers, prowled the closet and the bathroom. Nothing, absolutely nothing left behind to show that Casey had ever been there.

Everything was clean, with a depressing, sterile look, and smelled strongly of disinfectant.

And yet, underneath the stronger odor, Josh thought that he could smell something else, the faint scent of the floral perfume that Casey wore. He inhaled deeply, attempting to isolate the odor, but it was gone; or had it ever been there?

Slipping off his shoes, he threw himself across the bed; swept by a longing so intense, so powerful, that he was moved to tears.

Would he ever see Casey again?

Alive?

CHAPTER EIGHTEEN

It was mid-morning when Casey topped a small rise in the arrow-straight road going north, and saw the three mesas of Hopiland looming up in the distance. The air was crystal-clear, and the pink mesas looked to be only a few miles distant, yet Casey knew that they were at least twenty miles away.

Some ten miles apart, the three Hopi mesas loomed high, enormous rock-capped outthrusts, extending outward from the larger Black Mesa. The white man had named them First, Second, and Third Mesa. They were a part of the 4,000-square-mile Hopi Reservation, set aside by Executive Order in 1882. On the tops of the mesas, the little villages stood like small fortresses, lashed by bitter winds in the winter, baked by the blazing sun in summer. The reservation itself was like an island surrounded by the Navajo Indian Reservation. The Navajos were ancient enemies of the Hopi, and there still remained bad feeling between the two tribes, exacerbated by the Navajos' habit of encroaching upon Hopi lands.

Casey stretched, rotating her neck to ease the stiffness. She hadn't slept in over twenty-four hours, and she was dead tired. Donnie was asleep beside her, his head resting against the window, his small face appearing very vulnerable.

Simon must have called Josh by this time. She wondered if Josh was in Laughlin, looking for them.

Thinking of Josh, she felt a wave of longing for him; and with the Mesas in sight, she thought of what she had told him about her grandmother, and her tale of the Soul Eater.

Grandmother had to have been well up into her seventies the last time Casey had seen her; a tiny, wrinkled woman, who stood straight as a die, until the day she died. It was impossible to know her exact age, as the old Hopi did not record or celebrate birthdays, but the lines and wrinkles on her face and hands gave their own estimate of time. However, despite these signs of age, Casey remembered that her dark eyes had snapped with fire and intelligence; and her mind had been clear as a bell.

When Casey was a child, her mother had taken her to the reservation several times for visits. Casey's father had never accompanied them — he had not been welcome. As for

Casey and her mother, Grandmother always treated them as dear and special guests. She never mentioned her daughter's husband. For Grandmother, it seemed, he simply did not exist. As for Casey's mother, who often, in her own home, expressed her disdain for the old ways, she seemed to make an effort to hold her tongue, when in her mother's house. Although she often attempted, not too subtly, to get her mother to adopt more modern ways, the old woman always listened politely, then did as she pleased.

As for other relatives, although there were many distant cousins, Uncle Claude and his children were the only close relations. Uncle Claude lived next door to her grandparents, but Casey seldom saw him. Being a bright child, it soon became clear to her that her uncle was avoiding her, and her mother. She didn't mind. He seemed a very distant man; not pleasant to be around. She had been told that her uncle had been a movie actor — she had even seen some of the pictures he had been in — but although that seemed very glamorous, and he looked very handsome on the screen, he hadn't been very friendly in person. Her grandmother told her that Claude's wife was dead, killed by the same small-pox epidemic that had taken Grandfather.

Uncle Claude had three children, two sons

and a daughter. All were several years older than Casey, and while they had been carelessly kind to the younger child, they had all been busy with their own affairs.

One day not too long before her grandmother died, Casey overheard heated words between her mother and her uncle. Casey was in the bedroom of her grandmother's house, sitting by the open window; her mother and uncle were standing in the yard outside. Her uncle sounded very disdainful and angry. "You're a stubborn woman, filled with pride. You know that our mother is getting old and feeble now, but you won't return to the mesa because you won't leave your white husband. You were taught, just as I was, that a Hopi should never hold himself above his people. Why do you keep trying to be white? What makes you think you're better than us because you married a white man? You know the terrible things the white man has done to us. Why do you think they are so wonderful, and we are so worthless."

"I don't think that at all, and you know it," her mother answered angrily. "It's just that I live a different life now. And I resent what you say, and I resent your anger. I've worked hard for the life I have. I'm educated. I've seen something of the world outside the reservation, and that allows me to see the things that are wrong here, the poverty, the backwardness, the . . . squalor! I should think that you, of all people, would understand."

Claude Pentiwa gestured contemptuously. "Oh, I understand, all right. It's like I said, now you think you're too good for us."

Casey's mother stamped her foot. "And what about you, running around the world making movies; is *that* the Hopi way? You're a hypocrite, Claude."

Peeking around the edge of the window, Casey could see that her mother was crying, and her heart hardened against her uncle. Why was he talking so mean to her mother? What did he mean about the terrible things the white man had done to the Hopi? She made a mental note to ask her grandmother.

She watched as her uncle drew himself up. "I admit that I too was once attracted to the outside world; but I finally saw that what I was doing was wrong, and I came back to the Hopi Way."

Casey's mother sniffed. "Yes, after you made a bundle and saw all of the world you wanted to. Now you run around preaching the 'old ways' to everybody else, trying to set us back a hundred years. Well, I happen to think that the best thing for the Hopi would be to come down off of these mesas and get to be a part of the real world. Is that so terrible?"

Claude's face grew dark. "Yes. It would mean that we were totally beaten. It would mean that the white man had won."

Casey's mother shook her head. "Oh, Claude. The white man won long ago. Now the best thing is to just accept that, and go on from there and make something of ourselves, join the rest of the world, the modern age. And as for your anger at me, well, what do you want me to do, outside of leaving my husband, coming back to the reservation, and living in a shack?"

Claude glared at her. "Just stay away from here then. Why do you keep coming back?"

Casey's mother threw up her hands. "Because of our mother, of course. I come to see our mother. As you reminded me, she's old and frail, and she wants to see her granddaughter."

"Your daughter, yes, a white child who knows nothing about her people. A fine grandchild you have given our mother."

Casey's mother shook her head. "You seem to have forgotten one of the important teachings of the Hopi, Claude, that you should not harbor hatred and anger. You're full of it."

Turning, her mother had walked away, toward the house, and Casey had drawn back. She did not mention to her mother that she had overheard the argument, but now she felt she knew why her uncle was always so cold and distant. It was the two worlds again, this time fighting one another.

But most of her memories of Second Mesa were good. Casey smiled as she recalled a story her grandmother had told her of something that had happened some years before Casey had been born. Uncle Claude, who obviously was different then, had been making a visit to the mesa, between pictures. He had rented a pickup, and had purchased a bed for his parents.

Grandmother had been puzzled by the bed. Patiently, Uncle Claude had explained that it was to sleep on, that it would be much more comfortable than sheepskins piled on the often cold, and hard, floor. Grandmother listened politely, and tried the bed, pronouncing it very strange. Grandfather simply looked at the peculiar contrivance and grunted.

Later that night, Claude had looked in on his parents to see how they were sleeping in their new bed, but the old couple was nowhere in sight. Turning up his lamp, Claude had searched the room, and found them at last, rolled in their sheepskins, under the bed.

In time, Grandmother said, as her bones grew stiff, she had become grateful for the bed; but Grandfather had remained adamant, preferring his familiar sheepskin nest on the floor.

Casey did not remember her grandfather, for he had died when she was small; but from her grandmother and her mother, she had drawn a picture of him. He had been a short, broad-chested man who spoke seldom. To him the old ways were the best, and he had no interest in change. His wants were simple and elementary — food to keep his body alive and strong, heat in winter, a drink of water when he was thirsty, and his gods, to keep the world turning.

Casey smiled again, as she thought of the times she had squatted awkwardly on the rug opposite her grandmother, as the old woman told her tales of the past. Grandmother was talkative, and Casey loved to listen.

Grandmother's voice, dry and somewhat whispery, would rise and fall as she told of the old days and the old ways. She told of *Masau-u*, the God of Death, and of how he visited the villages, carrying away the souls of those he had chosen. He might appear at any time, even during the month of December, *Ka-muyau*, the Quiet Moon, or as some called it, the Moon of Dripping Blood, when the entire earth was sacred. All young Hopis were sternly instructed to observe this sacred month with respect, so that no evil would befall them. Digging into the earth was forbidden, as was stamping upon the earth. No drumming or loud talking was permitted; for *Muyingwa*, the Germinating God, must not be disturbed in his labors.

Maidens in the grinding room were forbidden to speak to anyone who appeared at the watching holes in the walls, and were not allowed to be courted by the young men. No one was allowed to cut their hair, for evil spirits might snatch the clippings to use in making their nests. If it was necessary to go out at night, crosses had to be marked upon the forehead and the soles of the feet, with ashes. And if, somehow, ghosts got into a house, and walked there, pitch was burned, providing a curtain of smoke through which the spirits could not make their way.

On one visit, when Casey was eleven, Casey had watched the women grinding corn and had asked her grandmother, "Grandmother, why do the women grind the corn by hand, on their knees all day? Aren't there machines that can do it?"

Grandmother had clucked disapprovingly. "Mother Corn has fed the Hopi people, child, since long, long ago. Mother Corn is food and life to our people. The women grind with thankfulness in their hearts for the richness of the harvest, not with the angry feeling of working too hard. As they grind, they bow their heads in prayer to the Corn God, so that he will see their gratitude, and make the next harvest good. You must not let the white man's way cause you to forget the Hopi way. I am sad that I could not have given you your first Mother Corn at birth."

She then told Casey of this birth ritual. A perfect ear of white corn was necessary, with straight rows of kernels growing up over the tip of the ear. The new-born infant was presented with the ear of corn, and the ear of corn and the baby were bathed in the same water. After the bath, the corn was cradled with the baby for the first twenty hours following birth. Then, along with the child, it was presented at the naming ceremony at the mesa's edge, as the infant received its spiritual "I am, I am" and a blessing of pollen from the sacred corn.

Casey, since she had been born off the reservation, had not gone through this ceremony, and had not had her ears pierced, as was the custom for baby girls. Looking up at her grandmother, she realized that this fact was a sadness to her grandmother.

As the flood of memories washed over her, Casey felt tears come to her eyes. She had almost forgotten how much she missed her grandmother, her stories, and her advice. Whenever there was a problem, Grandmother had an answer. There were stories to solve every problem, rules to tell you how to behave in any situation. Her grandmother's absolute confidence in these stories and patterns was, somehow, very comforting.

Only once could Casey remember her grandmother being angry with her.

On one of her visits, Casey was walking across a field, when she saw a *paho*, a prayer stick, sticking up out of a small hillock, its single eagle feather fluttering at the end of a short length of cotton string.

Pahos, made of short, sharpened sticks, were revered by the Hopi. For four days after the planting of a prayer stick, the Hopi believed them to hold the spirit of the offered prayer, and to be sacred and very powerful. To disturb one, they believed, before the stick had lost its power, would result in disaster for the unfortunate one who disturbed it.

Casey, although she may have been told this at some time, did not remember it, and with the insatiable curiosity of a child, pulled the stick out of the ground and took it to her grandmother for explanation.

Grandmother had recoiled in horror at the sight of it, exclaiming, "What have you done, Granddaughter?" Angrily she waved the stick away.

Casey lifted the stick and looked at it. "What's wrong, Grandmother? It's only a stick with a cornhusk and a feather on it."

"You have done a bad thing, child. Hasn't your mother taught you anything? Put it down, and I will tell you."

Feeling chastened, Casey complied.

"See the blue-green, chipped-off place at the top?" Her grandmother pointed a gnarled finger. "That's the face of the prayer stick. That means moisture, rain. Below is the body of the *paho*. It is painted red, that means the earth. This *paho* is a prayer for rain; but it is more than that, for it has a bundle on its back."

Casey, fascinated, said, "A bundle?"

Her grandmother nodded. "The cornhusk there, tied with string."

"What does that mean?" asked Casey.

"I would need to see inside," the old woman said. "But I will not do that. It probably contains things like — grass seeds, a bit of corn-meal, a pinch of honey."

"Why? Why good does it do?"

"What good? That would depend on several things. It would depend on how strong was the faith of the Hopi who made the prayer stick. And if all the things I told you are inside the bundle, it would mean that the Hopi who planted the stick in Mother Earth did so as a prayer for a good harvest, with rain enough to produce good ears of corn, good beans, and sweet melons."

Casey nodded. Grandmother's explanation sounded reasonable. "But what is the feather for?"

Her grandmother sighed. "Do you know nothing of the ways of our people, Granddaughter? The feather signifies the spirit that is in all things."

A few days later, while driving back home to Flagstaff, Casey told her mother what her grandmother had said. Her mother made a face. "That's all myth and superstition, Casey. Don't pay any attention to it. We are away from all that now. It is their way — I don't disparage them for that — but it's not for us. I want you to appreciate your Hopi heritage, of course, but you will grow up and live among white people. Their ways must be your ways."

During the rest of the drive, Casey thought about what her mother and grandmother had said. She loved both of them, but the things they told her were so different — as different as life on the mesa was different from the life in the city. They were like two separate worlds existing side by side. The things her grandmother told her often seemed to her like magic, and would seem out of place in the city; but the things her mother told her were out of place on the mesa. It was very confusing. She thought about it a while longer, then decided that despite what her mother said, she would not forget the things her grandmother told her. They were too interesting, and, there was the comfort in having something to do when you had a problem. She wondered if it would work if she made a *paho* to help her get good grades in math. It might be worth a try.

This was all magical, mysterious stuff; the stuff from which childish dreams might be fashioned, and Casey had been a dreamer. She often fantasized about living then, in the old days. There was always a handsome young Indian boy in the dreams, of course, and she always accomplished something heroic.

And now, here she was again, approaching Second Mesa but this time there would be no Grandmother to welcome her and to tell her stories. This time she wasn't even certain that she would be welcome at all.

Beside her, Donnie stirred and sat up. He yawned, stretching. "Are we nearly there, Casey?"

Startled out of her reverie, Casey took notice of their surroundings. The mesas now loomed large up ahead, and they were just rounding a curve. Ahead was an intersection with a few buildings; she slowed down. "Just about, Donnie." She pointed to the mesa directly ahead. "That's Second Mesa."

Donnie craned his neck to look. With something like awe he said, "We going up there? How come, Casey?"

"That's where my uncle, Claude Pentiwa, lives."

She made the stop sign, and turned left onto Highway 264. Within half a mile they began to climb the curving road to the mesa.

The last time Casey had been up this road had been just after her grandmother's funeral. That had been ten years ago, and she hadn't seen her uncle since that time. She had, however, kept up a sporadic correspondence with her cousin, Julia, and because of this had been kept more or less up-to-date on what was going on with the family. Julia had written her that Claude had built a new house and a shop, not far from the Hopi Cultural Center, on the highway near old Shungopavi.

On top of the mesa it was very quiet, and seemed several degrees warmer. The wind was strong up here; she remembered that there always seemed to be wind on the mesa. She noticed that there seemed to be more people about, and more traffic than she remembered.

She drove slowly, looking for her uncle's shop, and finally saw it — or what she hoped was it. She drove into the small parking lot, which was empty of cars. The shop appeared

294

to be closed. She turned off the motor and sat for a moment. Would her uncle help her, or turn her away? If he turned her away, what would she do?

"Casey?" Donnie said.

"Yes, kiddo," she said with a sigh. "Let's get it over with."

The door to the shop was locked, and the sign said "Closed."

She said, "Maybe he's around back."

Taking Donnie's hand, she led him around the small building toward the rock house that stood about thirty feet behind the shop.

As they approached the house, the door opened, and Claude Pentiwa emerged. He was wearing jeans, a tunic style shirt belted with a beautiful silver belt, and as he turned his head, Casey could see that his long hair was bound at the base of his neck in a bun. A blue, patterned head scarf was wrapped around his head. He looked much the same, thought Casey, as though ten years had not aged him; although he must be at least sixty years old now. His step slowed as he saw her.

Heart beating wildly, she said quietly, "Hello, Uncle."

He stood very still for a long moment, then came toward her slowly. When he was very close to her he stopped — his expression inscrutable — and looked deep into her eyes.

Clutching Donnie's hand, Casey stared back, attempting to judge his feelings. She felt as if an invisible hand was squeezing her stomach.

Then a slight smile lifted the corners of her uncle's mouth. "Oh-ee-e! *Nesseehongneum,*" he said in his resonant voice, "I've been expecting you."

Was that a smile? Was he being friendly? Tentatively, she smiled back at him. "Am I welcome, Uncle? It's been a long time."

He nodded, still looking into her eyes. "Yes, a very long time; but you are welcome. You look tired . . ." he looked down at Donnie, "and your friend looks hungry."

Donnie smiled. "Yeah. I'm starving."

"Oh," said Casey. "I'm sorry, this is Donnie, he's been travelling with me."

"Yes, I know."

"You know?" Suddenly she realized what her uncle had said earlier. "You've been expecting us?"

"Yes. Donnie, I am pleased to make your acquaintance." He held out his hand, and Donnie, looking shyly pleased, took it and shook it firmly. He seemed fascinated by Claude's clothing and the silver belt. Claude, Casey thought, seemed amused by the boy's interest.

"A white policeman, from Phoenix, was here," Claude said.

Casey felt stunned. "Josh was here? What was he doing here?"

"He was looking for you." Casey was desperate to know what Josh had been doing at the mesa, but Claude continued, "Come along. I was about to open the shop for business." He motioned for them to follow him.

The interior of the shop was cool, insulated from the blazing sun by thick stone walls. Glass cases ran the length of the structure on both sides. The cases were filled with silver jewelry; belt buckles; key-rings; and other items. Shelves behind and above the cases were filled with Kachina dolls; pottery pieces; basketry; and some leather-work.

"First, let me get you something to eat. I have some *pikami* pudding, *piki* bread, and I killed a rabbit yesterday, there is still some stew left. I think there's some fry bread too."

He turned to Donnie. "How does that sound, young man?"

"That sounds, great, I guess," Donnie said. He added dubiously, "What's *piki* bread and picka . . . that pudding?"

Casey laughed. "*Pikami* pudding. *Piki* bread is Hopi flat bread, made from sweet corn. *Pikami* pudding is made from sweet corn too, with some grass seeds and other ingredients added. Try it, you may like it."

"Okay," the boy said, his tone still dubious.

"You, niece?" Claude said.

Casey shook her head. She was too excited to eat. Claude led them to the rear of the shop where, in one corner, Casey was surprised to see a microwave oven and an electric coffee pot sitting brazenly on top of a small refrigerator. Looking up, she saw a small air-conditioner in the window.

Claude evidently caught her expression, because his own face assumed an expression of unease.

"I suppose you are wondering about the . . ." he gestured, "the modern contrivances."

Casey, not wanting to embarrass him further, shook her head. "Why, no. I mean why . . ."

He waved her words away. "I don't blame you," he said. "You must remember how I was, so set to follow only the old Hopi way. But things have changed, and so have I." His sudden, wide grin, showing strong, white teeth, made him look younger and very attractive. "I have learned the value of compromise. I keep my house in the old way, no electricity, no white man's appliances; but electricity is necessary for the shop. The tourists come here to savor history, but they don't want it to be *too* real, as in dark, hot, and uncomfortable. Also, sometimes a hospitable cup of coffee or a cold drink will close a sale. And since the electricity is here . . ." He shrugged. Casey wanted to hug him. The old so-and-so was human after all.

Claude lifted the coffee pot. "Coffee? It's fresh."

Casey nodded. "About Josh, Uncle. What did he tell you?"

Claude removed a covered dish from the refrigerator, placed it in the microwave, and punched the on button. "He told me only that he was looking for you, and he asked me to notify him if you came to the mesa. He also asked if I would take you in if you did come." His face quirked again in the almost-grin. "I'm afraid that I was not altogether polite to him. I gave him my strong, inscrutable Indian routine. I don't think he cared for it much."

Casey sighed. She could imagine how Josh might react to her uncle's seeming arrogance.

"And what did you say to that, when he asked you if you would take me in?"

"I told him I would consider it. He was arrogant, as are all the *Bahanas*."

That was the pot being hypocritical again, Casey thought, but she said, calmly, "I thought that you practiced the Hopi way, Uncle. As I remember, Hopi are taught not to feel anger and hate towards others. When he left, did you spit westward, over your shoulder, to rid yourself of evil?"

Claude looked surprised. "So you remember that?"

Casey smiled. "Grandmother told me many things, Uncle, and I haven't forgotten them all. Well, did you?"

Claude seemed embarrassed. "As a matter of fact, I did. It is not easy to be a good Hopi and live the balanced life."

He opened the door of the microwave, and pulled out the dish of rabbit stew, then heated some fry bread. When it was warm, he put some of the stew on a dish, and handed it to Donnie, along with a piece of the fry bread and a small dish of honey. "This policeman of yours also told me that you were in trouble, that you were an important witness to a crime, and that a madman, the man who committed the crime, was pursuing you. After the *Bahana* left, I talked to John Pela, the Criminal Investigator at Hopi Law Enforcement Services. He told me the details. I presume that this is all true?" His dark eyes narrowed as they looked into hers.

She nodded. "It sounds unbelievable, but it's true. This man, Ray Tibbets, is following us. He caught up to us in Laughlin, but Simon helped us get away. Tibbets seems to have an uncanny knack for finding us. Since, presumably, he doesn't know my background, I thought that he might not look for us here."

She paused, looking down at her hands, and then up at her uncle's face. "I'm sorry that I waited so long to come to you, and that it has to be like this, that I come only because I need help. I . . ."

Her uncle put his hand upon her shoulder. "It's all right, *Nesseehongneum*. We are all sorry for many things. Let the past stay past. You will be safe here. We will hide your car, and you and the boy will stay with me. We can darken the boy a bit," he smiled at Donnie, "and change your clothes and your hair. And if this man, this Tibbets, should come here, well, the Reservation Police are alerted, and I have my rifle."

Casey felt a belated misgiving. Was she putting her uncle at risk by being here? She said, "Josh and the other police in Phoenix tried to protect us, and they failed. One of the men who was supposed to be guarding us was killed. Maybe I was wrong to come here. I don't want anyone else to be hurt."

Her uncle shook his head. "The white police have grown soft, they can't handle the scum that infest the white cities, but now you are with your people. What will happen, will happen. You will stay here. Besides, among all the visitors that are coming to the mesa, it won't be that easy to find you."

Casey looked puzzled. "All the visitors, what do you mean?"

"Have you forgotten, or is that something my mother didn't tell you? It is the time of *Chu'tiva*, the Snake-Antelope ceremonies. It is only four days till the Antelope Dance, and the Snake Dance is the following day. The young men have already gathered the snakes and have them waiting in the Snake Kiva."

The Snake Dance! Dear God, she *had* forgotten. A convulsive shudder gripped her. Of all the times to come here . . .

Donnie said, "This bread is good stuff, Mr. Pentiwa. Could I have some more?" He held out his plate, then glanced from one to another of the adults, his face glowing with curiosity. "What's a Snake Dance, Casey? That sounds neat. Tell me about it."

CHAPTER NINETEEN

Despite his impatience, Ray Tibbets did not go immediately to the Hopi Reservation. He had decided that if a few days passed before he showed up, the woman might figure that she had lost him, and relax her guard a bit. That was, of course, supposing she was there. He had a strong feeling that she was.

He stopped in Williams for two days. He needed some time to rid himself of the anger and frustration caused by his errors in Laughlin, and to re-focus his purpose. He wouldn't be so hasty the next time.

While in Williams, he had the van repainted — brown this time, and stocked up on food and drinks. The area he was going to was thinly populated, and God only knew where he might find a grocery store. After he retrieved the repainted van, and again changed the license plate, he was well-rested and wired, ready for the final confrontation. The woman and the boy would be on the reservation. He was now certain of it.

When he reached the highway that led to the reservation, he was surprised to see the amount of traffic. He discovered the explanation when he pulled into the small service station at the intersection of Highways 87 and 264 for gas. The Indian manning the pumps told him that it was the time of the Antelope and Snake Dances. "This year the ceremonies are being held at *Shungopavi,* on Second Mesa. All the Hopi gather, and many people from other tribes: Zunis; Pueblos; and lots of Navajos. Visitors come from all over the world."

Tibbets cursed under his breath. Damn! Crowds of people would make it difficult to find the woman and the boy. On the other hand, they would provide good cover during his search.

He considered showing the woman's and boy's pictures to the attendant, but then thought better of it. He had read that these Indians were very clannish, and not overly fond of white people. He did not want to risk the possibility that the woman might be alerted. He said casually, "Many places to stay up there on the mesa?"

The Hopi laughed. "You're out of luck, friend. No way. The only motel on the mesa is the Cultural Center, and their rooms have been reserved as long as a year in advance. Even the rooms in Kearns Canyon and Tuba

City, miles away, are taken."

Tibbets thanked the man for his help. He wasn't too concerned about the lack of rooms. He could easily sleep in the van, and no doubt others would be doing the same.

As he left the intersection and headed toward Second Mesa, he shook his head. Why would anybody want to live in this godforsaken place? Dusty, dry, windy — it looked to him like the outskirts of Hell. He had no fondness for the outdoors — he was a city boy to the core — and all this emptiness gave him an eerie feeling. He hoped that he would find the woman and the boy soon; he didn't want to stay here any longer than he had to.

The main problem would be locating them. The newspaper article had been meager, mentioning only that the woman was half Hopi. From the map book he had bought in Williams, he had learned that there were three mesas and numerous small villages, but the Hopi Cultural Center was located on Second Mesa, as was this *Shungopavi,* and he had decided that that would be the most logical place to start. Perhaps they would be drawn to the festivities being held there.

He realized that it would be like searching for the proverbial needle in a haystack, but he did have one advantage — he had the license number and the color of the Mustang the woman was driving.

As Tibbets reached the top of Second Mesa, the traffic thickened. He found his way to the Hopi Cultural Center, and drove slowly around the main building, checking out the cars parked around it. The Mustang wasn't there.

Feeling the need for a hot meal, he parked in the lot in front of the Cultural Center and went in. It was well past the usual lunch-time, but the place was still crowded with tourists and Indians. He considered leaving, but decided to stay. Maybe the woman and the boy would show up here.

When he was finally seated at a table in a far corner, he scanned the room, but he could see no one who looked like the woman or the boy.

After his meal, he went looking for the village of *Shungopavi*. When he found it, he couldn't believe his eyes. It was a ruin. The place looked a thousand years old, yet it seemed people were still living here in the strange-looking little stone houses, some piled on top of one another, some falling to pieces. The place was full of tourists, stirring up the dust of the dirt streets.

The village was small, and it didn't take long to ascertain that there was no Mustang with the right license number parked by any of the houses.

By the time darkness fell, he had not become discouraged. He had known that it would not be easy. Besides, with every passing hour he became more certain that the woman was near. He could almost feel her presence, smell her fear. It was only a matter of time until he found her.

With the coming of darkness, he realized that he was tired. Pulling the van off the highway, he crawled into the back. He had seen other cars so parked, and felt that the reservation cops probably wouldn't bother him. Lying curled in his blankets, he squeezed the tennis ball, moving it from hand to hand, until he fell asleep and the ball rolled out of his lax fingers.

Casey arose early on her first morning on the reservation. Donnie, ablaze with curiosity, wanted to see everything, and she had promised to give him the royal tour.

Although her pallet of sheepskins and blankets had been hard, she had slept well for the first time in weeks, and felt well-rested and energetic.

Donnie — who had slept in the other room with her uncle — hearing her stir, was up and through the door only seconds after she was dressed, saying, "Casey, you promised to show me the reservation today."

She smiled at him. "Yes, kiddo, I did. But right now I'm going out to the shop and see if there is anything in Uncle Claude's refrigerator for breakfast."

She shook her head and looked around the simple interior of the stone house. "If ever a way of life had a split personality," she said, shaking her head.

Donnie looked puzzled, but seemed to grasp that her remark was disparaging. "I like this house, Casey. It's neat. It looks real Indian. I like all the stuff on the walls." He pointed to the hand-woven rugs and paintings. "Besides, I like sleeping on the floor. It's like camping out."

Casey grinned. "You can say that again. Is Uncle Claude still asleep?"

"I don't know. Let's go see."

They went into the other, larger, room, where they found Claude Pentiwa stirring beneath his blankets. Seeing them dressed, he asked Casey, "Are you going to take the boy out?"

"Yes, as soon as we have had some breakfast," Casey said. "I thought I'd show him some of the reservation. He's anxious to see it."

Claude grunted. "Do you think that's wise? What if that man is out there looking for you?"

"I don't think he'll find us here. And we

can't spend all of our time holed up indoors. Besides, there are so many people on the mesa for the ceremonies that we will hardly stand out."

Claude sat up. "Then I'll go with you."

Casey held up her hand. "That won't be necessary. I feel bad enough about crashing in on you like we did, and I don't want to cause you to lose business as well. You have a shop to run, and this must be the busiest time of the year for you."

Her uncle scrubbed long fingers through his thick, graying hair, scowling. "You're right. But I still don't like the idea of you going out alone. At least take my pickup. There's a rifle in the rack behind the seat. The keys are in my pants pocket." He reached into the trousers lying beside him, found the keys, and tossed them to Casey, along with another key on a separate ring. "That's the key to the shop. Lock it and bring it back when you're through."

As she and the boy turned to go, he said, "Be watchful out there."

Inside the shop, Casey made coffee. She found orange juice in the refrigerator, and half a large bowl of corn pudding. In the cupboard she found the *piki* bread and a jar of honey. It would have to do. She would pick up some milk for Donnie at the reservation store, while they were out.

As they waited for the coffee to process and the corn pudding to heat, Donnie bounced around the shop.

"You haven't told me about the Snake Dance, Casey. I want to hear."

Casey gave an involuntary shiver. "I'd rather not talk about that if you don't mind, kiddo. Snakes are not my favorite subject."

The boy's expressive face fell. "But how come, Casey? Why don't you want to talk about snakes?"

Casey sighed. "Because I'm afraid of snakes, that's why. I'm not proud of it, but that's the way it is. It's what doctors call a 'phobia.' "

"A phobia?"

"Yes, that means an unreasoning fear of something, like being up high, or being afraid of dogs, or cats or . . ."

"Snakes," said Donnie.

She nodded. "Yes, snakes."

Donnie looked thoughtful. "But talking about them isn't the same as seeing them, is it? Besides, Josh told me that if you're afraid of something that it's *good* to face it. If you tell me about the Snake Dance, maybe . . ."

Casey threw up her hands. "Okay, kiddo, you win. But you have to eat while I tell you."

He nodded and reached for the glass of orange juice and the bowl of corn pudding she handed him. She steered him to one of the two chairs behind the counter, then seated herself in the other, trying to decide just what she should tell him.

She had seen the Snake Dance only once, when the ceremonies coincided with one of her visits to her grandmother. It was still vivid in her mind. If she closed her eyes she could see the parade of painted, half-naked dancers, the snakes writhing between their teeth.

That year the ceremonies had taken place at Old Oraibi, and Grandmother had insisted that the whole family attend. She thought it would be a good chance for Casey to learn more about her Hopi heritage, and to witness the Snake Dance, she said, was a great honor.

Casey had still protested. "But I don't like snakes. They scare me."

Grandmother shook her head. "You should not fear the brothers of the underworld, but honor them. They help bring the rain. This has been a bad summer. No rain for months. We need rain now, or our corn will die!"

Then she had explained to Casey the deep purposes behind the ceremonies. So Casey and her mother had gone to Oraibi with the rest of the family, and it had proved to be a powerful and moving experience which Casey had never forgotten.

The people were all gathered in the *tipkyavi*, which Grandmother had told her meant *womb*,

311

the plaza in front of the Snake Kiva. When Casey and her family arrived, it was already growing crowded, but a friend of Grandmother's had saved them a place on the roof of her house. There were more Hopi gathered than Casey had ever seen in one place before, and many strangers as well, including other Indians. They were everywhere, squatting on the flat Hopi rooftops and walls, jamming terraces and doorways — any place from which they could see the plaza. She had clung to her grandmother's skirts, which smelled of smoke and corn, feeling nervous among so many strangers.

Grandmother, aware of her unease, had attempted to distract her, pointing out the *sipapuni*, a small hole dug into the ground, representing the place of Emergence from the underworld. "That cottonwood board over the hole is the *pochta*, the sounding board," she told Casey. "The little house behind it is the *kisi*, the shade house."

Casey liked the look of the small, green bower of cottonwood branches. It was hot in the plaza, and she would have liked to have been inside, in the shade. A blanket concealed the opening.

"That is where the snakes are now," said Grandmother.

Casey decided that she did not like the

bower after all.

By the time the ceremonies began, in the late afternoon, Casey was already tired, but when the dancers filed into the plaza, her interest was sparked. They were marvelously colorful and strange, like pictures from a book.

There were two rows of dancers. She counted them. There were twenty-four all together — twelve of one kind, and twelve of another. All had their bodies painted, but they all weren't the same. Half of them were painted in two shades of red, with large white ovals over their chests and shoulders, and a white strip across their upper foreheads and the fronts of their throats. The rest of their faces were blackened.

The others were painted ash-gray, with white zig-zag lines running from chest to shoulder, down the arms to the fingers, and down the fronts of their legs to the toes. White lines outlined their chins from ear to ear.

To Casey's question, Grandmother had answered that the red-painted dancers — who wore reddish-brown kirtles bearing the black design of a snake, and brown, fringed moccasins; both of which had seashells sewn onto them — were the Snake Dancers. The gray-painted dancers — who wore white kirtles, embroidered sashes, and carried gourd rattles — were Antelope Dancers.

She pointed the Snake Chief out to Casey. He was a big man, larger than most Hopi, and looked very fierce.

The watching crowd had grown very quiet, and Casey felt that almost inexpressible thrill of fear and anticipation that she experienced during a scary movie.

The crowd was quiet now, and in the silence the dancers began to circle the plaza, accompanied by the dry, eerie rattle of gourds and seashells. As the first dancer passed the *kisi*, he bent forward and stomped powerfully on the sounding board over the *sipapuni* with his right foot. Casey jumped. The sound crashed into the silence. After him, each dancer did the same, until it seemed that the plaza was filled with the roll and roar of thunder.

Four times in all the dancers circled the plaza, while the excitement of the watchers increased. Casey could feel it around her, like a tangible presence.

Sheltered behind her grandmother's skirts, Casey watched as Antelopes formed a long line extending from the *kisi*. They began swaying slightly to the left and right, like snakes. They were singing softly and shaking their rattles. Then the Antelopes straightened, and their voices grew louder. At that moment, the Snake Chief stopped before the *kisi*. He stooped down and reached inside. When he again stood, he held a large snake in his mouth. Casey felt her own mouth grow dry, and she shuddered. If Grandmother had not been with her, she would have been very afraid, but Grandmother *was* there, and Casey knew that she was protected. This allowed her to take a certain scary pleasure in the spectacle.

The Chief's jaws held the snake firmly, his teeth just below the snake's head. With his left hand, he held the upper part of the reptile's body level with his heart, and with the right hand, he held its lower length even with his waist. At once, another Snake Priest stepped up near the Chief. He had a feathered snake whip in his right hand, with which he seemed to be soothing the snake. He began to lead the Chief around the plaza. As they moved away from the *kisi*, the other dancers repeated the performance, until each dancer held a snake. Slowly they circled the plaza once again, then they placed the snakes upon the ground, and returned to the *kisi* for another snake.

Casey stared at the snakes lying on the plaza. Would they dart into the crowd. Why didn't somebody do something?

Then someone did. A short, squat man had entered the plaza and was picking up the snakes carefully, holding each one aloft to show to the crowd, then handing it to one of the Antelopes singing in the long line, who began to soothe it gently, still singing.

"The Snake Gatherer," whispered Grandmother. "He shows us that the snakes are being safely returned. That they are not coming among the people."

The dance went on until the last of the snakes had been danced with. As the last circle was completed around the plaza, several women made a circle beside the *kisi*.

"They are sprinkling corn meal," said Grandmother, "to pen the children of the underworld."

Casey wondered how corn meal could keep the snakes in. But strangely, it did. When the Antelopes deposited their armloads of snakes inside the circle, the snakes stayed there, until a group of men picked up as many of them as they could carry at one time, and went away with them.

Casey tugged at her grandmother's skirt. "What are they going to do with them?"

"Those men are members of the Snake Society. They will take the little brothers out into the desert and set them free, in all the four directions. This is done so that the snakes will carry to the four corners of the earth the message of the renewal of all life. The little brothers travel far . . ."

Her words were drowned by the rumble of

thunder. Casey looked up to see dark clouds gathering on the horizon. She was overcome by a feeling of awe. It worked. She smiled at her grandmother, who smiled back.

"You see, child, the old ways still have power."

Casey reached for the old woman's hand, full of the joy of having witnessed something wondrous. An hour later, the rain began to fall.

"Casey, I'm through with my orange juice. When are you going to start telling me?"

Casey, recalled to the present, looked down into Donnie's eager face, and took a deep breath. What would interest a nine-year-old boy?

"The purpose of the Snake Dance, Donnie, is to bring rain to the final phase of the corn crop. First the younger male members of the Snake Society go out on a snake hunt, carrying a snake whip and a sack."

Donnie leaned forward eagerly. "A whip? How come, Casey?"

"Well, you see, a snake can't strike very far unless it is coiled. When the young men come across a snake that is coiled, they wave their whips over the snakes until they uncoil, then they are captured and put into the sacks. This hunt lasts for four days, and the men capture all kinds of snakes: rattlesnakes, side-winders, bull snakes, racers. Some of them are poisonous, and some are not, but they are all put into large jars covered with deerskin, and are kept inside the Snake Kiva until it's time for the Snake Dance."

"What's a Kiva?"

Casey thought for a moment. "It's a holy place, where the men hold ceremonies and worship the gods, you understand?"

Donnie nodded. "I think so. It's an Indian Church, right?"

Casey smiled. "That's pretty much it. Anyway, before the Snake Dance, there is a ceremony held in the Kiva. It is a time for blessing and entertaining the snakes. Only the Snake chiefs and a few young men that the chiefs want to bring into the Snake Society attend. They aren't supposed to tell anybody what happens in the Kiva."

Donnie, licking the last of the corn pudding from his bowl, looked disappointed. "Heck. You don't know what happens next, huh?"

Casey looked down at her hands. "Well, I do, in a way — not everything, but some things."

Donnie put his bowl down on the floor. "Wow! Good! How did you find out? Did you peek through a hole in the wall or some-thing."

Casey waved away the suggestion. "No, not that. Somebody told me, a boy who was an initiate — one of the boys that the Snake chiefs were training to belong to the society — told me."

Donnie looked puzzled. "But you just said that they weren't supposed to tell anybody."

Casey nodded. "He was a bad boy, a mean boy. He knew that I was afraid of snakes, and he used to tease me. One day he caught me and held me down while he told me about what he had seen in the Kiva. Later he did some other bad things, and he was dropped from the society."

Donnie slid off the chair. "But what did he tell you? Come on, Casey, tell me."

"Well, a Kiva, you know, is partly underground, and the men enter by way of a ladder. This boy said that when the men were all inside, they sat down on the floor of the Kiva in a circle around the altar, cross-legged, knees touching the knees of the men on either side. In front of the altar was a bed of sand, which had been raked smooth so that the men could see which way the snakes were moving. Then the snakes were released from the jars, and the men began to sing, very softly. Then the snakes began to crawl, looking at the men, who sat still as statues, still singing."

Casey could still see the boyish face looming

over her, enjoying her discomfort. Drawing out the details.

"He said that there was one huge rattlesnake, and that it crawled up to an old man, who was singing with his eyes closed. The snake crawled up the man's leg, coiled in his lap, and went to sleep."

"Wow!" Donnie said. He seemed all eyes.

"And then other snakes did the same, until there were four or five of them on the old man's body. Then the other snakes did the same to the other men."

"Boy, I wish I could have seen that," Donnie said; but Casey's mind was elsewhere, she was remembering the final remark of that awful boy: "You would have screamed," he said, scornfully. Then his eyes narrowed and his grin grew wide. "I'll bet you'd be afraid to let my snake sleep in *your* lap," he said, and laughed.

At that moment she had managed to pull away from him. She had no idea what he was talking about, but she knew he was insulting her. It wasn't until years later that she understood what he had been implying. The little slime ball.

Donnie asked, "And after that they dance, huh? Are we going to get to see that?"

Casey nodded. "I don't think so; but we'll get up at sunrise and watch the Antelope Race and the Antelope Ceremony. But for now I thought we'd just prowl around for a while. I haven't been here myself in years. I'm curious to see what changes have taken place."

"Sure," he nodded. "That'll be interesting too."

As Casey locked up the shop, Donnie, his mind obviously on her story, said: "Casey, do people ever get bit? I mean the dancers and all. Don't the snakes bite them?"

Casey shrugged. "I guess they do, once in a while, but my grandmother told me that the dancers have a special substance, snake medicine. It comes from a certain plant they call 'stinking plant' and the roots and leaves of some other plants. She said they drink some of it, and rub it on their hands and arms."

Donnie looked puzzled. "But what good does that do?"

Casey shrugged again. "I don't really know, but I suppose it calms or drugs the snakes a little. Anyway, the Hopi say that if your heart, soul, and thoughts are pure, the snakes won't bite you."

Donnie thought for a moment. "They could take the snakes' teeth out, their fangs?"

Casey shook her head, feeling like her grandmother must have felt at Casey's own questions long ago.

"No," she said. "That would hurt the

brothers of the underworld and the ceremony wouldn't work."

This seemed to satisfy Donnie for the moment.

It was early in the morning. Ray Tibbets had breakfasted on crackers, cheese, apples, and orange juice. He was now trying to decide what to do. The methods he had used elsewhere were not going to be practical here; there were no convenience stores and there seemed to be only the one gas station. Also, he was hesitant to show his pictures at the Cultural Center or the shops. If he happened to hit on one of the woman's relatives, they would no doubt lie to him, and then tell her he was here. No, he would have to play it differently. Use a different story, a different approach. Well, he had been lucky so far, maybe he would get lucky again. The car was the key; find the car, and he would find the woman and the boy.

He would take the mesas in order; drive through them all, street by street, shop by shop; then, if necessary, he would do it again.

As he drove out onto the highway, he was dismayed by the amount of traffic coming toward him; then he remembered what the gas station attendant had told him, something about some kind of Antelope Ceremony being held today. Damn! Well, there was no help for it; and maybe the festivities would bring out the woman and the boy.

First Mesa proved to be something of a disappointment; the town itself — if you could call it that — looked smaller than the town on Second Mesa, a pile of decaying rock houses piled haphazardly atop the mesa. It didn't take him long to go through the whole place. Nothing.

There were not many shops, and they were scattered here and there, outside the villages, along the highway, small rectangular buildings with little pretension to beauty. He stopped at them all, searched the parking areas, went into the shops — and came up empty-handed.

It was still early when he returned to Second Mesa. The highway was clear now, although he saw many parked cars. Evidently whatever was going on at the village had started, and the tourists and visitors were all there. Despite his sureness that he would find the woman and the boy, he could feel the tension rising in his body and blood. He had to find them soon.

And then he saw two buildings off the road. Another shop — Pentiwa's Crafts. The building behind it seemed to be a residence.

He braked the van, and turned in. The dirt parking area was empty, and a sign on the door of the shop said "Closed."

The parking area seemed to circle the building, so he decided to circle it and get a look at the house.

When he spotted the Mustang behind the shop, he could not repress a shout. Yes! He had known they were here. He had been right.

Tibbets pulled his van in beside the Mustang, and took a good look around. He did not want a repeat of the incident in Laughlin.

There was no one in sight. He got out of the van, and quietly closed the door. As he did so, he noticed that the rear door of the shop was ajar. He moved toward it warily.

That morning Claude Pentiwa had risen before dawn and gone out onto the mesa, hunting rabbit. The white boy loved rabbit, and Pentiwa had grudgingly grown to like the boy.

Claude spent about an hour on the mesa, until well after sunrise, but had not seen one rabbit. Disappointed, he had trudged back to his house, and had found his niece and the boy gone.

In the shop, propped against the coffee maker, he found a note: "Uncle; Donnie and I have gone to the Antelope race. We'll probably stay in Shungopavi for the Antelope Dance as well. Since it isn't far, we decided to walk. We should be safe in the crowd, so don't worry about us. Love, *Nesseehongneum.*"

Claude's first reaction was amusement that she had chosen to use her Hopi name; then he felt a stab of annoyance. She had come to him with this disturbing story, that she was being pursued by a madman who might follow her here to the mesa, and then she tells him not to worry while she and the boy wander about the mesa unprotected. He would have to go find them; but first he must eat. He had left this morning without breakfast, and he was hungry.

As he was preparing his meal, the back door opened, startling him. He turned, and felt his heart jump in his chest, for he recognized the man instantly from Casey's description: square-built, powerful hands and arms, and a round, baby face wearing an innocuous smile.

The man approached, his eyes searching the room. "I apologize for coming in your back door, but it was open. Hope I didn't startle you."

As the man moved forward, Claude had to force himself not to back away. He nodded slightly, and said politely, "May I help you?"

The man smiled, and for a moment something dark flickered in his eyes. Claude felt his soul go cold. If he had ever had any doubts about the truthfulness of what Casey had told him, those doubts were gone. He could see

325

the madness in those eyes.

"Well, maybe, I don't know. You see, I was just driving by, and I saw a familiar car outside. It belongs to a friend of mine, and I thought she would be in here."

Claude shrugged and lifted his hands palms up. "As you can see, there's no one here but me, and I have not opened the store yet. That car out in back was parked here when I got up this morning. I guess it broke down, and the owner had to leave it."

Tibbets nodded slowly, his eyes again circling the room. "Or, it could be that she's in that house out back. Her and her son. Is that where they are?"

Claude had carefully lowered his right hand. He kept a rifle under the counter, and slowly he began to grope for it.

"I don't know what you mean," he said slowly. "There is no one in my house. I live alone. I told you that I don't know who the car belongs to." His hand closed on the butt of the rifle.

The man leaned across the counter. "Oh, I think you do," he said calmly.

Claude pulled the rifle out from beneath the counter, his finger searching for the trigger.

Hands braced on the counter top, the intruder vaulted over the counter in one smooth, rapid movement, his feet striking Claude at

326

the waist, sending him crashing backwards. The gun flew from Claude's hand, and Claude struck the floor on his right side. As he did so, he felt a sharp pain, and heard the crack of bone; the bastard had broken his arm! Then hands, solid as steel, were at his throat.

He struggled, attempting to knee his assailant in the groin, but the man had his legs pinned. Claude thought himself a strong man, but he was helpless against those hands. Fear began to fill him. Casey, and the boy. How could he help them now?

Looking up through misted eyes, he saw the distorted face above him smile. The face grew hazy, and then began receding down a long tunnel, receding, receding . . .

Tibbets, his hands strong around the Indian's throat, felt wave after wave of pleasure lifting him higher and higher. After the abstinence, after the frustration, this was what he had needed.

Then, abruptly, a noise caught his attention, distracting him. Not loosening his grip, he looked forward to the front of the shop. Three people were gathered before the door, knocking on the glass panel, their faces pressed close to the glass, trying to peer into the shop.

Startled, Tibbets relaxed his grip. What the hell?

He sat back, taking his hands from the

Indian's throat. The Indian was still as death.

"Hello. Anybody there?" The knocking at the door continued. Tibbets looked again at the Indian, and saw next to him on the floor a sheet of paper.

He picked it up and read: "Uncle . . ."

Tibbets didn't recognize the name signed to the note, but he was certain that it had been written by the woman, for it mentioned Donnie, the boy. One other word leaped out at him, Shungopavi, the village where the ceremonies were taking place. It was only a short distance away. Slowly he smiled.

Cramming the note into his pocket, he rose from the floor, the man beneath him forgotten. Exiting the shop the way he had come in, he got into his van and drove away, toward the Indian village. He had them now.

Claude Pentiwa swam up out of unconsciousness, momentarily puzzled to find himself on the shop floor. He struggled to sit up, and pain blazed down his right arm. As it did, he remembered the baby-faced madman. He groaned.

With great effort he finally got to his feet, clinging to the counter to stay upright. The shop was empty. The killer had gone. Why?

Looking down at the counter, Claude saw that the note that his niece had written was gone. Cold dismay weakened him, and he almost fell. The man must have it. He now knew where Casey and the boy were. That was why he had left.

He shook his head in an attempt to clear the dizziness that threatened to fell him. He had to do something, but with a useless arm, he was certainly no match for the muscular killer.

Unsteadily, he made his way to the desk where his telephone sat. Dropping heavily into the desk chair, he clumsily shuffled through the cards in his desk drawer, until he found the card of the white policeman. If asked, he could not have explained why he was calling this man first; it just seemed the right thing to do. As the number rang, he prayed that the man would be there.

At last a voice answered. "Sergeant Whitney."

Relief made Claude's voice weak. "This is Claude Pentiwa, on Second Mesa."

The policeman's voice quickened. "Mr. Pentiwa, is Casey there? Is she okay?"

Claude tried to speak louder. "She is here. So is the boy. But they are in terrible danger. The man you spoke of, the killer, he is here. My niece and the boy are at Shungopavi village for the Antelope ceremonies. This man has gone there. He broke my

329

arm. I am of no use to her. You must help them."

"I'll leave by chopper as soon as possible; but it'll take me at least an hour and a half to get there. Have you called John Pela?"

"Not yet."

"Then call him right away. Get him over there at once. I'm hanging up now."

Claude hung up the receiver. He was feeling very strange, very dizzy, and he could not recall the number of the reservation police. He fumbled with the telephone book, and dropped it. In reaching to pick it up, he struck his injured arm on the desk. Pain shattered him, sending him to his knees and then to the floor, as he washed away on a wave of darkness.

CHAPTER TWENTY

The sun was just coming up when Casey and Donnie found a spot on a rooftop from which to watch the Antelope Race. It was a little cool, though Casey knew that it would heat up quickly once the sun came up.

The village was crowded with people, but it would be much worse tomorrow, for the Snake Dance. The house on top of which they sat was perched on the cliff edge. The mesa fell away steeply to the desert below, which was slowly turning gold under the rising sun.

Beside her, Donnie said complainingly, "There's nothing to see, Casey."

She put an arm around his shoulders. "There will be, kiddo. Just be patient. The race starts about four miles out, too far to see from here."

She had brought along a pair of binoculars. She put them to her eyes and gazed out over the desert. Far out, she spotted the figure of an old man. He was dressed in nothing but a breechcloth, and his long, white hair flowed loose. Casey knew that he was an Antelope priest, and was carrying a bundle of prayer sticks and a small jar of water, which, as she remembered, would have been blessed in the kiva. He was jogging along slowly.

Casey handed the binoculars to Donnie. "See the old man jogging alone out there?"

Donnie peered through the binoculars, waved them around a bit, then declared excitedly, "I see him! But how come he's out there all alone?"

"He's an Antelope priest, and he's waiting for the first runner to reach him."

"Hey! I see one running up to him now; and some others out there behind. The first one must be fast, Casey."

Casey put her hand on his shoulder. "When the runner comes abreast of the priest, the priest will hand him the prayer sticks and the jar of water he's carrying. Then he will say, 'Thank you and bless you, my son. Carry these on to our home.' "

"He's doing that now. Now the runner is coming again, but he keeps looking back over his shoulder. Why is he doing that, Casey?"

"He's afraid that another runner will overtake him. If that happens, he must hand over the water jar and the prayer sticks, and bless the other runner as his successor. Here, let me look for a minute."

Donnie reluctantly handed over the glasses, and Casey put them to her eyes. The first runner was about a half-mile from the bottom of the mesa now, the next nearest runner about two hundred yards behind. The trail was now lined by men waving cornstalks and squash vines, urging the runners on to greater speed.

Casey could see the lead runner's face through her glass. It looked very young, and taut with concentration. He could not be more than sixteen or seventeen, Casey thought, young and agile. The other runners would have a hard time catching him. As she watched, the boy reached the base of the mesa, and began laboring up the steep slope. Men, whirling bull-roarers over their heads, lined his way; the sound of the roarers reverberating through the warming air like the low roll of thunder.

His chest laboring, the young runner reached the top of the mesa. The August sun was well up now, beaming heat down, and the tired runner's body was streaked with sweat and dust. The crowd, in a good humor, called out jokes to him as he made his way to the Kiva, and climbed down the ladder.

Casey lowered the glasses. "What happens now?" Donnie asked, as the young man disappeared into the Kiva.

"He will be blessed by the priests now,"

said Casey, "and later, while everybody is celebrating, he will slip out of the Kiva, go back down the mesa to his family's fields, and plant the prayer sticks and the jar of water, so that they will have a plentiful harvest."

Donnie sighed. "That wasn't so much."

Casey laughed, running her fingers through his hair. "Well, it may not be to you; but it means a lot to the Hopi. All this, the Antelope race and the Antelope dance, set the stage for the Snake dance tomorrow."

Donnie wrinkled his nose. "You said the snake brings rain, but what do the antelope do?"

"They bring the sound of thunder when they run. You've seen movies where there are large herds of animals running; doesn't the sound they make sound like thunder?"

Donnie nodded thoughtfully. "Yeah. I guess it does."

"And the sound of the running antelope, the sound of thunder, is supposed to bring the clouds. And when the clouds are here . . ."

"The clouds bring the rain," Donnie, said, pleased with himself.

"Yes," said Casey, "and the Hopi believe that the snake has the power to draw the rain from the clouds."

Donnie cocked his head. "It is kind of neat, sort of like a play," he said.

"Yes, it is," she said. "Now, I suppose you're hungry again?"

He nodded hopefully. "Can we eat our lunch now?"

"Well, how about brunch?" She held up the back pack from the rooftop. "I brought brunch, lunch, snacks, and drinks, knowing how you like to eat."

Donnie looked embarrassed. "Ah, I don't eat so much."

"No more than a football player," said Casey, putting her arms through the pack. "Now, let's find a shady spot."

Back on the ground, Casey stood for a moment looking around. People, both Hopi and visitors, were drifting aimlessly about, as the streets began to clear. Picture taking was forbidden, yet she saw some tourists furtively stealing shots. Looking around, Casey was struck again, as she had been yesterday while taking Donnie around Hopiland, by the signs of poverty in the village.

Conditions were worse in some of the other villages — Old Oraibi, for instance, was little more than a ghost town — but Shungopavi was far from prosperous.

Suddenly depressed, she said, "Maybe we should go back to my uncle's to eat, Donnie? There won't be anything happening here until much later, and soon the sun will be fierce."

"Yeah, I guess so, Casey," he said dispiritedly. Head lowered, he kicked at the hard earth with his toe.

Casey took his hand, and they started toward the plaza, weaving in and out of the thinning crowd.

Suddenly Casey stopped short, gripping Donnie's hand so tightly that he protested. "Hey, Casey . . ."

"Oh, God," Casey said. "It can't be!"

But it was. About fifty yards distant, coming down a side street, Ray Tibbets was moving steadily towards them, his head swiveling back and forth as his gaze swept over the faces of approaching walkers.

Casey's mind and senses felt frozen; while panic urged her to flight, she could not move.

Donnie, trying to pull his hand from hers, brought her back to reason. "Casey, what's wrong? You're hurting me."

Blinking, she tried to marshal her thoughts. Relaxing her grip on Donnie's hand, she said, "It's Tibbets. He's here!"

"What do we do, Casey?"

"I don't know. Hide," she said. "We need to find a place to hide."

Her mind seemed to be functioning again, and she scanned through the crowd for one of the reservation police. There were none in sight.

Would Tibbets dare attack them here, with people around? Reason said no, but experience said yes. Tibbets was like a shark cruising for food, nothing could or would stop him. And he was so convincing. With his baby face, and innocent smile, he would persuade bystanders that she was a run-away wife, or that she was insane, and he was taking her home. Or, he could kill them right there, and be gone into the crowd in an instant.

With a pang of bitterness she recalled the pledge she had made to herself after Laughlin, that she would not run from Tibbets again. The pledge had been easy enough to make at the time, but it didn't stand for much now that Tibbets was about to confront her again.

And then Tibbets saw them. She could see recognition and joy flare to life in his eyes.

Spinning around, turning Donnie with her, she gave him a hard push toward the plaza. "Run," she shouted at him, "run!"

Josh leaned forward in his seat alongside the chopper pilot, as though by doing so he could increase the aircraft's speed. It had been almost two hours since he had received Claude Pentiwa's phone call — a good portion of which had been spent attempting to requisition a helicopter — and the aircraft was still a distance away from Second Mesa.

In two hours almost anything could have happened to Casey and Donnie. If Tibbets had found them, they both could be dead by now.

Using the radio in the 'copter, he had contacted the dispatcher at the Hopi Law Enforcement Services, and been told that no call had come in from Pentiwa. He asked to speak to John Pela, but Pela was out of his office. In a fury of frustration he had told the dispatcher of the presence of Tibbets on the mesa, and impressed upon her the importance of protection for Casey and the boy. She told him that due to the influx of visitors all the cars were out on call, but that she would prioritize the search for Casey and the boy, and attempt to get in touch with Pela.

That had been three quarters of an hour ago. He was considering calling again, when a call came through from the investigator. "Sergeant Whitney, this is John Pela. I'm being patched through from my car. Sorry I couldn't get back to you sooner, but I was on a call, and was off the radio for a good spell. It's been madness here. But I have your message now, and I'm on my way to Second Mesa."

Josh said, "Thank God. Look, you'd better send someone out to Pentiwa's shop. When he called me, he said he was hurt, and the

338

dispatcher told me that he didn't make the call to you that he was supposed to."

"I'll get right on it. How far are you from the mesa?"

"About fifteen minutes, the pilot tells me."

"Then you may beat me there. Good luck, Josh."

Josh hung up the microphone and stared ahead. "There's a parking lot at Pentiwa's store where we can put down. We probably can't get much closer to the village because of the crowds."

The pilot nodded. But even as the mesa drew nearer, Josh had the sinking feeling that they were going to be too late.

Donnie was much faster than Casey and drew several yards ahead as they ran across the rapidly clearing plaza. Casey risked a glance back over her shoulder. Tibbets was gaining on them.

As she looked again at Donnie, she saw that he was now abreast of the Snake Kiva. He hesitated for a step, and then darted toward the Kiva. For a moment, she didn't grasp what he was doing, then a cry rose in her throat; he was going to enter the Kiva!

It all happened so quickly. Dismay washed over her. The Kiva was sacred, he would defile it; it was a dead end, there was no way out;

and the snakes were in the Kiva, many, many snakes.

Her cry of protest became lost in her throat. There was a large Hopi standing near the Kiva, perhaps he would stop Donnie; but he was looking the other way, and Donnie was so small and so quick! In seconds he had climbed on top of the Kiva, grabbed the ladder, and scurried down it.

She shouted, "No, Donnie, no!"

People turned to stare at her, but evidently no one had noticed the boy's entrance into the Kiva.

She looked back over her shoulder at Tibbets. He was still coming, directly toward the Kiva. If she ran in another direction, would he follow her, or go after Donnie? She remembered his words, "The smallest one first." She couldn't take the chance. She couldn't let Donnie face Tibbets alone; and surely if they all invaded the Kiva, someone was bound to notice, and try to stop them.

Praying under her breath, she ran for the Kiva, sprang up to the low roof, and headed for the ladder. As she reached the ladder, she heard an angry voice: "Hey, you can't go down there. Stop!"

Ignoring the voice, she hurried as rapidly as she could down the shaky wooden ladder. The Hopi had seen her. Surely he would see

Tibbets too, and stop him.

After the bright sunlight, the interior of the Kiva was like that of a cave, dark and musty. Halfway down the ladder, she heard the crash of breaking pottery.

As she stepped onto the hard dirt floor, she called, "Donnie?"

A small voice answered her. "Casey? I'm over here. I . . . I broke one of the jars."

Casey, her eyes not adjusted yet to the darkness, felt a wave of panic. The snakes!

From above came the sounds of a scuffle, and a man's voice. "What do you think you're doing? I said, hold it. You can't go down there."

"Donnie," said Casey softly, her voice echoing in the hollow womb of the Kiva, "stay where you are. Don't move. Stand very still. Do you hear me?"

A soft, frightened whisper, "Okay, Casey."

The scuffle was still going on overhead.

Casey's eyes had adjusted, and she could now see the outlines of the things in the room: the fire pit, the row of Snake jars, the Snake altar, the *pahos* planted in mud-earth containers. Queasily, she looked down and saw the broken jar, and, amid the shards, the pile of startled snakes. They appeared to be somewhat torpid, but how long would they stay that way? She could see

341

them beginning to move, to separate.

Looking around the room, she saw Donnie's small figure crouching on the seating ledge, against the wall.

There was a thud from the roof, and then the light was blotted out as someone began descending the ladder.

She prayed that it was the Hopi, but she knew in her heart that it wasn't.

Slowly she backed away toward where Donnie was standing, looking vainly about the room for anything that might be used for a weapon. She knew that she didn't stand a chance against Tibbets, but if she could delay him, perhaps help would come. She tried not to think about the thud on the roof.

The figure was now at the bottom of the ladder, and was turning. In the light from the entrance hole she could see that it was indeed Tibbets, and that he was smiling.

She thought her heart would stop. Never had she seen madness written so plainly on human features. He began to laugh, at first softly, and then the sound grew until it seemed to fill the Kiva. Stretching out his hands, he said, "You're mine now. You might as well come to me." The absolute assurance in his voice maddened Casey.

Her mind was racing. If she was going to do anything, she would have to do it now, while his eyes were still unaccustomed to the darkness. Where was help? Surely someone else must have seen them enter the Kiva. What could she use as a weapon?

Again her eyes searched the Kiva. There were the pots that held the *pahos,* but they would not stop him even for a few seconds. The larger pots containing the snakes; she didn't think she could lift them and throw them. There was nothing else but the snakes, which were crawling now, moving across the floor of the Kiva. She shuddered. One very large, heavy-bodied rattler was quite near her, crawling across the earth in front of her.

In an instant she made her decision. Thrusting aside her fear, knowing it was her only chance, she darted forward and grasped the big snake firmly by the tail, just above the large rattles. The snake's body felt dry and cool in her hand. Not giving the creature time to muscle back upon itself, she swung it around her head, once, twice, and then let it go, directly at Tibbets, who was slowly walking toward her.

The snake struck him athwart the upper chest with a flat sound. Tibbets, at the last moment, raised his hands and staggered forward toward the altar. As he did so, he tripped over one of the snake jars, and fell among them, breaking them. Casey ran to Donnie, and took his hand. Tibbets made no outcry, but began to kick and thrash, as if attempting to get to his feet.

Casey, avoiding the snakes, pulled Donnie over to the ladder, sure that Tibbets would be upon them at any moment.

There were noises from outside now, shouts and calls, and footsteps on the roof. She pushed Donnie up the ladder, and he disappeared into the light. Still Tibbets thrashed amid the broken jars.

She put her own foot on the first rung of the ladder, and feared that her legs would not hold her. The second rung, the third, and then she felt his hand on her ankle. It had been too much to hope for. But she wouldn't let him take her without fighting. Filled with equal parts of despair and anger, she kicked out, using all her strength. For a moment the grip clung, grew tighter, and then relaxed.

Unbelieving, she reached for the next rung, and felt hands grasping hers. In a moment she was blinking in the sunlight, attempting to understand what was happening. The roof was crowded with people, some of whom were Hopi police, and a tall figure that, despite the glare, looked very familiar.

"Casey, Casey," said Josh's dear voice, "are you all right?"

As she sagged against his chest, she tried

to nod. She didn't think that she could talk.

"Casey. Casey!"

It was Donnie. He was clinging to her legs. "You hit him, Casey. You were great!"

She felt Josh's hand lift her face. "My God, Casey. He could have killed you both."

Casey took a deep breath. "But he didn't," she said.

"You should have seen it, Josh." Donnie's voice was high with excitement. "She picked up that big snake and threw it at him, and it got him, pow! And then he fell over."

"Sergeant Whitney?" The voice came from behind her, but she was too tired to turn to see who was speaking.

"The man is unconscious. There was a big rattler coiled on his chest, and it got him right in the jugular. There were other bites on him as well. They're bringing him up now."

Josh held Casey away from him, and looked down into her face. "You threw a snake at him, at Tibbets?"

The look on his face was ludicrous, but she did not feel like smiling. She looked at him levelly. "I threw a snake at him. A big snake."

He drew her close again. "By God, Casey, you are some woman."

"Well," she said against his chest. "There was nothing else to throw."

CHAPTER TWENTY-ONE

The afternoon sun was kind to Josh's house, and Casey thought that she had never seen any place as beautiful in her life. Like the sea explorers in the history books, she felt like getting down on her knees, and kissing the ground.

Donnie bounced out of the car like a rubber ball. "Oh, boy, Casey. It's swell to be home. Wow!"

She smiled as she watched him bound across the yard and up the walk.

The last few days had seemed like weeks, but Donnie didn't seem tired at all. As for herself, she felt as if she had been dragged through the proverbial knothole. All the questions, the explanations to the police, the explanations and apologies to the members of the Snake Clan; and then the media people, and more questions and explanations. Visiting Claude in the hospital, then more media people. The media were in a feeding frenzy, making much of Casey's "heroic act."

She smiled thinking of Claude. He was back in his shop now, one arm in a sling. She had offered to stay, to help him, but he had declined. "My children will help me. You have your own life to get back to, *Nesseehongneum*. I can manage quite well with one arm. Besides, the media people would drive me crazy." He had added somewhat wistfully, "However, it would be nice if you would visit more often. And bring the little white boy. I will teach him of the Road of Life."

She had smiled and kissed him. "I will, Uncle. And thank you for everything."

He smiled a crooked smile. "I did very little. You handled the important part all by yourself, very well."

All during the long drive home, Donnie had been asking her and Josh the same question, could he stay with them. And it was a question that neither she nor Josh could easily answer. Since she had lost her job with the task force, they had agreed that she would continue to stay with Josh for a while, until she found a suitable place of her own; but neither of them could foretell what the boy's aunt would do, and for Josh to take on permanent care of the boy would be a big decision.

When Josh unlocked the door, Donnie dashed inside, leaving her and Josh, for the moment, alone. Josh leaned over and kissed

Casey's forehead. "Well, we're home, Casey, for now anyway, and it sure looks good. It's been some kind of hell we've been through, particularly you and Donnie. I hope it hasn't traumatized the kid."

Casey smiled. "I don't think so. He's tough, and resilient."

Josh nodded. "He's a great kid."

Casey looked up at him quizzically. "Does that mean you're going to take him on?"

Josh nodded. "I think I am. It's about time I started a family, and I like having him around."

"But are you sure you're ready for that kind of responsibility?"

Josh paused. "Yeah. I'm going to give it a try, if his aunt will agree. I don't think she'll be a problem. She wants to get rid of the kid, and the powers-that-be no longer disapprove so strongly of single parent adoptions."

Casey stood on tiptoe to kiss his nose. "And they say that *I'm* a hero!"

Josh laughed, Donnie came running into the living room, and the telephone rang.

Josh loped into the kitchen to answer it, and then called to Casey. "Casey, it's for you."

Wondering who it could be, Casey took the phone and put it to her ear. "Casey. You're home. I'm so glad. I can't tell you how much we've worried about you."

Casey widened her eyes in surprise. It was Tod Burns.

"We've been watching you on television. You're quite the heroine. Catching the Dumpster Killer, defending yourself and the boy."

Casey shook her head at Josh. "Well, I only did what any red-blooded American girl would do. By the way, Josh told me that you called while I was gone. I'll be down as soon as possible to clear out my desk . . ."

"Oh, no, no, no. Don't be ridiculous. Just ignore that call. It was a mistake on my part. We want you with us on the task force. We expect great things of you in the future. I know that you'll want to rest for a few days, but we hope you'll be back on the job Monday. Can we expect you?"

Casey let him wait a moment before saying "I think that that will be agreeable, Mr. Burns."

"Tod. Make it Tod, please."

"Alright, Tod."

Casey hung up slowly, shaking her head in wonder, and said to Josh: "He wants me back to work Monday. It's amazing what a little publicity can do."

Josh grinned, and held out to her the day's edition of the *Republic*. On the front page was an article quoting Tod Burns's assertions that he was very proud to have Casey Farrel as a member of his task force, and that she was a fine example of the quality of the people on the force.

"I don't think his actions are entirely the result of altruism," Josh said, then, "Look, I have to go out for a few minutes. Will you and Donnie be okay?"

She nodded. Now that Tibbets was out of the picture, she felt that she wasn't afraid of anything.

While he was gone, she parked Donnie in front of the TV, unpacked her and Donnie's things, and had a long, hot shower. She and Donnie were fixing some sandwiches in the kitchen, when she heard the return of Josh's car.

Feeling absurdly happy, she took Donnie's hand, and they went to greet Josh at the door — and were almost knocked over as the puppy in Josh's arms wriggled out of his grip and fell onto Donnie, who squealed in delight while falling to the floor under the dog.

Donnie and the pup — a small, spotted creature with enormous paws and ears — were up in an instant. "Is it for me, Josh? Is it for me?"

"Who else, sport?"

Casey took his arm and gave it a squeeze. "You're something else, Josh."

Josh shrugged and looked embarrassed. "What's his name?" said Donnie. "Does he have a name?"

"Well, I thought I'd leave that up to you," Josh said. "But I thought maybe Spot Two, or maybe Two Spot."

"Two Spot. Yeah!"

Casey, watching the boy and the dog, felt her eyes grow misty. She hugged Josh's arm again, leaning against him.

"You know," she said, "this may just work out all right, after all."

"Sure it will," Josh put his arm around her, drawing her close. "Depend on it."

The employees of THORNDIKE PRESS hope you have enjoyed this Large Print book. All our Large Print titles are designed for easy reading, and all our books are made to last. Other Thorndike Large Print books are available at your library, through selected bookstores, or directly from us. For more information about current and upcoming titles, please call or mail your name and address to:

THORNDIKE PRESS
PO Box 159
Thorndike, Maine 04986
800/223-6121
207/948-2962